Gabriel

The 4 Seats
Book 3

Cassandra Doon

Independently published by Cassandra Doon

Edited by TJ's Editing Services

Edition 2 2026

Cover design by ANK Book Designs

Interior design by Vellum

Author Website: Cassandradoon.com

Author's Note

Dear Reader,

Before you begin this journey with Gabriel and Alba, I want to take a moment to speak with you about the nature of this book and the subject matter it explores.

Books 1 and 2 in this series are dark and steamy. However, Book 3 takes a different approach. While it still contains romance and intimate moments, the heat level is significantly reduced. This is intentional.

On the Subject of Human Trafficking

Human trafficking is a global crisis that devastates millions of lives across countless countries every single day. It is not romantic. It is not glamorous. It is a horrific violation of human rights and human dignity. When I set out to write this story, I made a conscious decision; I would never romanticise the trafficking itself. The darkness, the abuse, the exploitation—these are presented as the grave injustices they are.

Instead, I have focused the romance, passion and the

relationship between Alba and Gabriel—on their love story, on their healing, on their journey toward redemption and hope. The steam in this book is reserved for their connection, for the intimacy they share as two people learning to trust again, learning to love again, learning to live again.

My Research and Responsibility

I have conducted extensive research into human trafficking in Australia, as it is the country I know best and the only nation I felt equipped to write about with the necessary depth and respect. Australia, like every country in the world, struggles with this epidemic. The statistics are staggering. The stories are heartbreaking. The need for awareness is urgent.

I have done my best to handle this subject matter with the gravity it deserves. I have tried to be gentle, while still exposing the true nature of what survivors endure daily— the fear, the trauma, the loss of autonomy, the fight for survival. If there are moments where I have fallen short, I take full responsibility, and I welcome feedback from survivors and advocates who can help me do better.

A Note on Content

If you are reading this series primarily for the steamy romance and intimate scenes, I encourage you to jump ahead to Catcher's story (Book 4) or Ruhn and Frost (Book 5), where the heat level returns to the intensity of Books 1 and 2. There is no judgment here—we all read for different reasons, and that's perfectly valid.

What I will promise you is this: every book in this

series ends with a Happily Ever After (HEA). You do not need to experience the journey in each book to appreciate the series as a whole. Each story stands alone. Every couple gets their happy ending. You can pick up any book and find a complete, satisfying conclusion.

My Commitment to You

My commitment as a writer is to tell stories that matter, to handle sensitive subjects with care, and to create characters you will root for, cry for, and ultimately celebrate. I hope that in reading Alba and Gabriel's story, you find not just romance but also hope—hope that even in the darkest circumstances, love can bloom; that survivors can heal, that redemption is possible, and a better world is worth fighting for.

Thank you for taking this journey with me. Thank you for caring about these characters. Thank you for standing with survivors of trafficking, whether through reading, advocacy, or direct support.

With gratitude and respect,

Cassandra XXX

If you or someone you know is affected by human trafficking, please reach out to local support services or organisations dedicated to survivor support and advocacy.

To the ones who loved us first—the high-school sweethearts who were kind, gentle, and sweet... and the ones we didn't marry.
This is the universe where you found me again—and did.
And to Heathcliff, patron saint of beautifully ruined hearts: you walked so dark romance could run.

Welcome Back, Dark Mafia Romance Readers.

Before you dive into the world of Gabriel and Alba, here is a list of what is inside this book. Please don't read if anything here bothers you. Your mental health and comfort are paramount.

- Abuse & Coercion
- Captivity & Loss of Autonomy
- Drug-Related Content
- Emotional Distress
- Intimate Content
- Pregnancy
- Strong Language
- Trafficking & Sexual Exploitation
- Trauma & PTSD
- Violence & Criminal Activity

To everyone who reads this, like a shipping list: Welcome back. This is the story of redemption, healing, and the kind of love that burns even in the darkness.

Chapter 1

Gabriel

17 years Old

The moment Alba's obnoxiously crooked gate comes into view; a grin, so wide, splits my face, and I know I probably look ridiculous. I pedal harder, the rusty chain of my bike groaning in protest as I race down the cracked pavement of her street, my legs scream out from the effort, but I don't care, not even a little bit. The Melbourne sun is doing its best to break through the clouds, casting a weak but welcome warmth across my shoulders, and I can't help but already picture the look on her face when she sees what I've got for her. A stolen treasure tucked safely in my backpack, something I've been planning for weeks, something that screams I am thinking about you.

It's a Saturday, and these few hours are just for us, before I have to head back into the suffocating quiet of my own house; where everything is measured, heavy and filled with expectations I'm meant to be living up to. It's where my father's voice echoes through marble hallways with commands about duty, legacy and the family business that I'm not even supposed to know about yet; but obviously do. It's where my mother watches me with this careful, worried expression; like she's waiting for me to become someone I don't want to be. But when I am here, with Alba, I can just be Gabe. Just a 17-year-old boy, who's completely and utterly obsessed with a girl who makes him feel like he can actually breathe.

I skid to a halt, letting the bike drop onto her overgrown lawn without a second thought. I don't bother with the front door, jogging straight around to the back where I know she'll be, because she's always there on a Saturday morning, curled up in her room with a notebook and a cup of tea; that has probably gone cold by now. The screen door squeaks open under my hand, a familiar sound that's become a soundtrack to all my best memories, my favourite moments. Her house is small, filled with the scent of laundry detergent and something uniquely Alba; like wildflowers, mischief and home.

"Oi, you're late," she calls out before I even see her, her voice laced with a playful sarcasm that makes my stomach flip, every single time. "I was about to send out a search party. Or, you know, eat your share of the biscuits. Actually, I already ate your share of the biscuits. Fair warning."

I find her lying on her stomach across her bed, chin propped up in her hands as she scribbles in her worn leather notebook that she carries everywhere; one she's filled with sketches, thoughts and probably things about me that I'll never get to read. Her red hair is a messy halo around her head, falling across her face in a way that makes my fingers itch to brush it back, the old band t-shirt she's wearing is way too big for her, and hangs off one shoulder in a way that's somehow more distracting than it has any right to be. She glances up at me, her green eyes sparkling from the fun she was just poking at me, a mischievous glint that I've come to recognise as her being in a good mood.

"I had to make a detour," I say, my voice coming out softer than I intend, betraying how nervous I actually am about all of this. I walk over and drop onto the edge of her bed, the old springs creaking under my weight in protest. "A very important, top-secret mission was undertaken. Government-level classified stuff. I probably shouldn't even be telling you about it."

She rolls her eyes, but she's smiling, a real smile that reaches all the way to her eyes. "Does this top-secret mission involve actual secrets, or did you just get lost again trying to find that one bakery you like? Because I'm still not over the fact that you managed to get lost in a suburb you've walked through a hundred times."

"Hey! I only got lost that one time," I protest, shoving her foot gently, my hand lingers on her ankle for a moment longer than necessary. "And no. This is much better. This is significantly better, actually. This is the kind of mission that required planning, strategy and me riding my bike across half of Melbourne in the heat."

"Oh, so you're sweaty," she observes, wrinkling her nose; but her eyes are dancing with amusement. "Fantastic. That's exactly what I want on my quiet Saturday morning.

My bedroom smelling like sweaty teenage boy and desperation."

"Your bedroom already smells like that," I shoot back, but I'm grinning because this is what I love about her, this easy banter that flows between us like we've been doing this forever. "I'm just adding to the ambiance. Consider me a contribution to your interior design."

She laughs, a bright, genuine sound that fills the small room and makes something in my chest feel like it's expanding, like it might burst right out of me. "You're an idiot. A sweaty, desperate idiot. Now, are you going to tell me what this mission was, or are you going to keep being mysterious and annoying?"

I shrug off my backpack, trying to play it cool; even though my heart is hammering in my chest like it's trying to escape. I pull out a slightly squashed box of cannoli from a bakery two suburbs over—her absolute favourite, the one she's always complaining is too far to walk to, the one she mentions every single time we talk about food.

Her eyes widen, and a genuinely breathtaking smile spreads across her face, the kind that makes everything else fade away. "You didn't."

"I did," I say, watching her reaction like it's the most important thing in the world; because to me, it is. Because she is.

"Gabe, you absolute legend!" She scrambles up, abandoning her notebook to snatch the box from my hands; one already in her mouth before I can even laugh, a dusting of icing sugar on her nose that I want to kiss off, but I'm not brave enough for that yet. "You are officially forgiven for being late. You're also officially my favourite person in the entire world. Just don't tell your mum."

"Your standards are concerningly low," I tease, but I'm pleased; pleased that it is me who can bring her something that makes her this happy. "I'm glad the cannoli are winning me points though."

"Cannoli win all the points," she says with her mouth full, in a completely unladylike and absolutely perfect way. "Cannoli are the way to my heart. Forget flowers, chocolates and all that romantic nonsense. You want to impress a girl? Bring her cannoli from across the city."

I watch her eat, completely content just being here with her, and I realise that my heart is doing a weird thing, where it feels too big for my chest. It's been doing that a lot lately, especially around her. I've been trying to ignore it, trying to convince myself that it's just friendship, just a normal kind of closeness that comes from knowing someone your whole life, but I know that's a lie. I know exactly what it is, and I've known for months now.

"So," she says, her mouth still full of cannoli, completely unaware of the internal crisis I'm having, "what's the occasion? Or did you just miss my stunning personality that much? Because if you did, you should probably know that my personality is even more stunning today. I'm at peak form."

I can't help but laugh, reaching out to wipe the sugar from her nose with my thumb. Her skin is soft, impossibly soft, and the simple touch sends a jolt straight through me that makes my breath catch. She goes still, her eyes meeting mine, and I can see the moment the energy between us shifts into something different, something charged and real, and terrifying.

"I just wanted to see you," I admit, my voice quieter and more honest than I meant it to be. The words hang between us, heavy with meaning, and I'm suddenly very aware of how close we are, how I could reach out and pull her closer if I was brave enough.

She swallows her bite of cannoli, her own playful energy softening into something else, something more serious and vulnerable. "Yeah?"

"Yeah," I breathe out, my mouth suddenly dry. My heart starts to beat a little faster, as a nervous flutter starts up in my stomach, feeling like a thousand butterflies are trying to escape all at once. I've been thinking about this for weeks, months even. Thinking about how to say it, when to say it, whether she even feels the same way or if I'm about to completely ruin the best friendship I've ever had. But there's never a perfect moment, there's only now, and I'm tired of waiting, tired of pretending that this is just a friendship, when it's clearly so much more than that.

"Alba, I..." I start, but the words get stuck in my throat, tangled up in fear, hope and this desperate need for her to understand what I'm trying to say.

She just waits, her gaze unwavering as she's completely patient with me. She always gives me the space to figure out my own jumbled thoughts without judgment or pressure. It's one of the things I love most about her; a quiet acceptance that she offers so freely.

"I really like you," I finally manage to get out, the words feeling both huge and ridiculously small at the same time. "More than just as a friend. I think I have for a long time. And I know this might ruin things, and I know you might not feel the same way, and I'm probably going to regret saying this, but I can't keep pretending anymore. I can't keep acting like you're just my best friend when you're so much more than that to me. You're everything to me, Alba. You're the only thing in my life that feels real and true and good, and I need you to know that."

The words tumble out of me in a rush. I'm terrified, absolutely terrified of what she's going to say, of the look on her face. But then a slow smile spreads across her lips, and it's not the teasing one from before. This one is gentle, and it makes my heart do a complete flip inside my chest; a somersault that leaves me breathless.

"Took you long enough, Gallo," she says softly, her eyes shining with something that looks like relief, happiness and maybe even love. "I was starting to think I was going to have to spell it out for you. Like, literally write it on a banner and hang it from your window or something."

"Wait, what?" I ask, my brain struggling to catch up with what she's saying. "You… you like me too?"

"Of course I like you, you idiot," she says, and there's exasperation in her voice but also affection, so much affection. "I've liked you for ages. I was just waiting for you to figure it out. I was starting to think you were never going to get there."

Relief floods through me, so intense that I feel almost dizzy from it. She likes me. She actually likes me. This beautiful, snarky and incredible girl likes me back. I feel like I might actually explode from happiness.

"So, what happens now?" I ask, my voice uncertain

despite the relief; I want to get this right. I want to know exactly what this means for us.

"Now?" She reaches out and takes my hand, threading her fingers through mine in a way that feels so natural and so right. "Now you kiss me, you absolute moron. Unless you've changed your mind and you actually don't like me that much."

"I haven't changed my mind," I say quickly, maybe too quickly, but I don't care. I lean in, and she meets me half-way. Her lips are even softer than I imagined, and taste like sugar and her, like cannoli and the girl who's become my entire world without me even realising it was happening.

It's not a big, dramatic movie kiss. It's clumsy, and sweet, and a little bit hesitant because neither of us really knows what we're doing, but it's perfect. It's ours. It's the beginning of something that feels like it might be everything.

We pull apart, both a little breathless, and I'm grinning so hard my face hurts. I rest my forehead against hers, bringing my hand up to cup her cheek, and I can feel her smiling against my lips.

"That was nice," she whispers, her eyes still closed.

"Yeah?" I ask, needing reassurance, needing to know that this is real and not just something I'm imagining.

"Yeah," she confirms, opening her eyes to look at me. "Really nice. We should do it again."

"I can definitely arrange that," I say, pulling her closer. "In fact, I'm planning on doing it a lot. Like, a concerning amount. You might get sick of me."

"Impossible," she says, her eyes shining with amusement. "I could never get sick of you, Gabe."

And then I kiss her again, this time it's less hesitant. It feels like coming home, like finding something I didn't even know I was looking for. I know I have to leave soon, back to the quiet order of my life, back to my father's expectations and the weight of my family's legacy, but for now, I'm exactly where I'm supposed to be. Wrapped up with my snarky, beautiful girl in her small room that's filled with sunlight and the sweet taste of our beginning.

"So, does this mean I can officially call you my girlfriend?" I ask when we finally break apart, a hopeful grin takes over my face, despite the nervousness still fluttering throughout my stomach. I need to hear her say it, I need to know that this is real and not just something that's happening in this moment; I need her to confirm it officially.

She laughs, a bright, happy sound that fills the small room and makes everything feel right. "Only if it means more secret missions for cannoli," she says, her eyes serious despite her playful tone. "Because I'm going to have very high expectations now. You've set the bar extremely high with this one."

"For you?" I say, my voice thick with an emotion that feels bigger than like, an emotion that feels like, forever. "I'd go to the ends of the earth. I'd ride my bike across the entire state of Victoria if you asked me to. I'd do anything for you, Alba."

"Good," she whispers, her eyes shining with unshed tears that she's trying to blink back. "Because you're stuck with me now. And I'm not letting you go, Gabriel Gallo. Not now, not ever."

I pull her in for another kiss; this time it's tender, deep and filled with all the things that I'm feeling but I can't quite say yet, it's so intensely it's almost painful. It feels like a promise, like the start of something that's going to change everything; like our new beginning.

We spend the rest of the morning wrapped up in each other, talking, laughing and kissing, learning the feel of each other's hands and the taste of each other's lips. We eat the rest of the cannoli, and she tells me about the sketches in her notebook, and I tell her about my week at school, just existing in this bubble of happiness and newness and possibility.

But as the clock on her wall ticks closer to noon, reality starts to creep in at the edges. I can feel it, the knowledge that I have to leave soon, the weight of my other life pressing down on me, that I have to go back to being the dutiful son, the heir to something I never asked for.

"I have to go soon," I say reluctantly, my arm around her as her head rests on my chest. "My father's expecting me for lunch. Something about discussing the business."

She tenses slightly, and I feel her pull back a little. "The business," she repeats, her voice carefully neutral. "Right. The thing we don't talk about."

"We don't have to talk about it," I say quickly, because I don't want anything to ruin this; I don't want the darkness of my families world to touch this perfect moment we've created. "We can just… not. We can pretend it doesn't exist when we're together."

"Can we though?" she asks, a sadness to her voice that breaks my heart a little. "Because I know what your family does, Gabe. Everyone knows. And I'm not stupid enough to think that's just going to go away or that you're going to be able to keep me separate from all of that forever."

"I know," I say, pulling her closer and pressing a kiss to the top of her head. "But right now, in this moment, we don't have to think about any of that. Right now, it's just us. Can we do it? Can we just have this?"

She's quiet for a long moment, then she nods and burrows deeper into my chest. "Yeah," she says softly. "We can have this."

We stay wrapped up in each other for a while longer, trying to hold onto the moment before the real world comes crashing back in. I know this bubble of happiness is only temporary. I know that eventually, the darkness is going to find its way in, and that my world is going to collide with hers in ways neither of us can predict or control. But for now, for these precious hours, I get to have her, get to hold her, and be the kind of person she deserves.

"I'll see you tomorrow morning at mine," I tell her, my hand still holding hers as I reluctantly stand to leave, not wanting to let go. "Don't forget, yeah? Sunday breakfast is sacred."

"Wouldn't miss it for the world," Alba replies, her smile tinged with sadness as she walks me to the door. "Especially cause your mum makes the best pancakes. And because I'll get to see you again."

"See you, Alba," I say, leaning forward for one last kiss, I savour her sweet taste and commit it to memory. I want to remember this forever, want to hold onto this feeling of pure happiness and rightness.

"See you, Gabe," she says, and I can hear the smile in her voice.

With that, I step out of her fibro house and head back to the life I've been born into—one of power, violence and bloodshed, one where I'm expected to become someone I'm not sure I want to be. I pedal away on my bike, the image of her waving from the doorway becomes seared in my brain, burnt there like a brand. It know that no matter how deep I sink into the darkness of my families affairs, she's the shining star that guides me home, and I will burn the whole city down to keep my star shining.

Chapter 2

Alba

The ghost of Gabe's kiss still tingles on my lips as I'm lying on my bed, staring up at the ceiling but not really seeing it as my mind replays the last few hours on a continuously, giddy loop. He likes me. Gabriel Gallo, the boy I've been hopelessly and secretly in love with, for what feels like my entire life, actually likes me back. A laugh bubbles up out of my chest, a real, happy sound that feels foreign inside the usual quiet of my house. I press my fingers to my lips, still tasting the sugar from the cannoli, and still feeling the clumsy, perfect pressure of his mouth on mine. He brought me cannoli, from the other side of the city. That thought alone is enough to make my stomach do a backflip. He's my boyfriend. The words feel huge, sparkly and terrifyingly wonderful at the same time. I say it out loud, just to hear how it sounds in the empty room. "Gabriel Gallo, is my boyfriend." It sounds like a secret I've been waiting my whole life to tell.

I roll onto my stomach, grabbing the notebook he was teasing me about. I flip to a fresh page, my pen hovering over the paper as I try to capture the feeling and the look in his eyes when he finally said it. But the words feel small and inadequate. How do you draw a feeling? How do you sketch your heart feeling like it's going to beat right out of your chest? I end up just writing his name, over and over, the letters looping together like our fingers did. Gabe. Gabe. Gabe. It's a prayer, a song, a promise.

A floorboard creaks somewhere in the house, and the happy bubble I've been floating in, pops with a sharp prick of anxiety. I glance at the clock on my bedside table. It's past four. A familiar knot of worry tightens in my gut. Dad. He's usually home by now, nursing a beer at the kitchen table, either grumbling about a bad hand or boasting about a small win. His gambling is a constant, humming anxiety in the background of my life, but he's a creature of habit. He always comes home.

I try to push the worry away, trying to sink back into the warm, fuzzy feeling of Gabe's confession. It's probably nothing. He's probably run into a mate or lost track of time. It happens. But the silence within the house feels different today. It's heavier, more suffocating. Usually, I can hear the low murmur of the TV from the lounge, but today there's just nothing. The quiet pressing in on me, amplifies the frantic ticking of the clock.

I get up, my bare feet cold against the worn floorboards, and wander into the kitchen. His favourite mug is sitting by the sink, unwashed from this morning. His newspaper is still folded on the table, the crossword half-finished. Everything is exactly as he left it, and that's what scares me the most. It's like he just vanished. I tell myself I'm being ridiculous. He's a grown man, he can take care of himself. But I know the kinds of places he frequents and the kind of men he owes money to. I've seen them before, lurking in cars at the end of our street, their faces hard and unforgiving.

Just as I'm about to give in to the panic and call Gabe —a thought I immediately dismiss, because the last thing I want is to drag him into my messy life on our very first day as a couple—the front door groans open. Relief washing over me so fast, it makes me dizzy. See, he's fine. I've been worrying for nothing. I open my mouth to call out a sarcastic comment about the time, but the words die in my throat as he stumbles into the hallway.

"Dad?" The word a choked whisper. It's him, but it's not. His face is a swollen, bruised mess; a grotesque mask of purples and red. His lip is split, and a trickle of dried blood crusting the corner of his mouth. He's leaning heavily against the doorframe, his whole-body trembling, and his eyes clouded with a shame so deep, it makes my own stomach clench in sympathy.

"Jesus, Dad! What happened?" I rush to him, my hands hovering, unsure of where to touch him without causing more pain. The sharp metallic smell of blood fills the air, and it's sickening .

He shakes his head, a slow, defeated movement that seems to take all of his energy. "No, princess," he rasps, his voice a gravelly, broken thing. He won't look at me, his gaze fixed on the floor, like he can't bear to see the horror on my face. "I fucked up… and now I've lost it all."

Lost what? The question screams in my head, but before I can ask, the door behind him swings open wider as three men step into our small house. They are so out of place it's like a scene from a movie. They're huge, all of them are dressed in immaculate black suits, that probably cost more than our entire house. They fill the hallway, their presence sucking the air out of the space, and their shadows swallow what's left of the afternoon light.

My eyes snag on the one in the middle, and a cold, sharp spike of fear pierces through the panic. I've seen him before, at Gabe's house. He's one of them. One of Gallo's men, a bodyguard or an enforcer or whatever they call the men who do their dirty work. He's always lurking in the background, his face a mask of indifference, but I've seen the way people flinch when he looks at them. And now he's in my house.

"Is she the one?" His low and gravelly voice asks, the question directed at my father, but his cold, empty eyes are locked on me. They're assessing me, weighing me, and I suddenly feel a desperate urge to cover myself, to hide from his gaze.

My dad gives a tiny, almost imperceptible nod. It's a small movement, but it feels like a gunshot. A betrayal so profound, it knocks the breath from my lungs. What is happening? What has he done?

The man's gaze lingers on me for a moment longer, a flicker of something unreadable in their depths, before he gives a curt nod to the men beside him. And then they're moving towards me. I take a step back, my heart hammering against my ribs like a trapped bird, but there's nowhere to go. My back hits the wall, the rough plaster scraping against my t-shirt.

"What's going on?" I demand, my voice shaky but

laced with a defiance I certainly don't feel. "Who are you? What do you want?"

They don't answer. Instead, Strong and unyielding fingers wrap around my upper arms, the sheer force of the grip is terrifying. They start to pull me towards the door, and in a pathetically futile attempt to resist, I dig my heels. "Dad!" I scream, my eyes finding his. "Dad, do something! Tell them to let me go!"

But he just stands there, his face a mask of misery as tears stream down his bruised cheeks. He doesn't even look at me. He just stares at the floor while they drag his only daughter out of his house.

They drag me outside, the cool evening air hits my face as They drag me towards a black BMW that's parked at the curb, its engine humming and its tinted windows like black holes. They shove me into the back seat, and I land awkwardly on the plush leather. I'm sandwiched between two of the mountains as the doors slam shut with a heavy and final thud, the familiar man slides in behind the wheel.

"Wh-what is going on?" My voice is small, like a child's voice that is lost in the sudden, terrifying silence of the car. The world outside the window is still the same—kids riding their bikes, a woman watering her garden—but my world has tilted on its axis, and I don't know which way is up anymore.

I catch the driver's eyes in the rearview mirror. They're the same cold and empty eyes from before, but now they hold a flicker of something else. Pity? Maybe, regret? But it's gone before I can be sure. He just looks away, his jaw tight.

"Your father owes us a lot of money," the man to my

right says, in a flat, emotionless rumble. "He gambled more than he had and lost. And now…" He turns his head to look at me, his gaze is so cold it burns. "…he put you up to pay for it."

The words don't make sense. It's like he's speaking a different language. Put me up? Pay for it? The blood drains from my face, a ghostly chill settling in its place. My mind becomes a frantic, buzzing mess, as I try to piece together the impossible.

"I do hope you're a virgin," the man continues, his tone so casual, like he's commenting on the weather, it's obscene. "That's the price he's selling you for."

And there it is. The ugly truth, so monstrous, it's almost unbelievable. A silent scream builds in my throat, but no sound comes out. My father sold me. He sold me to these men to pay a gambling debt. And the price… the price is something I can't even comprehend. The cannoli I shared with Gabe, the sweet and innocent taste of our first kiss, it all turns to ash in my mouth.

The initial shock gives way to a white-hot rage, burning through the fear and disbelief; for the first time since they grabbed me, I feel a surge of strength. My snark, my defiance, it's all I have left. "You've made a mistake," I state, my voice surprisingly steady. "A very, very big mistake."

The man beside me actually chuckles, a low, humourless sound. "I don't think so, little girl."

"You don't know who I am," I spit, my eyes flashing. "You have no idea who you just kidnapped."

"We know you're the daughter of a degenerate gambler," he says, his amusement fading.

"Call Luca Gallo," I say, the name a weapon on my tongue. "Call Aubrey. Call Gabriel. Call them right now, and you'll see what a mistake you've made."

The men exchange uneasy glances at the mention of the Gallo names. The driver's eyes meet mine in the rearview mirror again, and this time there's a definite flicker of uncertainty. But the man beside me just shakes his head.

"I can't do that," he says, his voice flat again, all traces of emotion gone. "Orders are orders."

"Let me out!" I shout, my voice cracking with desperation. I start to struggle, to fight against their hold, but it's useless. They're like unmovable and unyielding walls of muscle. "Just call Luca, please! Call him! You don't understand—Luca Gallo would never allow this! I'm… I'm with Gabe!"

The words hang in the air, a desperate and pathetic plea. But they don't listen. They don't care. They're just following orders, cogs in a machine that's chewing me up and spitting me out. As the car speeds away from my street, from the only home I've ever known, a single, hot tear escapes and traces a path through the grime on my cheek. The life I had this morning, the girl who was giddy over love and a box of cannoli's, she's gone. And I have no idea who or what is going to be left in her place.

Chapter 3

Gabriel

The clink of silver on porcelain is the only sound in the cavernous dining room. It's a sound I hate, a sterile, soulless noise echoing throughout the expanse of this house. My stomach twisting into a tight, anxious knot as I stare at the empty chair across from me, a place I'd insisted my mother set for Alba. She should be here. It's Sunday morning, and Sunday breakfast is our thing. It's the one time a week she gets a proper meal, the one time I get to see her bright, happy face across this ridiculously long mahogany table, a splash of vibrant life within the monochrome world I live in.

My mother shoots me a sympathetic look from the head of the table, her perfectly manicured fingers wrapped around a cup of tea she's not drinking. My father, on the other hand, may not have looked up from his newspaper, but I can feel his disapproval radiating across the table. He hates when I bring Alba here. He thinks she's a distraction, a common girl from a bad family who has no place inside our world. He doesn't understand that she is my world.

"She's probably just running late, darling," my mother says, her voice a soft, placating murmur.

I nod, but I don't believe it. Alba is never late for Sunday breakfast. She's usually the waiting on my doorstep, her face scrubbed clean, and a teasing smile on her lips as she complains about how early I make her get up. After yesterday… after the kiss, after everything, I expected her to be here before I woke up, her eyes sparkling with the secret we now share. The memory of her lips on mine, the taste of sugar and her, is so vivid, it's like it just happened. I want her here. I need her here.

Every tick of the grandfather clock in the hallway is another hammer blow to my already frayed nerves. The pancakes my mother made, Alba's favourite, are getting cold. The joy and anticipation I woke up with this morning, the floating and giddy feelings of being in love, are slowly being replaced by a cold, creeping dread. Something is wrong. I can feel it in my bones; a deep and primal instinct screaming at me.

"Maybe she's not feeling well," my mother suggests, but her voice is laced with a worry that mirrors my own.

I push my chair back, the legs scraping against the polished floorboards with a sound that makes my father flinch. "I'm going to go check on her," I say, my voice tight.

"Gabriel, sit down," my father says from behind his newspaper, his voice a low, dangerous rumble. "You will finish your breakfast."

"I'm not hungry," I snap, my hands clenching into fists at my sides. For the first time in my life, I don't care about his orders or about the consequences. All I can think about is Alba. "Something's wrong. I have to go."

I don't wait for his response. I turn and walk out of the dining room, his muttered angry words following me down the hallway. I grab my bike from the garage, my heart pounding in a frantic, terrified rhythm against my ribs. The Melbourne streets are a blur as I pedal, my legs pumping with a desperate, adrenaline-fueled energy. The world feels tilted, off-kilter, and the only thing that can set it right is seeing her, seeing that she's okay.

I throw my bike onto her overgrown lawn, the same way I did yesterday, but the memory of that happy, hopeful moment is now a bitter taste in my mouth. Her dad's rusted-out Holden is in the driveway, which means he's home. A fresh wave of anxiety washes over me. He's a useless, gambling drunk, but he's still her father. He should know where she is.

I barge through the front door without knocking, the stench of stale booze and regret hitting me so hard, I almost gag. The house is dark, the curtains drawn against the morning sun, and the air is thick with the smell of decay. Alba's father is sprawled out on the couch, a half-empty bottle of whiskey dangling from his limp fingers, and his mouth hangs slack jawed as he snores. He's a pathetic, broken man, and I hate him for the life he's forced onto her, for the constant worry he puts her through.

"Mr. Baker!" I shout, my voice raw with a mixture of anger and fear. He doesn't stir. "Alba?" I call out, my voice echoing through the suffocating silence of the house. Nothing. Just the sound of her father wheezing.

My feet carry me towards her room, the dread inside of me so thick I can barely breathe. The door is slightly ajar, my heart lodging in my throat as I push it the rest of the way open. Her bed is made, the quilt pulled tight and smooth, not a single wrinkle in sight. It's too neat. Alba's bed is never this neat. It's always a chaotic mess of blankets, pillows and open books. Her few possessions are in their place—her worn-out copy of 'Wuthering Heights' on the bedside table, her collection of smooth, grey stones lined up on the windowsill. But the room is empty. The life, her spark, the very essence of her is gone. It's just a room, a cold space that feels like a tomb.

"Where the hell are you, Alba?" I whisper, a desperate plea into the empty room. I spin around, my eyes scanning every corner as if she might be hiding, playing some kind of stupid joke. But she's not here. She's gone.

I storm back into the lounge, my panic turning into a blind, helpless rage. I grab her father's shoulders and shake him, harder than I probably should, but I don't care. "Where is she?" I demand, my voice a low and dangerous growl. "Where's Alba?"

His bloodshot eyes crack open, bleary and unfocused. He squints up at me, a flicker of confusion in their depths. "Gabe?" he slurs, his voice thick and raspy. "What're you doin' here?"

"Where is she?" I repeat, my grip tightening on his shoulder. "Where is your daughter?"

He blinks slowly, his brain struggling to catch up. Suddenly, a strangely sad smile plays on his lips, a smile that makes my blood run cold. "She's gone, mate," he mutters, his words sloshing out of his mouth. "Ran away last night."

"What?" The word explodes out of me, a raw, incredulous sound. "What are you talking about? She wouldn't run away! We... she wouldn't." We just got together. We just had our first kiss. She wouldn't leave. Not now. Not after that.

"She's gone," he says again, his voice flat and resigned. He pulls his shoulder from my grasp and takes a long swig from the whiskey bottle. "And she won't be back."

The room starts to spin, the edges of my vision blurring. It can't be true. It's a lie. A sick, drunken lie. Alba wouldn't leave me; she wouldn't just disappear without a word, without a note, without anything. My mind becomes a chaotic storm of confusion and denial, as it flashes with images of her face, her smile, and her eyes when she looked at me yesterday. It doesn't make sense. None of it makes sense.

Panic claws its way up my throat, hot and suffocating, making me feel like I'm going to be sick. I stumble back, away from the stench of him, away from his poisonous words. I feel like the walls are closing in on me as I look around the small, dingy room, at the peeling wallpaper and the stained carpet. This can't be happening. This can't be real.

"Dammit, Alba..." I mutter, my voice breaking. I clench my fists so tight, my knuckles turn white. I have to find her. I have to know why. Because I have a bad feeling in my gut, and a gaping, black hole where my heart used to be, that will swallow me whole if I don't. The love I felt this morning, the bright, shiny hope I had for our future, is gone; it's all been replaced by a cold and terrifying certainty. Something terrible has happened to her. And I'm going to find out what, no matter what it takes.

Chapter 4

Alba

Present day

"Yes, Master," I whisper as I slip out of the room, the words taste like ash on my tongue; they're not even my words anymore, just sounds that I make. they are the right sounds, the expected sounds, the sounds that keep me breathing, fed and alive in the twisted, hollow version of what alive means here. My footsteps are silent on the plush carpet, a skill I've perfected over time, ensuring I move like a ghost through spaces that don't belong to me. Nothing belongs to me anymore. Not even my own name.

This is my fifth owner; or it may be my sixth. The faces all blur together now, a dizzying carousel of cruelty and indifference that I can't quite keep track of anymore. They all have their own names for me, their own brands that they want to stamp onto my skin, like I'm cattle at a market. This one calls me Anna. Anna, the name sits wrong on my tongue, foreign and cold, like wearing someone else's clothes that don't quite fit. But I answer to it because that's what I do now. I answer to whatever name they give me, whatever identity they want to impose on me, because Alba… Alba is dead. Or at least, I've tried very hard to kill her.

The door to my room closes behind me with a soft and final click, as I allow myself exactly three seconds to breathe. Three seconds where I can let the mask slip, where I can feel the weight of this new identity pressing down on me like a physical thing that is suffocating and heavy. I catch my reflection in the mirror, and for a moment, I don't recognise the girl staring back at me. She's hollow. There's nothing behind her eyes anymore, just an empty void in place of where a person used to be. My auburn hair falls past my shoulders now, longer than Alba ever wore it, a deeper shade than natural, dyed by hands that weren't mine. My green eyes, the ones Gabe used to say were like emeralds, look dead. Completely, utterly dead.

I trace my fingers along my jaw, feeling the sharp angles of a face that's become unfamiliar to me. My skin has been through too much pain and too many touches, from too many hands that didn't ask permission before they took what they wanted. Dan's hands. The hands of the men before him. The hands of strangers whose names I never learnt and whose faces I've trained myself to forget the moment they leave the room. I've become very good at forgetting. I think it's a survival mechanism. If I don't remember them, if I don't see them as real people, then maybe I can pretend that what happens inside those rooms, isn't real either.

Dan, my current owner, isn't the cruellest I've had. That distinction belongs to a man named Viktor, a Russian with cold eyes and even colder hands, he liked to leave marks in places where they wouldn't show. Dan is different. He's indifferent. He looks at me like I'm a piece of furniture, something to serve a purpose but not warrant any real attention. Sometimes I think it's worse than the cruelty; at least with Viktor, I knew where I stood. With Dan, there's a constant uncertainty. I don't know what will set him off, what small thing I might do wrong that will earn me a backhand or a night locked down in the basement. The not knowing is its own special kind of torture. I'm the only girl who lives with Dan, the rest just work at his club. But I get the luxury of both - I work at the club every night, then come home and be his plaything as well. Oh how lucky I am.

I sit on the edge of the bed that isn't mine, in the room that isn't mine, in a life that isn't mine, and I try to remember what it had felt like to be Alba. It's getting harder. The memories fading, becoming dreamlike and insubstantial, like they happened to someone else in another lifetime. I remember my tiny house with the crooked gate. I remember my useless and broken dad. I remember the way the sun felt on my face on Saturday mornings. And I remember Gabe.

The thought is like a knife through my chest, and I have to grip the edge of the bed to keep from falling apart. Gabe. His name is a wound that never heals because I keep picking at it, even though it only makes it worse. I wonder if he ever looked for me when I went missing. He probably thinks I ran away. He probably hates me for leaving him without a word. Or worse, he's forgotten about me entirely, cause he knows I was sold through his father shady dealings and he just doesn't care; That thought alone is almost worse than the pain.

I stare at my reflection, whispering the name they've given me to this time, testing it against my lips like I'm trying to learn a foreign language. "Anna." It sounds hollow. Empty. Like a name for someone who doesn't exist. But beneath the surface, Alba is still there, buried so deep that sometimes I can barely feel her anymore; like a spark that refuses to be completely extinguished, no matter how many times they try to snuff it out. It would be easier if I could just let her die completely, but I'm trying to hold onto that spark, even though it makes things harder. It's my only lifeline back.

I notice the neon lights flickering outside the windows in the club, casting garishly, sick colours across the grimy cityscape. I move through the back hallways like I'm underwater, like I'm moving through a dream I can't seem wake up from. The club is Dan's empire, his temple to carnality and exploitation; a place where fantasies are bought and sold with women like me as the currency. I'm part of the inventory now. That's what they call us. Inventory. As if we're stock to simply be managed, rotated and replaced when we wear out.

The air inside the hallway is thick with the smell of perfume, sweat and something else, something darker that I've learnt to not think too much about. I pass the main stage, where girls in various stages of undress are gyrating for the hungry eyes of the crowd. I feel a strange mix of pity and relief at the sight, at least they're still on the stage and they haven't been moved to the back rooms yet. But I know it's only a matter of time; All inventory ends up in the back rooms eventually.

My place is further in, behind another set of doors that only certain people are allowed to pass through. The special rooms. That's what they call them, like there's something exclusive and luxurious about them. But there is nothing luxurious about them. They're just cells dressed up with velvet and silk, designed to hide the screams, the tears and the desperation of the women trapped inside them. They're designed to hide the truth of what happens behind closed doors.

I move through the hallway with steady hands and a blank face, a mask of impassivity that I quickly perfected during my first few months. I've learnt to lock away the fear, to bury it so deep that sometimes I can't even feel anything anymore. I've learnt to separate myself from my body, to float somewhere above it, while things I don't want to think about are happening to it. Alba might tremble. Alba might cry. Alba might beg. But Anna? Anna is a fixture here; a ghost, who's presence exists only to serve the desires of men with money and empty souls.

"Anna." A voice cuts through my thoughts. It's the woman at the mahogany desk, the keeper of keys and schedules, her eyes sharp and knowing in a way that suggests she's seen things that would break most people. "Blue Room, in ten."

"Understood," I say, my voice sounding like it belongs to someone else.

I move past her, each step taking me closer to the room where I'll spend the next few hours. The Blue Room is Dan's favourite. He likes to assign colours to the rooms, like he's an artist, like there's something beautiful about what happens within them. But there's nothing beautiful about the Blue Room. It's just a space where men come to use me, to take whatever they want, to hurt me and leave me more broken than they found me.

I prepare myself in the dim light, slipping into the costume of flesh and feigned pleasure. The silks feel like chains against my skin. I look at myself in the mirror, at the expensive fabric that's meant to make me look desirable, and I feel nothing. I'm a puppet. I'm an unwilling performer in a show that never ends, a blank canvas for other people's fantasies; a receptacle for their cruelty.

"Tonight," I whisper to my reflection, my voice is hollow even to my own ears, "you are Anna. But remember, beneath it all, you are Alba. And they cannot take that from you." The words feel like a lie because they take everything from me. Every night, they take a little bit more. But I have to keep holding onto the lie because it's all I have left.

The door clicks shut behind me, sealing my fate for the evening. But inside, buried so deep, my spark of defiance is still flickering. I know it's weak now, barely a whisper of what it used to be, but it's still there; it has to be. Because if that spark dies, if Alba dies completely, then there will be nothing left of me to save at all.

The Blue Room never changes. The walls are painted a

soft, mocking shade of blue, as if colour can somehow make this place less horrifying. Heavy drapes block out the world, in an attempt to keep the secrets of what happens inside these walls locked away, where no one can hear them. There's a bed, a chair, and a rolling table with various instruments of pain arranged on it like a surgeon's tools. This is my realm now. Tonight this is where I exist.

I trace my fingers along the cool, light azure paint, and I think about when Dan explained how he chose this colour, he said it represented depth and stability. The irony is so sharp it cuts. There's no stability here, no depth either, just an endlessly suffocating emptiness. The only thing stable about this place is the constant stream of men who come through that door, each one's pockets full of money while their souls are full of darkness.

A fresh bruise flowers beneath my sleeve, hidden by the fabric of my costume. A reminder from last night, or the night before, I can't quite remember; the days seem to blur together now. The men all leave marks. Some are visible, while some aren't. The ones you can't see are the worst because they stay with you, they are the ones that burrow into your mind and never quite leave.

I've been beaten, whipped and degraded in ways that should have broken me completely. And yet somehow, I'm still standing. Not because I'm strong, but because I've learnt to not feel anything anymore. My body is a simply a vessel once I enter these rooms, not something I want to inhabit. My mind is a safe place I can escape to, somewhere far away from this room, these walls and these men.

The door opens, and a man walks in. His face is forgettable, interchanging with all the others. He has the swagger of someone who's paid for the right to do whatever he wants to me. He looks at me like I'm just a piece of meat, while I stare back at him with the detached curiosity of someone who's seen too much to be surprised by anything anymore.

"Quite the premium you fetch, Anna," he says, and his words an attempt at a compliment, but they land like a whip across my back. A reminder of my value as a slave in a world which is measured only in what I can endure.

"Yes," I murmur, thinking about how my ability to suffer silently has become my most lucrative asset. Men pay more for me because I don't scream, because I don't cry, I just lie here and take whatever they give me. "I suppose that's true."

His hands eagerly prepare the instruments he's selected. Whips, ropes, and things designed to inflict pain, but also extract sounds from women who haven't yet learnt how to disappear inside themselves. But I've learnt. My silence is now as much a part of me as my heartbeat is. I won't give him the satisfaction of hearing me break.

I drift away thinking about how I used to believe that places like this were a necessary evil, that they kept women safer by choice rather than coercion. I was so naive. So impossibly stupid and naive. But that girl is gone now. The girl who believed in things like choice, consent and fairness. She died the moment my father sold me to the highest bidder.

My ex-best friend's father. The thought twists in my gut like a knife. Gabe's father. Luca Gallo. The kingpin of this entire merciless trade. I used to sit at their dinner table, laughing and oblivious to the empire of suffering he lorded over. I used to think the Gallos were good people, that they cared about me. The irony is a bitter pill that I swallow every single day along with my pride, my dignity and my humanity.

"Shall we?" His voice slices through my thoughts, bringing me sharply back to the present.

"Whenever you're ready," I answer, my voice steady even though inside I'm a mess. Inside, I'm begging, I'm screaming, I'm dying a little bit more each day. But on the outside, I'm Anna. Just a girl, in a blue room, waiting for whatever comes next.

He begins, the lashes falling upon my skin, each one a note of brutality, a symphony of pain. But I remain still and silent. I give him nothing but a blank canvas, a body without a soul inside of it. He'll leave disappointed, like so many before him, never understanding that it's not the numb, brokenness keeping me quiet. It's strength. It's an iron will forged within a fire so hot, it's burnt away everything except my core, a part of me that refuses to break, no matter how hard they try.

As I mentally float away to endure this, somewhere above my body, watching it all happen from a distance, I hold tight to the one thing they can never take from me. The knowledge that while they can break my body, while they can steal my name, my freedom and my future, my soul is mine alone to command. It's all I have left. It's everything I have left. And I'm terrified that one day, even that won't be enough.

Chapter 5

Gabriel

The bass thumps through the marble floors in the old mansion, creating a pulsating heartbeat that matches the rhythm of my own dead heart. I toss back another shot, the burning in my throat now a distant sensation that barely registers against the numbness that has become my constant companion. The crowd roars my name, and I smile because that's what I'm supposed to do. That's what Gabriel Gallo must do at his own birthday party. He smiles. He drinks. He pretends like there's not a gaping hole, he's been bleeding out of, where his soul used to be.

I'm 30 years old today. Nearly half of that 30 years has been spent, breathing, existing and slowly dying from the inside out. The voices around me are a cacophony of loyalty and fear, a symphony of people who don't actually know me at all. They see the prince of a twisted realm, the heir to an empire built on blood and suffering. They see power, potential and a future that stretches out like a golden road. They don't see the walking corpse standing in front of them. They don't see the man who hasn't slept properly in years, who can't remember the last time he actually felt anything real.

The sea of well-dressed mobsters and their dolled-up companions parts like I'm Moses parting the Red Sea, and I move through them like a ghost, like I'm not even really here. I grin, a predator among sheep, because that's the role I'm supposed to play. But inside, I'm screaming. Inside, I'm falling apart.

I step out onto the balcony, needing air that isn't tainted with the stink of cologne, desperation and the weight of expectations; I never asked for. Melbourne's skyline sprawls out before me, a kingdom of lights spread out in all its glittering glory. But I don't see the beauty of it anymore. All I can see is the darkness lurking beneath the glow, the festering wound that no amount of neon's can disguise. All I can see is the place where Alba disappeared.

Two streets away, the world isn't so bright. Kids born into poverty and crime have nothing to hope for but a quick fix or a fast bullet. Their homes, if you can even call them homes, are stacked high and packed tight; cages really, where the stench of poverty permanently clings to peeling paint. Alba's street is somewhere inside the maze of desperation. I've been there a thousand times, standing outside her house, trying to figure out what happened to her. Trying to understand how the girl I love could have just vanished into thin air.

"Living the dream, huh, Gabe?" The words slip out of my mouth, bitter like bile, and I don't even realise I've said them out loud. Funny how the drug-afflicted bastards claw at life with everything they have and fail, while we dance on their graves, sipping champagne and trading lives like baseball cards. Iconic how I've become exactly the kind of person I used to despise. And I don't, seem to even care anymore.

I lean on the railing, the metal cold against my palms, as I look down on my concrete empire. There's a hunger inside of me, a craving for violence that feels as natural as breathing. It's the same hunger that has me reigning over these streets, indulging in the carnage, while demanding obedience and ruling with a velvet wrapped iron fist. But the hunger is hollow now. It's become a reflex, a fixation, a way to keep moving forward even though everything inside me is screaming to stop.

I've been searching for Alba for years. Years of using my family's resources, years of interrogating people, years of following leads that end up nowhere. I've torn through the city looking for her, and all I've found is silence. The kind of silence that tells me she's either dead or something worse has happened to her. And I can't decide which possibility is more terrifying.

Even as the power courses through me, even as I feel the weight of my father's empire settle on my shoulders, there's a shard of ice in my heart, a sliver of doubt that cuts so deep, I sometimes think I might bleed out completely. Am I any better than the monsters lurking in alleys, waiting to pounce? Or am I worse because I wear a suit and call it business? And more importantly, am I somehow complicit in whatever happened to Alba? Did my family do this to her? The thought is a poison I can't quite flush out of my system.

"Fuck," I shout into the night sky, my voice sounding

hollow and empty, like it's coming from someone else. Nobody will hear it, and even if they do, what would they care? They're all too busy kissing the ring of the soon-to-be Don, too busy revelling in the glory that is the Gallo family, too busy pretending like the world isn't rotting from the inside out.

"Gabriel, time to come inside." A voice, smooth as silk and twice as dangerous, calls from the doorway. I don't need to turn around to know it's my father. Luca Gallo. The man who built this empire on the backs of people like Alba. The man who owns half the city and doesn't give a shit about the cost for anyone else. The man I'm supposed to become.

"Coming," I say, pushing off the railing. I throw one last glance at the blight just beyond our palace gates, at the place where Alba used to live, and the life I used to have before everything went dark. Then I turn my back on it all and step back into the den. It's where I belong, after all. It's where I've always belonged. It's just taken me this long to realise that belonging somewhere doesn't mean it's where you want to be.

The manor is alight with decadence, but outside these walls, the city is bleeding. And one day, it'll be my hands holding the knife. The thought used to excite me, but now it just makes me feel sick.

I follow my father through the dwindling crowd, past the drunken laughter and clinking glasses that have now grown tired. The music is a heartbeat that's lost its rhythm, and the mansion—the damned gilded cage—feels more like a mausoleum with every step we take away from the party. We walk down corridors lined with portraits of my dead ancestors, their eyes following us like they know what's coming, like they're judging me for becoming exactly what they once were.

We reach his office, the heavy door with intricate carvings stands like a gatekeeper for all the secrets of the Gallo empire. He pushes it open and gestures for me to enter before him. It's respect, but a kind that's laced with expectation, heavy like the gold watch on my wrist—a gift for my 30 years on this earth. 30 years of being groomed for this moment. Thirty years of being shaped and moulded into a weapon.

The office smells of leather and scotch, the air thick from the heavy decisions that have built and broken lives. He goes straight to the decanter, pouring two fingers into a glass, and doing the same in another. Offering one to me. I take it, the glass feeling heavy in my hand, like it's weighted down with all the blood spilt to get us here.

"Sit," he orders, nodding towards the chair in front of his desk. It's not an invitation; it's a command, and I obey because that's what sons do when their fathers are Luca Gallo. That's what you do when your entire life has been a series of commands, each one designed to slowly strip away your humanity and replace it with something harder, colder, more useful.

He doesn't sit behind the desk. Instead, he leans against it; a monarch in his court looking down at his heir. There's a weight in his glare, something that makes the alcohol in my hand feel like lead. I can feel his expectations pressing down on me, suffocating me, drowning me in a sea of responsibility I never asked for.

"30 years," he says, his voice the voice of a man who's

broken countless lives and never lost a moment of sleep over it. "And you've proven yourself time and again. You've got the respect of our men, the fear of our enemies." He stops to take a breath and a mouthful of scotch. "Which is why it's time. Time for me to step aside."

I nearly choke on the scotch. The statement is blunt, no pomp or ceremony, just a stark truth laid bare between us. This isn't some distant promise anymore—it's real, tangible, like the cold steel from a gun pressed against my temple. My father is handing me the keys to the empire, and I feel absolutely nothing about it. It's how I know I am truly broken.

"Handing it off?" I ask, though it's not really a question. The words are edged with a sharpness of the reality I can't escape.

"To you," he confirms, his eyes never leaving mine. "You're ready to run this business. To lead our family."

"Lead," I repeat, the word tasting like ash in my mouth. I'm supposed to feel something about this. I'm supposed to feel hungry for the power he's offering me on a silver platter. But all I feel is tired. So incredibly, bone-deep tired.

"Make no mistake, Gabriel," he says, and his voice is cold, clinical, like he's explaining the rules of a game. "This life, it's blood and bone. You'll bleed for it, kill for it, live and die by it."

"Wouldn't have it any other way," I reply, because that's what he expects to hear. That's what a Gallo son is supposed to say. But inside, I'm wondering if Alba is still alive. Inside, I'm wondering if she ran away because of my family. Inside, I'm wondering if I'm going to spend the rest of my life searching for my soul mate.

"Good." There's a hint of pride in his tone, or maybe relief. "Because come tomorrow, we start preparing you to take over. Everything you thought you knew about our operations—you're about to learn a whole lot more."

A grin breaks on my face, a rare moment of actual satisfaction, but it feels like a mask I'm wearing. 30 years I've waited, each one a rung of a ladder slick with blood and sweat. This was supposed to be it. This was supposed to be the moment I finally reached the top. But all I feel is hollow. All I feel is empty.

"12 months, Gabe," Luca says, his eyes sharp as he studies me across the expanse of polished mahogany in his office—a throne room for the king of Melbourne's underbelly. "Then it's yours. All of it."

"About time," I mutter under my breath, but there's no real bite to it. My hands itch for control, for the reins to this empire, but not because I want them. Because if I'm busy running the family business, maybe I won't have time to think about Alba. Maybe, I won't have time to fall apart.

"Matteo and Antonio will be working closely with you." His voice is matter of fact, like he's discussing the weather or the quality of wine. But we both know it's a calculated move. Chess pieces being positioned before the endgame. "They know the ins and outs, the players, the stakes."

Matteo runs Sydney like a well-oiled machine, and Antonio the Gold Coast. Working with them means more than just oversight; it's an alliance, a triad of power poised to dominate Australia.

"Remember, though," Luca adds, and there's something in his voice that makes my blood run cold. "Power isn't given—it's taken. Keep that hunger alive."

"Always." My response is a promise, an oath carved into my soul. A vow to rule, to protect, to never forget where I came from or who I am. Gabriel Gallo—30 years old, born of violence, baptised in blood, and absolutely ready to reign over the chaos that is my birthright. But I'm also a man who's lost the only thing that's ever mattered to him, and I'm starting to think that maybe I deserve this. Maybe I deserve to be consumed by this empire. Maybe I deserve to become exactly what my father is.

The old man finally takes his seat and leans back in his chair. "There's one more thing," he says, and I can feel something shifting in the air between us.

"Yes…," I prompt him, my patience running as thin as the gold leaf on these old walls.

"Your friends," he says, pausing as his eyes narrow in a way that makes my stomach clench. "Catcher and Aurelio. They've been your sidekicks since you were all snot-nosed brats stealing cigarettes."

I can't help but smirk at the memory, even though the smile feels wrong on my face. "Yeah and look how we turned out."

"Exactly." Luca's face is stone, his eyes betraying the hint of a smile. "They could serve as your right-hand men if that's what you want. If you trust them."

"Trust them?" A laugh rips from my throat, harsh and genuine, but it sounds hollow even to my own ears. "With my life, old man. They're my brothers, not just by choice, but by the shit we've waded through together." The shit that's left us all broken, numb and incapable of feeling anything real.

"Then it's decided." He nods once, and it feels like a gavel slamming down, finalising a verdict. "But remember, they may be your brothers, but this is a business. It's up to you to train them and shape them into the lieutenants you need."

"Consider it done." The words are like a blade sliding home—smooth, precise and with deadly intention. "I'll mould, sharpen, and point them where we need them most." Just like my father did to me. Just like I'm going to do to everyone who comes after me. The cycle continues, generation after generation, each one more broken than the last.

Chapter 6

Alba

The air is thick with the scent of musk and bourbon, a sure sign that tonight The Velvet Chamber will be hosting the city's elite. I trace my fingers along the cool surface of the bar, the varnish smooth against my skin, as I try not to think about how many times I've stood in this exact spot, how many times I've watched politicians and businessmen walk through those doors; men, ready to purchase whatever depravity they're craving, this is the bar out the back, the one for the most depraved and cruel.

"Anna." Dan's voice cuts through the low hum of conversation, and my entire body goes rigid. He's leaning against the mahogany door frame, his eyes piercing in a way that makes my stomach churn with a sickening mixture of fear and resignation. "You're up tonight."

I know exactly what he is saying; the wealthy politician is back for more. The one with the smile that's all teeth and no heart, the one whose reputation for cruelty precedes him like an unshakeable shadow. I've seen him many times, and the memory of our last encounter is a wound that's only just starting to heal. It took 3 days before I could walk without wincing, before the bruises faded enough that I could hide them under long sleeves. The thought of spending another night with him makes my skin crawl, makes me want to claw my way out of this place and never look back.

But I can't do that. I've been trapped in this world for 13 years. since I was 17 years old and my father decided to sell me to the highest bidder. 13 years of being passed around from hand to hand, of learning to disappear inside myself, of becoming less and less human with each passing day. 13 years of wondering if Gabe knows what happened to me.

Thinking these things always cuts deep. These are the things I try not to think about because it's too painful, too complicated, too wrapped up in hope, despair and a love that feels like it happened in a different lifetime. Does he know that his family did this to me? Is that why he never came for me? Or does he simple not care?

I want to believe he doesn't know. I need to believe he's never known. Because if Gabe knew what is happening to me, if he knew his father's empire has been built on the suffering of girls like me, and he's done noth-ing…Well, I don't think I could survive that knowledge. It would destroy the tiny part of me that's left.

"Of course, Master," I reply, betraying none of the turmoil that swirls within me, like a gathering storm. My submission is a performance, knowing full well the conse-quences should I ever miss a step. Dan has taught me well.

He's taught me that resistance only brings pain and compliance is the only way to survive.

"Get changed," he instructs, tilting his head towards the back where a myriad of costumes await, each one a different level of degradation. "The pink latex tonight. He's specifically requested it."

My stomach drops. The pink latex. The gimp suit. The one that leaves me completely exposed, vulnerable, and makes me feel like I'm suffocating even before the night begins. I nod, unable to trust my voice, as I turn towards the dressing room, I feel his gaze lingering on me like a brand.

My steps are heavy and deliberate, the illusion of choice is sometimes the only armour one has in this world. If I take my time and move slowly enough, maybe I can convince myself that I'm choosing this, that I have some agency in what's about to happen. It's a lie, but mentally, it's a necessary one.

Inside the dressing room, I stare at my reflection in the mirror for a long moment. I take two seconds to breathe through the panic, before I push it all inside where it is safe and can't come out to play.

I begin the familiar ritual, slipping away from Alba and into the role that this cruel stage demands. Tonight, I will wear a facade, a counterfeit version of myself, tailored to the desires of a man who sees me as nothing more than a toy to be broken.

The other girls help me, their hands moving with practiced motions as they slip the pink latex over my limbs. We don't talk much anymore; all too broken for any actual conversation. But there's a silent understanding between us, a shared knowledge of what it means to exist in this place. One of them, a girl named Sophie who's been here almost as long as I have, whispers encouragement as she tucks every stray strand of my auburn hair out of sight.

"Easy," she says, her hands gentle despite the cruelty of what we experience. "You've got this."

But I don't got this. I'm not sure I ever did. The latex clings to my skin, suffocating me, and I feel the claustrophobic heat building beneath it. It's like being buried alive, like being entombed in my own skin. I think about Gabe, about that kiss we shared when we were 17, when the world seemed vast and full of possibilities. I think about how he tasted of sugar and hope, and how that moment felt like the beginning of something beautiful.

I wonder if he remembers that kiss. Its seems to be the only thing I think about these days. Maybe because it was the last time I felt loved, or needed, maybe I think of it and him daily because I like to torture myself, longing for a man who's family sold me into the sex trafficking trade.

I hope he searched for me, because at least if he looked, it means I mattered. It means the moments we shared meant something. But if he's forgotten about me, if he's moved on with his life while I've been trapped in this hell... that would be a different kind of torture altogether.

I stand before the full-length mirror, taking in the grotesque caricature I've become. My body is segmented by the suit's cruel design, left vulnerable at the nipples—an objectified offering for the lustful gaze of a man whose appetite runs darker than most. I look like a piece of meat, like something to be consumed and discarded. The memory of our last encounter pulses with pain, and I have to grip the edge of the vanity to steady myself.

"Looking good, Anna." Dan's voice slithers into my ear, his breath hot against the exposed nape of my neck. His words wrap around me like chains, laden with implications I can't dwell upon. I nod, mute behind the mask, my agreement as hollow as the echo of footsteps down an empty hall. His hands linger at the small of my back in mocking reassurance, and I have to fight the urge to flinch away from his touch.

"Make sure he's satisfied," he orders, his voice carrying an edge of threat. "I don't want any complaints."

"Yes, Master," I reply, the muffled voice that emerges foreign to me. It's the voice of the compliant creation that has been shaped by necessity, for survival, after 13 years of learning that resistance only brings pain. It's a lie we both believe, for different reasons. He sees only what he desires—a reflection of his own twisted dominion. I see the unspoken truth, that each night spent in his bed, any demand met with reluctant acquiescence, chips away at the facade I present to the world.

Yet, even as I bend to his will, there remains a part of me untouched by his claim. A secret alcove buried deep within my mind where I keep the remnants of who I once was, and who I still long to be. There, amidst the memories, in that safe place, is Gabe.

I turn towards the abyss that awaits, and each stride is an act of rebellion, though Dan will never know it. With each breath, I retreat further, away from the gaping maw of the Blue Room and its Saint Andrew's Cross, away from the politician with his cruel hands and insatiable hunger.

Instead, I escape to Gabe, to that stolen moment when we were 17.It's in that fleeting memory I find solace, strength, and hope against the darkness seeking to consume me.

The heavy door to the Blue Room swings open with an ominous creak, the sound is a prelude to the night's grim show. I step inside, the latex of my suit clinging and contorting with my every move, suffocating me in its pink embrace. The scent of musk and leather greets me, wrapping around my senses like a shroud. The room is dimly lit, designed to cast a shadow on the worst of what happens within these walls.

He's already here, his presence an oppressive ghoul in the shadows. My heart hammers against the restrictive material as he motions towards the Saint Andrew's Cross, positioned like an altar at the centre of the room; it looms over us, its purpose clear and unyielding. I've been tied to this cross more times than I can count. I know every inch of it, every splinter, every cruel angle designed to maximise vulnerability and pain.

With reluctant steps, I approach the cross, each footfall a drum against the cold, hard floor. Once I reach it, I turn my back towards the wooden beams, raising my arms in silent surrender. I can feel his eyes on me, studying me as if I'm some prized animal he's preparing to exhibit. The objectification is complete. I'm not a person anymore. I'm just a thing to be used.

His hands move to secure mine, and I notice the rings of gold that adorn his fingers, symbols of his wealth and power. The rope snakes around my wrists as he fastens me to the top of the cross, pulling the knots tight until they bite into my flesh. I wince inwardly but keep my face impassive, refusing to give him the satisfaction of seeing my discomfort.

I hate rope. I despise how it confines and labels me as something less than human—a commodity to be used and discarded on a whim. But today, the latex serves as my ally; its sleek barrier preventing the harsh twine from tearing into my skin as it has done before. I'm grateful for the small mercy.

"Good," he murmurs, a serpent's hiss of approval, and I can't help but wonder if he senses my inner rebellion. "Very good."

I remain silent, my eyes fixed on a point far beyond the walls of this cursed room. In my mind, I cling to the fragments of another life, one where I am not a marionette performing for the whims of men like him.

His cold fingers command my limbs with a familiarity that makes my stomach churn. The metal of the spreader bar is icy and unforgiving against my sweltering skin; the cocoon of pink latex causing me to overheat. He adjusts the bar mercilessly, pulling it to its maximum length. The strain tugging at my muscles, a dull reminder of my own fragility. And yet, no pain sears through me as it should have; I've disassociated already, drifting far from here, sailing on the wings of my mind to the only thoughts that once made me smile, and it's here I'll stay, while my body is broken once again.

Chapter 7

Gabriel

9 Months later

The buzzing of my phone cuts through the silence like a knife, an all too familiar name flashes across the screen. Dad. I know what this call is about before I even answer. Although I've been expecting it, dreading the moment when I'd have to walk into that warehouse and do the one thing I don't want to do in the job I'm about to inherit.

I answer, "Shipment's in," he grunts without preamble. His voice cold and businesslike, as if he's discussing the weather instead of human beings.

"Got it," I reply, my voice hollow even to my own ears. I tap the end call button and shove the phone back into the pocket of my jacket. My hands are shaking slightly, and I grip the steering wheel of my black Mercedes G-class to steady them. The engine roars to life, eager to devour the distance between me and the warehouse, I can't help but feel like I'm driving towards my own execution.

The Melbourne night is a shroud of darkness as I drive, the city lights flicker like distant stars slowly being snuffed out. My mind is a whirlwind of thoughts, each one darker than the last. It's been 9 fucking months since I've gotten sucked deeper into this twisted world, 9 months since my father began handing me the keys to an empire built on blood and suffering. Every day feels like I'm wading through a swamp—mud sucking at my boots, trying to drag me under, and I'm not even sure I'm fighting anymore.

Only 3 more months. 90 days until every decision, every life, every illegal operation falls squarely on my shoulders. 90 days until I become the man I've always feared I'd become. 90 days until I'm officially responsible for the human trafficking shit show that makes my stomach turn and my soul scream.

I park outside the non-descript building that houses more than just crates and boxes, and the steel door slams behind me with a finality that makes my chest tighten. The warehouse is dimly lit, the stench of fear and despair hanging in the air is almost suffocating and I have to force myself to breathe.

My eyes adjust quickly to the darkness, and that's when I see them. 20 or so women huddled together like cattle waiting for slaughter, their faces etched with terror and confusion. Their ages range from 16 to 40, but in here, age is just another thing that means shit—just another detail for inventory; they are now just another piece of merchandise to be catalogued and sold.

One of them is 17. The same age Alba was when I kissed her for the first time. The same age she was when she disappeared. The sight hurts my already battered heart, and I have to grip the edge of a nearby crate to keep from falling to my knees.

"Fuck!" I mutter under my breath, the surge of anger boiling up inside me is so intense, I think it might consume me whole. I swallow it down and lock it away in the deepest part of myself, a part that's already dead. I can't afford to show weakness here, not in front of them, not in front of my men. They look up at me with wide, pleading eyes, but they don't see Gabe Gallo, the boy who once believed in love, hope and a future that didn't involve this nightmare. They see their captor; an executioner: a monster.

"Line up!" I demand with a false authority that leaves a bitter taste in my mouth, like I've eaten ash and broken glass. In a mix of sobs and whispered prayers, they scramble to obey and I feel something inside me die a little bit more.

I walk past them, each face is a mirror that reflects back a piece from my dark soul. This isn't the life I wanted; it's the one I'm chained to—a legacy written with blood, tears and the screams from women like this. And as much as I used to revel in the violence and control, as much as I used to think that I wanted this power, a part of me, the tiny part that's still human, is screaming on the inside.

"Keep it together, Gabe," I whisper to myself, clenching my fists until my knuckles turn white, until the pain becomes something I can focus on instead of the horror surrounding me. "Just a little longer."

But even as I say it, I know the truth. It's not about

time; it never has been. It's about the chains and whether I have the balls to break free of them before they drag me into hell with every other degenerate. And I'm starting to think I don't. I'm starting to think I'm already in hell, and I've been here so long that I can't remember what the outside world looks like.

Jesus Christ, I think as I scan the sea of faces before me. Most of them—perhaps Thai or Chinese—have a similar hollowed-out expression. They were sold a dream, signed their names on dodgy contracts, with bastards who promised them the world only to deliver them straight to hell. I know their story because I've heard it a thousand times. I also know what's going to happen to them because I've seen it happen to countless others.

It doesn't matter if they've been smuggled in crates or waltzed through customs with forged papers. They're here now, and this is business. My business; or it will be, once the old man fully hands over the reins. Once I officially become the monster he's been slowly transforming me into.

I pace down the line, my polished shoes thumping against the cold concrete floor, and I have to keep the disgust off my face. I can't let these girls see the rage brewing inside me, can't let them see that I'm just as trapped as they are, just in a different way. Because deep down, where the darkness curls around my heart, I know I'm part of the problem. I'm about to become the head of this whole twisted circus, and I'm not sure I can stop myself from becoming exactly like my father.

"Move!" I snap. "Let's get this over with."

The women flinch, shuffling obediently as I walk by.

This is my inheritance: a legacy of flesh and fear, nothing but broken lives and shattered dreams. And even as my gut twists, even as I loathe the thought of taking over the throne in this vile kingdom, a part of me gets off on the power. A part of me is already sitting on that cold and unyielding throne, and that's the part that terrifies me the most.

This isn't just taking over a business—it's a fucking descent into madness, and I'm falling faster than I ever thought possible.

I look over to see Catcher lounging against a crate with his inked arms folded, there's something different about him, like an electric energy radiating off him. His eyes are bright, almost feverish, and his predator's smile is sharper than I've ever seen it. This bastard loves violence more than anything else in this world. He thrives on it, lives for it, breathes it in like oxygen.

"Looks like you're in a good mood," I note, watching him practically vibrate with anticipation. "What's got you so wired?"

"Fight tomorrow night," Catcher says, his voice dripping with excitement. "Some bastard's been talking shit, and I finally got him to agree to step into the ring with me." He cracks his knuckles, the sound echoing throughout the warehouse like a gunshot. "I'm gonna break every bone in his fucking face. Make him regret he ever opened his mouth."

He's completely lost in the anticipation of it, his pupils dilate, his breathing hitches. This is what turns him on— the promise of violence, the chance to hurt someone, to dominate them physically. He's my brother, my best friend, and he's a monster. We all are.

Aurelio is here too, leaning against a stack of crates, but his attention focuses on one of the younger girls. He's got a look of disgust on his face, one that makes him look like he's not just a predator, but a man with secrets.

"Got a date tomorrow night," he says to me, his eyes gleaming with a sick kind of anticipation. "Remember that politician's daughter? The one from the charity gala last month? Her father owed me a favour, I finally called it in. She's all mine for the evening." He licks his lips, Aurelio has had his eyes on that girl for years, but she's turned him down again and again; well until now that is.

I shove past them both, pushing open the door to my father's office with more force than necessary. The old man sits behind his desk, a king surveying his corrupt kingdom. His cold and calculating eyes meet mine, and I see my future reflected in them. This is what I'm going to become. This is the man I'm going to end up.

"Gabriel," he says, and his voice is calm and measured, like he's not about to ask me to do something that will strip away another layer of my humanity. "You need to go take polaroids of the women."

"Isn't that what we have minions for?" I challenge, my anger now simmering just beneath the surface; threatening to boil over.

He levels a hard stare at me. "Today, it's your job. Learn every aspect of the business, figlio. You need to understand what you're inheriting. You need to know exactly what this life costs."

Without another word, I grab the camera, heavy in my

hand—a tangible reminder of the legacy I'm about to inherit. Walking out, I can't shake the feeling that each snap of the shutter will capture a piece of my soul to be sold alongside these women. I'm going to become a merchant of human suffering, and there's nothing I can do to stop it.

"Alright, one at a time!" I bark, my voice hard and cold, the voice of a man I don't recognise. They obey, their eyes hollow, resigned to their fate. As I raise the camera, I feel the monster inside of me stir, feeding on the power, even as I loathe myself for it. The two parts of me are at war, and I'm not sure which one is going to win.

"Face!" I order, snapping the first picture. *"Now turn!"*

Their compliance is mechanical in its efficiency. Each click of the camera is a gunshot in the quiet of the warehouse, each flash a brief illumination of the darkness we're all trapped in. I'm documenting their bodies like they're merchandise, like they're not human beings with hopes, dreams and families who are probably looking for them.

"Next!" I mutter, moving to the next woman in line I feel the silent accusation in each of their eyes. They know what I am. They know what I'm doing. And I know too. I know exactly what I am, and I'm starting to think that knowing doesn't make it any better.

"Real name?" I ask, not sure why I bother. It doesn't matter. Nothing matters anymore.

"Have you been sold before?"

"Age?"

Their answers are murmurs lost in the vastness of the space, carried away on the stale air as if the universe itself is trying to forget the horrors within these walls. But I can't forget. I'm going to carry this with me forever.

"Strip!" I command, devoid of emotion. The camera feeling like a brick in my hands, a tool for torment as I document their exposed vulnerabilities for future transactions; it's like creating a catalogue of suffering, and I'm the one holding the pen.

"Turn around!"

Snap. Flash. Another soul stolen. Another piece of me gone. This is the inferno where my humanity has come to die. And I'm voluntarily standing right at its centre, waiting for the flames to consume me whole.

The shutter snaps again, another face and body frozen in time—commodities in my father's twisted empire. I don't know how many I've done now; their all starting to blur together. Every click, every whir of the Polaroid as it spits out another image, is like a fucking dirge for the dying pieces of my conscience.

"Name!" I bark at the next one, refusing to look her in the eye. She's just another number, another product, and knowing her name makes it personal, so I try and block out her answer. I can't afford personal connections—not in this business, not in this life. Personal connections are what destroy you.

"Li Hua," she whispers, quivering like a plucked string on a broken violin.

"Age?"

"22," she replies, eyes darting to the floor.

"Previous owner?" The words scald my throat as they come out, each syllable a betrayal of what little humanity I have left.

She nods, a slight jerk of the head, giving all the confirmation I need. I scribble something nonsensical on the clipboard—it doesn't matter. None of it matters. Or it will matter too much, and I can't afford to let myself think about it.

"Take off your clothes!" My command is stripped of emotion, but inside I'm seething; a volcano ready to erupt. I'm so angry I can barely see straight, but the anger isn't directed at her. It's directed at myself, at my father, at this entire fucked-up world that I'm trapped in.

I watch this girl named Li Hua as she sheds her layers, and I feel the heat rising behind my eyes, a rage so potent it could set the world ablaze. But it's concealed with the cold exterior I've had to perfect over the years, the mask I wear so no one notices how broken I really am.

Click. Whir. Another piece of someone's soul torn away, filed under 'G' for Gallo, for guilt, for the grave we're all heading towards.

"Turn around!" I say with disgust, directed more at myself than her.

She turns and the camera captures the curve of her spine, the vulnerability of being exposed and alone in this warehouse of horrors. I'm documenting her suffering, and I'm going to have to live with that for the rest of my life.

Chapter 8

Alba

Dan called me into his office just after we arrived tonight. Normally I help the girls get the club ready before I'm shoved out the back with one or two men for the night. He swivels in his chair, a predator surveying his domain, and fixes me with a look that hints at the oil-slick nature of his authority. I've learnt to read the micro-expressions on his face, the small tells that indicate whether I'm about to be rewarded or punished. Today, I'm not sure which.

"Anna," he begins, his voice low and deceptively soft, the kind of voice that makes my entire body go rigid with anticipation. "You'll be working the floor tonight."

A flicker of surprise appears on my face before I can stop it, but I'm quick to squash it, schooling my features back into the mask of compliance. The floor. Not the Blue Room. Not one of the private chambers. The floor is a reprieve, a lighter sentence in this prison, and it seems almost like a reward—if anything in this place could be called such.

But relief is a dangerous thing. Relief means letting my guard down, means thinking I might have a moment to breathe, and in this world, those moments are usually followed by something worse.

"Is there a particular reason?" I dare to inquire, but with respect. It's not like Dan to shuffle the deck without cause. There's always a reason, always some angle. Nothing he does is random or kind.

He leans back, fingers steepled and regards me with cool green eyes that never seem to miss a beat. Those eyes have watched me suffer countless times. Those eyes have seen me at my most vulnerable and broken, and they've never shown a shred of mercy.

"The Blue Room's out of commission; one of the pipes sprang a leak," he says, and there's displeasure in his voice at the inconvenience. "And just to sweeten the pot, two of the girls are off sick."

The Blue Room is prime real estate in this establishment, its absence from tonight's roster is a definite thorn in Dan's side. As for the girls, sickness is a luxury few can afford here. We don't get sick days. We don't get time off. We just keep working until our bodies give out completely. But I can't help the pang of concern for them anyway. We're all bound by invisible chains, but some are heavier than others.

"I need you to bus drinks to the VIP area and entertain the men there," he sneers at me, and the words a command wrapped in velvet but the edges could slice through bone.

I nod again, managing to keep my expression neutral, my mind carefully partitioning away the dread that seeps at its edges. A breath I hadn't realised I was holding escapes in a silent sigh of relief. The simple task is a reprieve, a small mercy. I can serve drinks. I can paint my lips with smiles and fill the air with laughter, as light as champagne bubbles. It requires only charm.

As I turn to leave, a flicker of gratitude ignites within me. I got off easy tonight. The thought brushes against my consciousness like a feather over raw skin. The whip marks on my back still throb with a persistent ache, making every movement a study in pain management. They're hidden beneath my clothes, but not from my mind's relentless replay. Two days have passed, yet the healing has barely begun. Usually when I am injured from a client this badly dan would leave me home and make me service him. Or he will only hand me out to clients who want me fully dressed.

"Wear something that hides your back, but leave every-thing else on display," Dan orders. I nod, not trusting my voice without betraying the quiver of unease along my spine. The fact that he's thinking about my wounds, that he's aware enough to know I need to hide them, is somehow more terrifying than if he'd just ignored them. It means he's invested in my appearance, in my marketabil-ity. It means he is always thinking of my resale.

In the changing room, the fluorescent lights hum a monotone lullaby above me. My fingers trace the hem of the high-necked one-piece laid out before me. It's an unapologetically designed outfit, its purpose solely for the seedy eyes of men, who hunger for flesh like piranhas. Slipping into the garment feels like sliding into an alter ego, becoming Anna instead of Alba, becoming the thing they want me to be, instead of the person I actually am.

The fabric clings to my curves, concealing the crimson lines etched into my flesh and with each movement, the g-string back teases the thin line between pain and sensuality. It's a clever costume; it covers the evidence of my transgressions while presenting the only asset I'm supposed to own—my body—to the world. Or rather, to the VIPs who will see what I 'choose' to show them, which is everything.

I study myself in the mirror, turning slowly to ensure the marks are indeed invisible. Although the whip marks are hidden, the emotional scars are written all over my face if you know how to read them. I've learnt to hide those too. I've learnt to make my eyes empty, my smile hollow and my entire presence a blank slate for men to project their fantasies onto.

A cool and gratifying wave of relief washes over me. Tonight, my body will be on display, but my wounds will remain my own. At least for a few hours, I won't be tied to a cross. For a few hours, I won't be at the mercy of someone's cruelty. For a few hours, I can pretend that I still have some small measure of control.

Placing the black velvet mask on my face, the one all floor workers are made to wear, I turn and walk out. The mask is supposed to protect my identity, to give me a sense of anonymity, but it's just another layer to the performance, another way to hide who I really am. Beneath the mask, I'm still Alba. Beneath the mask, I'm still screaming.

The clink of glasses and the murmur of conversations swell as I push through the velvet curtains that separate the VIP floor from the rest of the establishment. A dim, amber glow bathes the room, casting long shadows that slither across the plush carpet like silent serpents. The scent of expensive cologne and anticipation hangs in the air like a toxic cloud, suffused with the subtle notes of aged whiskey and Cuban cigars. I navigate the maze of leather sofas and mahogany tables with familiarity, a tray of crystal flutes balanced in my hands. With careful steps, I move with grace, the high neck of my one-piece brushing against my throat—a choker created from the fabric meant to protect and tantalise. I feel eyes on me, heavy and expectant, tracing the outline of my body as if their gazes alone could cut through the cloth and reveal the secrets it guards.

These men are powerful. I can tell by the way they carry themselves, by the expensive watches on their wrists and the casual way they discuss deals that probably involve millions of dollars. They're the kind of men who are used to getting whatever they want. They're the kind of men who see women like me as commodities to be purchased, used and then discarded.

I wonder if Gabe is like these men now. I wonder if he sits in rooms like this, discussing business over expensive whiskey and treating women like they're nothing more than an object to be owned.

"Drinks, gentlemen?" My question weaving into the baritone hum of negotiations and illicit deals. My voice is smooth, practiced and designed to be pleasing without being memorable. I'm a ghost, a phantom, a presence that's meant to be felt but not acknowledged.

A hand, adorned with a ring that catches the light with its audacity, waves me over. I approach, my smile never reaching the sanctuary of my eyes; a sanctuary hiding the cyclone of emotions I truly feel. I pour the amber liquid with a precision that betrays none of the terror running through my veins. My hands are steady, even though on the inside I'm falling apart.

"Thank you, darling," the man says with a predatory grin, his words dripping with an innuendo that doesn't require decoding. He's already undressed me with his eyes, already imagining what he could do to me if he had the chance. And the terrifying part is, he probably could. If he wanted me badly enough and if he offered Dan enough money, he could probably have me for the night.

"Of course," I reply, my voice a perfect blend of warmth and distance. I'm good at this. I've had 13 years to perfect the art of being present while being completely absent.

One of them reaches out as I pass, his hand brushes against my hip in a way that's meant to be casual but feels like a violation. I don't flinch. I don't pull away. I just smile and move on, because that's what I do. That's what I've learnt to do. I endure to survive. I let my body be used while I disappear into myself, my mind retreating to a place where none of this is real.

As I move through the VIP area, refilling glasses and accepting compliments that feel like insults, I catch sight of my reflection in one of the mirrors. The mask covers half my face, but I can still see the emptiness in my eyes. I can still see the ghost of the girl I used to be, fading a little bit more with each passing day.

A man notices my moment of weakness and mistakes it for something else entirely. He reaches for my hand, his fingers trailing up my arm in a way that makes my skin crawl.

"You okay, beautiful?" he asks, his voice dripping with false concern.

"Of course," I say, pulling my hand away gently, maintaining the smile that's become my armour. "Just thinking about how thirsty you gentlemen must be."

He laughs, and I move on, disappearing back into the performance, back into being Anna, back into being the thing they want me to be. Because that's all I know how to do anymore. That's all I'm allowed to do.

Chapter 9

Gabriel

T he last click of the camera bounces off the cold warehouse walls, feeling like a gunshot in the silence. I lower it, my fingers linger on the edge as if it's the trigger of my Beretta. The room falls quiet for a moment, the only sound is the ragged breathing of the women huddled together. They may be merchandise to be bartered over, but it cuts into my core seeing them like this.

"Alright, that's enough," I mutter, mostly to myself. I can't look at their faces anymore. I don't want to see the fear, the resignation, or the tiny sparks of defiance that some of them still cling to. It's too much.

"Get them out of here!" I order, rubbing the back of my neck where tension has knotted my muscles into concrete. The air feels heavy, charged with despair and the sour taint of guilt that clings to my suit like cigarette smoke.

"Sure thing, boss," someone replies, and I don't bother looking up to see who. The shuffle of feet and quiet words of command fill the space as the women are herded out.

My job may be done, but it leaves a bitterness in my mouth, with the images forever imprinted in my mind's eye, like scars that will never fully heal.

I shove the camera into its case with more force than necessary, and I can feel the walls closing in around me. Each desperate face is another brick entombing me, another reminder of what I've become. They aren't supposed to get to me. They are another chess piece in a game that pays in blood money and broken spirits. But here I am, standing in the middle of the board, feeling every bit the pawn myself.

My father's voice echoes in my head, his lessons etched deeper than the ink on my skin. "We're predators, Gabe. Not prey. You show any cracks in that armour, and they'll tear you apart." He's right. Weakness has no place in the Gallo bloodline. And this—this feeling of revulsion, this guilt, this need to see them as human—this is weakness.

I straighten up, clenching and unclenching my fists. Money. Power. Control. That's what matters. That's what I'm bred for. Feeling sorry for anyone—especially those caught in our web—is a distraction I can't afford.

I shove the door open, the camera bag in my hand feeling like an anchor as I cross the threshold into my father's office, the photos of tear-streaked faces and defeated eyes clasped in my grip.

"Here," I drop the stack of glossy misery onto the mahogany desk. My father barely glances up from the papers he's perusing as he reaches for the photos.

"Good," he grunts, his fingers flipping through the images with clinical detachment. "Any issues?"

"None," I lie smoothly. Issues? Yeah, there are issues. But none that would interest the old man, unless it messes with the bottom line. And my conscience isn't about to make us lose a single dollar.

My father's hand is steady as he keys in the combination, the tumblers of the safe clicking like the bones of our enemies under pressure. The thick metal door swings open with a groan—a sound as familiar to me as my own heartbeat.

"Here are the old reports," Luca says. He doesn't need to look at me; I know what to do. "If any of them are resales, you update the file. If they're new meat, fill out a fresh form and add them to the pile."

I nod, a mechanical gesture devoid of feeling. The safe is a monster, housing hundreds of folders, stuffed with details about the lives we trade like stocks. Every new entry is another soul caught in our web.

"Last known name is your guide for the resales," he continues, stepping aside to let me dig into the abyss of records. "You know the drill."

"Got it," I mutter, my hand diving into the cold metal mouth. My fingers brush against the edges of countless folders, each one a story of a life bent beneath our will. The M section is towards the back. As I flip through the names, the paper cuts remind me that even in this line of work, there are still ways to bleed. I pull out the new files, counting them off. 20 in total; fresh meat for the grinder. 19 of them will be simple: fill out the form, add the pictures, done. But it's the repetition of it all, the sheer volume of human suffering being catalogued and filed away like it's nothing, makes my stomach turn.

"Remember, time is money, Gabe," my father says, his impatience a living thing in the cramped office. "And money is something we don't piss away."

"Understood," I reply automatically, but my mind is elsewhere. Somewhere darker, somewhere deeper, where the lines between right and wrong blur into nothingness. A place where humanity is non-existent and monsters like us thrive.

I scribble on the forms, my handwriting a jagged line of contempt. Dates, places, prices—the banality of evil distilled into bureaucratic bullshit. With each stroke of the pen, I feel the darkness growing within me, the beast fed by every transaction I record. Paper trails for human souls. There's irony here, or maybe just the universe's cruel sense of humour. Either way, it's all part of the gig, part of the legacy I'm bound to inherit, whether I like it or not.

The last folder snaps shut with a finality that brings temporary relief, my hands feel dirtier every time they touch one of the godforsaken files. I push back from the desk, the chair squealing under the abrupt movement, and I stand up, shaking off the restlessness crawling under my skin.

I need to get out of here. I need to get away from the weight of what I've done today, from the faces of the women, from the knowledge that I'm becoming exactly what I swore I'd never become. The walls of this office feel like they're suffocating me, and I need air that doesn't taste like guilt and despair.

"Hey, Gabe," Catcher says, sauntering in with Aurelio close on his heels. Both men's footsteps are heavy and purposeful against the marble floor, the energy radiating from them is electric, manic and dangerous. "You keen to go out? I wanna hit Velvet."

Aurelio's eyes are alight with the same manic energy that always precedes a night of indulgence. He's practically vibrating with anticipation; probably thinking about that politician's daughter he's got lined up for tomorrow night.

Under any other circumstances, I'd need convincing. But right now? Right now I need Velvet more than I need my next breath. I need the noise, the chaos and the beautiful oblivion that comes with the darkness of that club. I need to lose myself and forget about today. I need to forget about the photographs, the files and the women whose lives I've just documented like they're nothing more than inventory.

"Fuck yeah," I say, and I can see the surprise flash across both their faces. They weren't expecting me to say yes so quickly. They were probably preparing their arguments, the persuasion tactics. But I'm already grabbing my jacket, already heading for the door. "Let's go. I need to get out of here before I lose my fucking mind."

"That's what I'm talking about," Catcher grins, his predatory smile widening. "Knew you'd be up for it."

"The women," Aurelio adds with a leer, "are going to be absolutely fucking stacked tonight. I heard they've got some new dancers from overseas. Fresh meat, if you know what I mean."

The phrase makes my stomach clench, but I push the feeling down. I can't think about that right now. I can't think about anything except getting to Velvet and losing myself in the booze, the bodies and the beautifully terrible chaos of it all.

"Perfect," I say, and I mean it. "Let's get out of here before my old man finds something else for me to do."

We head towards the door, and I can feel the tension starting to drain from my shoulders. Velvet is exactly what I need. The club is a place where the rules don't apply, where the darkness is celebrated instead of hidden and where I can be exactly who I am, without pretending to be anything else.

"You good, man?" Aurelio asks, glancing at me with a hint of concern. "You look like you're about to explode."

"Just need to blow off some steam," I say, it's not entirely a lie, I do need to blow off steam. I need to forget about the day, about the photographs, about the hollow eyes of the women I documented. I need to become someone else for a few hours, someone who doesn't carry the weight of the world on his shoulders.

Chapter 10

Alba

The clink of ice against glass punctuates the low hum of conversations as I weave through the crush of bodies, holding my tray high above the fray. The VIP room is a den of lecherous stares and wandering hands. I feel them trailing over me like slithering serpents, each touch igniting a spark of revulsion that flickers across my skin. I dodge another unwelcome advance, slipping away with a smile that never reaches my eyes.

"More champagne, love!" A man in an expensive suit waves me over, his hand already reaching for my hip.

I sidestep him with practiced ease, setting down fresh glasses on his table. "Of course, sir. Can I get you anything else?"

"Just you, darling," he says with a wink that makes my stomach turn.

I smile and move on. This is a dance I know. This is the rhythm I've learnt to move to. The men here are all the same—powerful, wealthy, and convinced that money gives them the right to touch whatever they want. I've learnt to navigate their advances without making them feel rejected, a delicate balance between compliance and self-preservation.

"Anna!" Sophie, one of the other girls calls me over to help her with a tray that's too heavy. I grab the other end, and we move together through the crowd. "These guys are fucking animals tonight," she mutters under her breath. "That one over there tried to put his hand up my skirt."

"Did you report it to Dan?" I ask, though I already know the answer. Dan allows the men to touch, but if they go for places that cost him money he doesn't like it. He usually comes out and tells the men they need to book us for private time if they touch the no-no areas.

"And get whipped for not being friendly enough?" She laughs bitterly. "No thanks. I'll just keep my distance."

We set the drinks down at a table of businessmen who barely acknowledge us. They're too busy talking deals, money and things that don't matter to people like us. Sophie and I exchange a look—the kind of understanding that only comes from shared suffering—and we head back to the bar.

"You good?" she asks, studying my face.

"Yeah," I lie. "Just tired."

"Aren't we all," she says, and she's right. We're all tired. Tired of the hands, the smiles, tired of pretending that this is any kind of life.

I load my tray with fresh drinks, moving on autopilot. A businessman tries to grab my wrist as I pass, and I pull away smoothly, maintaining my smile. "I'll be right back with your order, sir."

The night stretches on like this—drink after drink, hand after hand, smile after smile. I've become a ghost in this place, present but unseen, heard but not listened to. The men here see me as a service, not a person. And today I'm ok with it. I've learnt to make peace with being invisible.

I'm heading back to the bar when I notice the entrance. The heavy door swings open, admitting a blast of cooler air and three silhouettes cut through the club's smoggy atmosphere like sharpened steel. The crowd seems to part for them instinctively, and I can feel the shift in energy. These are not ordinary men.

They move with a predatory grace, their tailored suits screaming of power and an insidious kind of elegance. Even from this distance, I can tell they're different from the usual clientele. They carry themselves with an authority that makes everyone else in the room seem small.

I retreat to the bar, loading my tray with fresh drinks as my gaze lingers on the three men taking their seats in the VIP area. There's something about them that makes my skin prickle with warning. They're the kind of men who are used to getting what they want, the kind of men who see the world as something to be conquered.

I navigate back through the minefield of groping hands and leering smiles, setting drinks down before expectant men with a grace born from necessity. The lewd voices claw at my skin, leaving invisible marks that burn hotter than any physical touch could.

"Here you go," I murmur above the cacophony.

Their nods are curt, distracted by the new apex predators that have claimed their territory.

I steel myself for the short journey to the new arrivals. My heart drumming a relentless rhythm against my ribs, heavy with an anxiety I can't quite name. There's something about these men that feels different; something that's making every nerve ending in my body stand on alert.

"Good evening, gentlemen," I greet, careful to keep my voice steady. "Can I get you anything?"

I look directly at the men, my pulse quickening and my breath catches in my throat. For a moment, everything blurs, and the world seems to tilt on its axis.

The man in the centre, something about him feels impossibly familiar. The way he carries himself. The cut of his jaw. The colour of his eyes.

No. It can't be.

But as clarity pierces the dim lighting, the truth reveals itself like a raw and undeniable wound reopening.

It's Gabe. Gabriel Gallo.

The boy whose laughter once filled my summers with warmth now sits before me, a man carved from the recess of my most haunting memories. He's older, harder and a lot darker. But it's unmistakably him.

My first kiss. My first crush. My soulmate. The boy I loved with my whole heart.

And he's here. In this club. In this place where I'm nothing more than a piece of meat to be used and discarded.

The tray in my hands trembles. One misstep, a single falter on the plush carpet, and the illusion of poise I've so carefully constructed over the years threatens to unravel in a microsecond. My foot catches on an invisible thread of fate, gravity pulling me towards an unwanted destiny.

In the space of a heartbeat, Gabe surges to his feet. His hand shoots out, the blue of his eyes piercing through the dimly lit ambience as he reaches for me. Instincts honed by years of evasion kick in, and I jerk away, my voice a razor-sharp whisper, "Don't touch me!"

A frown forms between those familiar eyes as they narrow—a hint of confusion, maybe even offence, registering in their icy depths. "Okay," he says with a patronising edge as if reprimanding a wayward child, "Kind of your job, but okay."

The words hit like a slap. He doesn't know. He has no idea who I am. He's looking at me like I'm just another girl in a club, just another piece of merchandise to be used and discarded. And the pain of that—the absolute agony of realising he's forgotten me, that the boy I loved has become a man who sees me as nothing—it's almost more than I can bear.

I force a smile. "Can I get you anything?"

He's changed. The boy I knew is gone, replaced by this towering presence in a suit that's tailored to perfection. His dark hair is styled with precision, and his jaw is set in a hard line. But it's his eyes that destroy me. Those blue eyes that once looked at me with tenderness, now look at me with nothing but casual indifference.

"We'll take a bottle of gin. Nolet's, thanks," he says, his voice smooth and commanding. He doesn't even look at me as he speaks, his attention already turned back to his companions.

"Of course," I murmur.

I turn and march away, every muscle coiled tight. Behind the bar, my fingers brush against the chilled

surface of the Nolet's bottle, the frosty glass a balm to the
fire licking beneath my skin. My hands are shaking so
badly I can barely grip it.

He's here. Gabe is here. And he doesn't recognise me.
He doesn't know who I am. He's become exactly what I
feared he'd become—a man of this world, a man who sees
women like me as nothing more than servants to be
ordered around.

The bottle feels impossibly heavy in my hands as I
place it on my tray with three glasses, I can feel his eyes
on me from across the room, but when I look up, he's not
looking at me at all. He's talking to his friends, laughing at
something one of them has said, completely oblivious to
the fact that the girl he once loved is standing ten feet
away, serving him drinks.

And that's what breaks me. Not the fact that he's here.
Not the fact that he's become a monster. But the fact that I
meant so little to him, he doesn't even recognise me. That
our love, that moment under the glow-in-the-dark stars in
my bedroom, meant so little that he's forgotten me
completely.

I carry the tray back to their table, my movements
mechanical, my smile painted on like a mask. I set the
glasses and bottle down in front of them, and when I do,
Gabe finally looks at me. For just a moment, his eyes meet
mine, and I see a flicker of something—recognition?
Confusion? But then it's gone, replaced by the cold indifference of a man looking at a servant.

"Will there be anything else?" I ask, my voice steady
even though I'm falling apart inside.

"That's all," he says, and he turns away.

The pain is exquisite, a knife straight through my chest, twisting, turning, and tearing me apart from the inside. Because the worst part isn't that he's forgotten me. The worst part is that some small, foolish part of me still loves him. Some small, foolish part of me still remembers that kiss, the moment when the world felt infinite and full of possibility.

But that girl is gone. She died 13 years ago, the moment my father sold me to the Gallo's.

Chapter 11

Gabriel

I watch her strut away, hips swaying with a rhythm that twists my gut in a way I can't explain. The dim lighting of the club hangs over her like she's some kind of angel meant for trouble. I feel a strange pull towards her, like an invisible string's tied around my chest and she's yanking on it hard. It's a sensation I'm not used to and a sensation I don't fucking like.

"Who the fuck is she?" Catcher growls beside me, his eyes burning with a familiarly manic glint as he watches her disappear into the crowd. "Do we know her?"

I turn to look at him, catching the predatory leer on his face. Catcher Calcone is built like a tank and inked from his jaw to knuckles, he's just shy of being labelled a psychopath. Women are just another conquest to him, wearing their names like badges of honour under his skin. But this girl, she's not just another name. There's something about her that's gotten under my skin, and I can't shake it.

"Can't remember the face of every girl you fuck?" Aurelio chortles, his laugh bouncing around the table.

I don't join in with their laughter. Instead, I'm anchored to my seat, my eyes drifting back to where she disappeared. It's like she's left a trail of gunpowder and I'm one spark away from being blown to pieces. I hate it. I hate this feeling of being pulled towards something I can't control.

"What about you, Gabe?" Aurelio nudges me, his voice slicing through my thoughts.

I realise I've been silent for too long, stewing in the tumult of my own head; her image branded behind my eyelids. But what am I supposed to say? That she's left an indelible mark on me? That I can't stop thinking about the way she moved, the way she looked at me with something that felt like recognition mixed with fear?

"Something like that," I mutter as my fingers drum on the table.

The truth is, I can't make sense of the magnetic pull that has her at the centre of everything and me spinning. It's not like me. I've spent the last 13 years making a point to not feeling anything for anyone. I've spent 13 years proving that I don't need anyone, that I can take what I want and walk away without looking back. Women are a dime a dozen. I see one I like, I take her for the night, and then I move on. No strings. No complications. No one getting under my skin.

But this one? This one's already burrowing so deep I can feel her in my bones.

I snag on her as she moves with a purpose that doesn't include pandering to the likes of us. A strange ache persisting in my gut, and I don't like it. I don't like the way my eyes continue to follow her around the floor. I don't like that I'm thinking about booking her for the night— something I've never done before. Something I've never even considered before. But my dick is hard from that small encounter.

I've always been the kind of man who takes what he wants, when he wants it. I don't ask for permission. I don't make arrangements. I just take. But with her, I'm actually considering going through Dan, actually considering paying for a private room; which is something I've never done. I traffic women for a living, paying for women in a club like this just doesn't sit right with me, but I can't seem to stop the thought of doing exactly that right now.

It's insane. It's a weakness.

And yet, I can't stop thinking about it.

She appears again, moving between tables like she owns the place. Confidence rolling off her, but it's not the arrogance you see in most—it's quieter, deeper. There's something about the way she carries herself that suggests she's been broken and put back together so many times that she's learnt to hold herself together through sheer force of will.

"Here we go, gentlemen," she says with a well-rehearsed smile, setting down the bottle and three glasses with care. Her fingers brush the back of my hand as she hands me my drink, and for a split second, there's a spark of electricity that surges up my arm and jolts me right in the chest.

I grasp the glass, its coolness pulling me back from the brink of self-absorption. It's just a touch, nothing more. Yet it feels like a challenge, a call to something inside me I've been trying to suppress for years.

Catcher's hand shoots out like a viper, his fingers closing around her delicate wrist with a kind of casual brutality that's always been second nature to him. He yanks her down onto his lap, his arm snaking around her waist to keep her in place.

"Sit tight, doll," Catcher growls against the pulsing beat of the music.

I watch the whole scene unfold, a spectator to the predator-prey dance that we're all too familiar with. She goes rigid on his lap, her body tensing like a bird caught in a snare. But she doesn't say a word. That's the unspoken rule here; the girls who work the floors know their role—to be used by men like us, men with power, who take what they want without asking.

Her obedience should be expected, routine even. But something about it niggles at me, burrowing under my skin and festering there. She's just another girl in a sea of many, yet she isn't. Something about her silence and her stillness, grips me. It must be the hair, I have a weakness for red heads, and she has the type that sends me to my knees.

I lean back in my chair, drink forgotten, as I watch Catcher's hand roam. My jaw tightens, a coil winding up inside me ready to snap. This game, this hunt—it's wearing thin. And for the first time in years, I wonder what the fuck we're all doing.

The girls usually flit around us like moths to a flame, eager to bask in our dangerous allure, in the promise of greenbacks and the high of being chosen by men like us.

But this one is different. She's prickly, like a damn thistle among roses, her edges sharp enough to draw blood.

Catcher, with his devil-may-care smirk, seems to take her resistance as a personal challenge. As his hand slithers up her thigh, a possessive grin plays on his lips, I feel something twist inside me again—a warning signal, maybe, or just the bitter taste of our sick reality.

"Stop it, Catcher!" she yells. Her palm comes down hard against his wrist, slapping it away with a force that makes heads turn. My heart hammers against my ribcage, echoing the shock that ripples through me.

How the fuck does she know his name?

No one calls Catcher by his name, not unless they want it to be their last word. Eyes blazing with defiance, she uses his name like a weapon, and suddenly, the room feels too small, the air suffocating. The curiosity claws at me, a relentless itch demanding to be scratched. Who is she? How does she know us?

I watch Catcher as realisation dawns in his eyes, dark and dangerous as storm clouds.

"Fuckin' hell!" he growls. His hand shooting out, lightning fast as fingers close around her slender neck like iron bands. "How do you know my damn name?"

I lean forward, the edge of the seat biting into me, my ears straining to catch every syllable above the music. Her face, inches from his, masks her true feelings.

She shakes her head, vehemently denying him an answer, her lips pressed into a thin line. With a fierce jerk, she wrenches free from his grasp, her movements swift and desperate. The sight of her fighting back sends a jolt through me—a mix of respect and something darker, something hungry.

"Get your fucking hands off me!" she hisses, venom lacing her words. For a moment, she stands there, a warrior queen surrounded by wolves, before she spins on her heel and storms away, cutting a path through the sea of bodies back to the bar area.

"Figlio di puttana," Catcher mutters, *son of a bitch*. He slams his fist onto the table, sending the glasses to their demise. I remain silent, the echo of her refusal ringing in my ears like a siren song winding its way through the messiness of my thoughts. Who is she? Why did her resistance feel like a challenge meant just for me?

An hour drags by, every tick of the clock mocking me with her absence. She avoids our table as if it's cursed, slinking through the tables, ducking heads, and dodging grasping hands that aren't mine. It niggles at me, this chase without movement, this hunger without satisfaction.

I need to see her again. I need to understand what it is about her that has me so twisted up. And I need to do it in a place where she can't run away.

"Hey, darling," I call to one of the other girls—a brunette with a smirk that could cut glass. She sashays over, her hips promising sins that don't interest me. Not tonight. "I need to put a request to Dan. Tell him I want the red head for an hour."

Her eyes widen for just a heartbeat before the professional glaze slips back in place. She leans forward, her breath a soothing warmth against my ear. Her fingers trace a path down my chest, bold as brass, but I feel nothing.

"Sure thing, handsome," she coos, her lips curl into a smile that knows too much. "I'll put it through for you."

With that, she turns on her heels, hips rolling like the waves of a dark ocean as she retreats to make arrangements. I watch her go, my body tight with anticipation. A private room means no distractions, no interruptions—just me and the woman who's sparked a flame in the cold hearth of my soul.

"Since when do you hire hookers?" Catcher taunts, his voice drips with derision.

I shoot him a glance sharp enough to draw blood. "Call it curiosity," I say, fixing now on the darkness she's vanished into.

The door swings open, and the girl struts back to us. "It's set up," she announces with a smirk. "Sixty minutes in the Red Room."

Her words slither through the din of the club, wrapping around me like a venomous snake. A hot and relentless surge of satisfaction roars through me as I lean back against the plush leather of the booth, a predator's smile curling my lips. She can't run from me in there. And maybe, just maybe, I'll finally understand what it is about her that has me so completely undone.

"It's the red hair isn't, you're always a pussy for red heads mate," Aurelio chuckles, ripe with curiosity. He isn't wrong, If I stood up right now, I would tent my pants, showing off just how hard I get for anything with fiery red hair, and creamy skin.

Chapter 12

Alba

Melissa's footsteps pound the plush carpet as she approaches me. The air carries a chill, prickling my skin, despite the warmth of the dimly lit corridor. I turn, and she says, with the weight of inevitability, "Dan would like to see you."

My heart clenches—a small, rebellious bird within its cage—knowing the summons is not a request but an order. With a nod that feels more like surrender, I gather the tattered edges of my composure around me like a shawl and walk into his office.

The door swings open with a hush, revealing Dan, a man who wears power as comfortably as the tailored suit that clings to him. His desk is a monument of dark wood and authority, serving as his throne. A woman is on her knees in front of him, her movements desperate to satiate his demands. Dan's head rises, cold and calculating eyes the colour of storm clouds bore into me with the precision of a marksman taking aim..

"Anna," Dan murmurs. Without breaking his gaze from

mine, he delivers his judgment with the imperious flick of his wrist, dismissing the woman at his feet as if she's nothing more than a misstep in his choreography of control.

"You need to teach this one better," he says. "Her technique is abysmal." The woman stumbles backward, her eyes downcast in humiliation and fear as her form crumples to the floor.

With an invisible force compelling my steps, I breach the distance between us. "Come here, pet," he commands with an expectation that refuses to be ignored. "Show her how it's done. I cannot have her out there making me look bad when she can't execute even the most rudimentary of tasks."

Resentment rises within me, a silent rebellion against the role I'm perpetually forced to play. And yet, the insidious tendrils of my own survival instincts wrap around my will, guiding me to him.

"Of course, Master," I reply, my voice steady despite the storm of indignation raging inside.

With resignation heavy in my limbs, I sink to the cool floor, a willing captive of Dan's twisted desires. My fingers brush against the warmth of his skin, tentative at first before wrapping firmly around him. Muscle memory guides my touch as I engage my experience, feeling the familiar pulse beneath my grip. The air reeks of lust and power—Dan's favourite perfume.

I massage the head of his penis, each movement purposeful yet detached, as if my hands belong to someone else. With a sigh that never reaches my lips, I lean forward and allow my tongue to trace the slit at the tip. I loathe the reduction of my being to an instrument of pleasure, but it's what he craves, and survival dictates I indulge him.

My lips part as I envelope him, pushing forward until the back of my throat constricts around his girth. There's no pleasure in this for me, only the cold calculus of necessity. But with each motion, I perform with a grace that belies my internal contempt. It's a performance where I'm both the marionette and the puppeteer, choreographing my movements to the silent rhythm of subservience.

Time has eroded the reflex meant to protect, leaving behind a void where instinct once lived. As I hold him in deep in the cavern of my throat, a low hum vibrates from my chest—a counterfeit moan designed to stroke his ego as much as his shaft. It's a calculated mimicry of pleasure, a ruse crafted through years of unsavoury servitude.

Feeling him harden even more, I recognise the signs of his nearing climax. Methodically, I withdraw before enveloping him once more, repeating the motion with the precision of a well-rehearsed routine. My hand, an extension of this choreography, reaches out, finding his balls, and applies pressure that I know will hasten his release.

It isn't long before he succumbs and his body tenses as he spills into me. The taste of cum assaults my senses, always so jarringly salty and disagreeably slimy. I cling to the silent mantra that has become my anchor in these moments. *This is just a moment; it does not define you.* Resistance against the crushing tide of degradation that seeks to claim me.

As the final shudders of his pleasure fade, I remain motionless until I sense his relaxation, the signal that I can finally let go. I disengaged from Dan and watch the string of saliva break as I pull away. "Thank you, pet," he says hoarsely, his eyes already scanning over some document on his desk. "You are needed in the Red Room. You have been booked."

The words 'Red Room' ignite a familiar spark within me—a mixture of relief and resignation. Here is another escape, another role to play in this grand charade. I nod, my smile hollow.

"Cover your back," Dan continues. "Find something crotchless so it can stay on. Don't gross him out."

His words remind me of the marks that mar my skin, vestiges of previous encounters where pleasure and pain intertwined. I turn on my heel and walk away from Dan's office, feeling like I'm reclaiming my composure.

The reflection that greets me in the changing room is both familiar and estranged. My fingers skim over the outfits that hang meticulously in a row, each one a different mask to wear. I select a piece that conforms to Dan's specifications—the ensemble bears semblance to my current attire, but leaves nothing to the imagination where it matters most.

The fabric clings to my curves, accentuating them while strategically covering the past transgressions etched upon my flesh. The need to appear untouched, despite my battered body, is a cruel irony.

I take a deep breath, steeling myself for what may be ahead. There's no room for hesitation or doubt. In the Red Room, I will once again transform into the enigmatic Anna, who wields her sensuality like a weapon, even if beneath it all, she's fighting to preserve the tattered remnants of her soul.

And so, donning my new outfit, I march towards the designated chambers. The door looming before me, promising another round of this twisted game.

Each step towards the red room takes me further from the main floor; away from prying eyes and the covert comments that breeze past like unwelcome spectres. Away from the man with the dark hair and piercing blue eyes. Away from Gabe.

The thought of him being here makes my chest tighten. I can't afford distractions. Not now. Being booked means safety in obscurity, a temporary reprieve from the grinding reality of my existence. It means I don't have to think about the fact that he didn't recognise me. It means I don't have to think about the way he looked at me.

But even as I try to push the thought away, it lingers. He's here. In this place. In this world that destroyed me. And he's become exactly what I'd feared—a man who sees women like me as nothing more than an object to be used and discarded. I wonder how often he comes to the club, I never get to work the main floor, always in the back rooms, booked nightly for the most depraved men in Melbourne City. Is he here all the time and I've just never known?

Entering the red room, my heels sink into the plush carpet, muffling the sound of my steps as I approach the bed. I lay down upon the satin sheets and begin to position myself as expected, legs spread, back arched, sprawled out with an artful grace that belies the screaming silence in my mind.—I'm the very picture of availability, an offering to the insatiable appetites that haunt this place.

My eyes are fixed on the ceiling, tracing patterns in the

intricate plasterwork as if I could conjure some sort of escape within its swirls and flourishes, the sheets are cool against my heated skin, the fabric whispering across my body like a lover's caress that I could never truly welcome. Time slows to a crawl, each second stretching into infinity as I wait for the door to open and the faceless client who will see only what he wants to see: not a woman, but a fantasy made of flesh.

The door clicks open, then closes again, before I hear the words, "Stand up, I want to see what I booked."

My blood instantly runs cold. That voice, I know that voice. It's the voice of the boy I loved, now deepened by years and hardened by the darkness he's embraced. It's Gabe.

Oh God. It's Gabe.

Chapter 13

Gabriel

"Stand up, I want to see what I booked."

The sight that greets me as I step into the Red Room is as deliberate as it is unashamed. There she is, sprawled across the bed like some kind of offering to the gods of lust—legs wide, her pussy on display without a hint of modesty. The dim bedside lamp casts shadows in all the right places, turning her body into a landscape worth conquering, the sight has my cock hardening, pressing against my zipper.

She's wearing the kind of lingerie that leaves nothing to the imagination, a delicate crotchless piece that frames her perfectly, and even from here, I can make out the delicate folds of her pussy, the way the fabric curves around her like it's worshipping her. It's enough to coax a growl from the pit of my stomach, awakening a hunger that demands I take what's so provocatively offered. My hands clench into fists, and I have to remind myself to breathe.

I step forward, my hand instinctively reaching inside my tailored suit jacket adjusting the gun holstered against my ribcage. The weight of it is a comfort, a reminder of who I am and the power I wield. The heat of desire is laced with something else—something I can't quite name, something that makes the back of my neck prickle with warning. There's something about her that feels familiar in a way that makes my entire body tense with anticipation and dread.

Her elbows dig into the mattress as she props herself up, her gorgeous eyes finding mine, and for a fleeting moment, I see something in them—a flicker of recognition that sends a jolt through me, so powerful it nearly brings me to my knees. It's like a ghost has entered the room, like the past has suddenly become present, and I can't quite process what I'm seeing.

And then, like a switch has been flipped, she freezes. Her entire body going rigid, and I watch as the colour drains from her face like someone pulled a plug, letting all her blood run out onto the floor. She looks like she's either seen a ghost or she's looking at death itself.

"Shit!" she hisses between gritted teeth, her voice a razor-sharp whisper cutting through the heavy silence of the room. The word is barely audible, but it carries so much weight, so much fear, that it causes me to pause.

In one clumsy, desperate scramble, she claws her way back up the bed, as if distance can somehow shield her from the inevitable, from me and whatever it is she thinks is about to happen. The sheets tangle around her limbs, the fear giving her graceless movements an urgency that nearly matches my racing pulse. Her retreat is a silent plea, a desperate attempt to put some form of space between us, and yet, there she is—still as much on display as before, still caught in a snare of this twisted game we're playing.

I feel something shift inside me, something dark and possessive that I've been trying to suppress since the moment I saw her on the floor of the club. I want to pin her to that bed. I want to make her understand that there's nowhere to run, nowhere to hide. I want to take what I came here for and make her forget about everything except the feel of me inside her.

But there's something else too, something making me pause, something making the predator in me hesitate for just a moment. The way she's looking at me, the raw terror in her eyes, . Like it's trying to tell me something I should know, like it means something.

"Easy there," I say, my voice rougher than I intend, betraying a hint of my own surprise, my own confusion. "It's just you and me in here."

I watch her— a tangle of lace and raw fear, her body trembling like a leaf in a storm as she tries to shrink into herself at the top of the bed. It's obvious by the way she's cowering that she fears me, that she's terrified of what I might do to her. I'm a well-known figure in these parts with a reputation for ruthlessness that precedes me like a shadow. She probably knows my name and that I'm about to inherit my father's empire, knows that I'm feared by the entire city, not just her.

But her breath hitches, her eyes wide like those of a cornered animal, but there's something else there too, something that makes my blood sing. There's a fire in her gaze, a searing disobedience making my blood hum with need, hunger, and something I can't quite name.

"I thought I asked you to stand?" I say, as I climb onto the bed and lean over her, caging her with my arms on either side of her body. I'm close enough that I can feel the heat radiating off her skin, close enough that I can see the rapid rise and fall of her chest, close enough that I can smell her—a mix of terror and something sweetly floral that's intoxicating and making me want to bury my face in her neck, breathing her in until I'm drowning in her.

Her chest rises and falls rapidly, the pulse at her throat fluttering like the wings of a trapped bird. I can see the fear written all over her face, but underneath the fear is something else. There's something that looks almost like longing mixed with despair and recognition.

She opens her mouth as if to speak, but nothing comes out. Her lips part, her jaw working, but no sound emerges. It's like she's trying to say something but can't find the words, like there's something caught on the tip of her tongue.

"You know me?" I say as I hover inches from her face, our breath mingling in the space between us, the air thick with tension, desire and something darker that I can't quite identify. "Voglio sapere come." *I want to know how.* How does she know me? How did she know Catchers name?

Her eyes blaze as she gathers herself, a flicker of anger flashes across her face like lightning illuminating a dark sky. The fear doesn't disappear, but it's joined by a fierce, burning rage that makes her look dangerous, like she's capable of tearing me apart with her bare hands.

"You're fucking kidding me, right?" she says, her voice shaking with emotion. "I'm that easy to forget?"

"Easy to—what?" I say, tension coiling in my muscles,

my jaw clenching so hard my teeth might crack. This isn't how it's supposed to go down. She's meant to cower and break under the force of my presence, submitting to me without question. Instead, she's throwing my own game back in my face, making me want her even more, to dominate her and sink into that tight pussy of hers.

"Me!" She says, her fragility instantly transforming into a fierceness as her body straightens and her eyes blaze with a fire that's almost beautiful in its intensity. "You and your family fucking took me as payment, Gabe."

The words threaten to unravel everything, to tear apart the carefully constructed walls I've built around my heart. There's something about the way she's looking at me, the way she says my name feels like it should mean something. It's like her tone is trying to tell me something important, something that I've clearly fucking missed since seeing her. I can't place it. I can't remember. My mind is a blank slate she's trying to write something on , but I can't seem to read the words.

I scowl, the confusion gnaws at my insides, biting at me like a rabid dog. "I have no fucking idea who you are," I say, , each word a cold and sharp blade designed to cut. It's true; her face is just a blur in a sea of many, an imprint on the canvas that is my fucked-up life, plus it's half covered by a fucking mask. There have been so many women, so many faces, so many bodies that I've used and discarded without a second thought. How am I supposed to remember one girl among thousands?

But even as I say it, I feel like I'm lying, like I'm missing something crucial, something right in front of my face that I'm too blind to see. Something about her is familiar, tugging at the edges of my memory, trying to break the surface.

With a trembling hand, she reaches up, her fingers grazing the edge of her mask—a flimsy veil of black velvet that's hiding far more than it's revealing, that's been protecting her identity, making her anonymous, making her just another girl in a club full of girls. The fabric slips away, revealing the contours of a face that should've been lost to me—like so many others, so many faces that have passed through my life and left no impression.

But this face; this face is different. This face is familiar in a way that makes my entire world tilt on its axis.

"Your father took me as payment from my dad," she says, her voice steady despite the tremor I can see running through her body. It's a pointed accusation, a branding iron searing into my skin, burning away the last vestiges of my denial.

Time stands still, the very fabric of reality seeming to warp and fray as the pieces click into place like a lock opening. Her face is no longer a blur from the past, but a vivid memory clawing its way to the surface, demanding to be acknowledged, demanding to be felt. Those eyes like emerald pools that have haunted the edges of my dreams for 13 years. That face. That beautifully broken face I've been searching for, that I've been mourning, that I've been trying to forget.

"Alba?" I gasp, the name ripping from my throat like it's dragging over broken glass, tearing me apart from the inside out. My heart hammers against my ribcage with the fury of a caged beast, desperate to break free from the sins of my bloodline, desperate to escape the knowledge that I'm about to receive.

Alba. It's Alba. After 13 years of searching, 13 years of believing she was dead or gone forever, 13 years of trying to numb myself to the pain from losing her, she's here. She's here, in front of me, sprawled across a bed in the Red Room like she's nothing more than merchandise to be used and discarded. And I had purchased one hour with her, the thought makes me want to shoot myself.

"Alba!" I repeat, louder this time as if saying her name will somehow ground me, somehow allow me to make sense of the fact that the girl I loved, the girl I've been searching for, is trapped in my family's hell. My voice cracks on her name, and I can feel something breaking inside me, something that I've been holding together with duct tape and prayer for over a decade.

"Fuck me!" I mutter under my breath, staggering back off the bed, my hand reaching out to steady myself against the wall. Her name is a bullet, and it's hit its mark with lethal precision. I'm supposed to be untouchable, unshakable, a man carved from stone, ice and darkness. But those eyes... the emerald eyes I've dreamed about a thousand times... they unravel my composure completely, tearing apart everything I've built, reducing me to nothing but a man who lost everything and just found it again.

She's here, in front of me, not a ghost or a figment of my imagination, but flesh and blood—a debt personified, a living reminder of the darker workings of my family's empire. And she's been here all along. She's been trapped as a slave, being sold, used and destroyed by the very family I belong to, by the very empire I'm about to inherit.

The realisation hits me like someone's driven a knife straight through my chest. My father took her. My father bought her like she was nothing more than a piece of property, like she was a commodity to be traded and sold. My family has been using her, breaking her, destroying her. And I've been complicit in it. Every time I've walked through these halls, every time I've participated in this business, I've been part of the machinery that's been grinding her into dust.

"Alba?" I say again, my voice rough with emotion, rough with the weight of 13 years of searching, of mourning and of trying to forget. "Jesus Christ... how did I not see it?"

The room spins around us, and for a moment, nothing else exists but the two of us. My pulse races, the darkness pumping through my veins, part hunger, part rage and part something else entirely, something that I don't have a name for.

Chapter 14

Alba

Gabe's silhouette is framed by the soft light of the room, his features carved in a mixture of disbelief and something akin to horror, making my chest tighten with a pain I thought I'd learnt to suppress years ago. I can see the tumultuous storm of questions swirling in his stare, the way his adam's apple bobs like a buoy on rough seas, the way his entire body seems to be warring with itself, trying to reconcile what he's seeing with what he thought he knew.

His stance is rigid like he's been petrified by the sheer sight of me alive and breathing, it's like he's looking at a ghost that shouldn't exist, like the universe has just played the cruellest joke imaginable on him. And something twisting inside me, something that I've been trying to keep locked away for 13 years, something whispering that maybe, just maybe, he doesn't know. Maybe he really has no idea what his family did to me.

But I can't afford to believe that. I can't afford to hope

that the boy I loved is innocent, because if I do, if I let myself believe it, then the pain becomes unbearable. The betrayal becomes absolute. The loss becomes total.

"Alba..." His voice cracks the silence, rough with an emotion I can't quite decipher and hearing him say my name—my real name, not the fake one I've been forced to answer to—does something to me that I'm not prepared for. It breaks something open inside me that I've been holding together with sheer force of will. "What the fuck? You ran away?"

I remain still, watching as he steps closer again, my body tense and ready to move, ready to run, to do what-ever it takes to protect myself. The tension is palpable, thick enough to cut with a knife, a standoff neither of us had prepared for, yet here we are, caught in a surreal moment that feels like it's happening to someone else; it's like I'm watching the whole thing unfold from outside my own body.

"I went and saw your dad," Gabe adds, his eyes searching mine for any telltale sign of deceit or confusion; He went to see my father? "He said you ran away."

The simplicity of his statement belies the complex web of lies that entangle our lives, the intricate dance of decep-tion his family has to have orchestrated to hide what they've done. The reality causes me to snap. Laughter, dark and devoid of any true mirth, erupts from my chest—a cruel sound that seems foreign even to my own ears, it's a sound that doesn't belong to me, that belongs to someone else, someone harder, colder and more broken than I ever thought I'd become. I can see the way it jars him, the way he flinches like I've struck him, like the sound of my laughter is more painful than any punch could ever be.

"Don't play dumb with me, Gabe," I say, the bitterness coating each word like a poisonous venom, as all the rage, pain and despair that I've been swallowing for 13 years finally pours out of me. "Your dad took me as payment for my father's gambling debt! He sold me. He sold me like I was nothing more than a piece of property, like I was a commodity to be traded and exchanged."

I watch as his expression morphs, confusion gives way to anger, his piercing blue eyes simmering with an anger that's directed at me, at the situation, at the world, at everything. The air around us shifts, becoming heavy with unspoken accusations and denials.

"Alba, that's bullshit!" he yells, shaking his head vehemently, causing the strands of his dark hair to fall across his face. His voice holds a tremor of disbelief and denial of a man who's being confronted with a truth that he doesn't want to accept. "My father would never take you. He looked after you, fed you, and treated you like his own daughter!"

The words hang between us, unwelcome truths and comforting lies battling for dominance within the charged silence, and I feel something break inside me even further. Because a part of me—a small, foolish part of me—wants to believe him. Part of me wants to believe that his father took me in out of kindness, that he fed me, clothed me and sheltered me because he cared about me. But I know better. I know what I've lived through, the cold touch of reality that has painted my days in shades of grey long before Gabe had found himself standing here, wrestling with an image of a man he thought he knew.

But in the end, it's not about what he believes. It's not about what he wants to be true. It's about the scars that mar more than just my skin—the kind of scars that tell stories no one wants to hear, least of all the son of my keeper, the son of the man who destroyed me.

Traitorously hot tears begin their descent down my cheeks, carving clear paths through the makeup clinging to my skin, like a mask I can't remove, even when I'm alone. The tears feel foreign.

"I don't know what to tell you," I say, my voice barely above a whisper as my eyes lock onto his—those deep pools of cerulean that once promised safety but now seem to question the very essence of my being, that seem to be asking me if I'm telling the truth, if I'm lying or if I'm crazy.

The room seems to close in around us, crushing the chasm of understanding that lies between Gabe and I, the vast distance that 13 years has created between us. The smell of tobacco and old wood serves as a reminder of the world that has ensnared us both, but in drastically different ways. He's been living in luxury, working the family business and becoming a monster. While I've been trapped in a cage, being used, broken and destroyed, piece by piece.

"Alba, this... it's..." He struggles for words, but none can bridge the gap or unwrite the history that's etched into my flesh and soul, none can undo what's been done, none can bring back the girl I used to be.

"The truth is the truth," I say, having survived years of silent battles fought in the dark corners of rooms where hope seldom reaches, where light seldom penetrates, where I learnt to disappear into myself, just to survive. "Do with it as you please." My look does not falter, even as a fresh wave of sobs threatens to break free from my chest, threatening to drown me and pull me under.

There's a rawness to the moment, the kind that reveals the bones of who we truly are beneath the veneer of our positions within this criminal network. I'm a pawn, moved and used according to the whims of men like Luca Gallo; while Gabe stands on the precipice, caught between the love for his father and the moral quagmire that comes with the family name, caught between the boy he used to be and the monster he's becoming.

In the silence that follows, the sound of my own heartbeat thunders in my ears, a wildly frantic rhythm matching the panic rising in my chest. And in that fragile silence, I see something shift behind Gabe's eyes—a flicker of doubt, perhaps, or the dawning realisation that the world he thought he knew is built on a foundation of lies, that his father is not the man he believes him to be, that everything he's built his identity on is crumbling.

I draw a shallow breath, the chill of the room clinging to my exposed skin like frost on a winters morning, like ice water running through my veins. The fabric of my lingerie brushes against my back as I shift position, a deliberate act mocking the notion of choice in a world where choice is just an illusion, where I have no agency and I'm nothing but a body to be used and discarded.

My arms tremble slightly, not from fear, but from the effort it takes to maintain the façade as I try to hold myself together, attempting to keep myself from falling apart completely. I feel the cracks forming, the pieces of me that I've held together for so long beginning to crumble and break.

"So, how do you want me?" It's a question drenched in bitterness, a challenge laid bare before him in the waning light of the room, a question asking him to choose, to decide what he's going to do with me, if he's just going to take what he came here for. Because that's what men like him do. They take. They use. They destroy.

Gabe's jaw clenches visibly, his piercing blue eyes darkening. His eyes rake over me, taking in the sight as if it's a grotesque tableau he wishes he could unsee, as if looking at me causes him physical pain, as if the sight of me, is more than he can bear.

The veins on his hands stand out, taut from him clenching and unclenching, trying to hold onto some semblance of the man he believes himself to be. I can see the war happening inside him, the battle between what he wants to do and what he knows he should do.

"I'm not touching you," he says, venomously with revulsion, the words crumbling what is left of my heart. Why would he want to anyway, I've been fucked, whipped, and used up more times than I can count. I knew he wouldn't want me now anyway.

With that, he turns sharply, the tension in his frame speaking volumes of the turmoil that's raging inside him, of the war being fought in his soul. He strides towards the door, the conversation having torn open old wounds and inflicted new ones, destroying whatever fragile hope I might have been clinging to.

The click of the door closing echoes through the

hollow space, leaving me alone with the chilling embrace of truth and his lingering disgust, leaving me alone with the knowledge that even the boy I loved, can't stand to look at me, because even he sees me as nothing more than a broken and damaged thing.

Chapter 15

Gabriel

The neon lights blur into streaks as I storm out of the club, my blood boils with a fury that feels like it might consume me from the inside out. The night air does nothing to cool the fire raging inside my chest, an inferno that's been ignited by the knowledge that Alba—my Alba—has been trapped inside that place all along, trapped in a nightmare I should have protected her from.

"Jesus, Gabe," Aurelio grunts, hustling to keep up with my frenetic pace, his breath puffing out in quick, visible bursts due to the temperature of such an early hour. He's struggling to match my stride, struggling to keep up with the storm that I've become, but I don't slow down. I can't slow down. If I slow down, I'll have to think about what I just saw, what I just learnt, what I just did.

Catcher is on my heels too, his heavy boots clomping against the footpath with the subtlety of a sledgehammer, his ever-present scowl etched deep into his face like it's carved from stone. But right now, I'm not thinking about Catcher. I'm thinking about Alba. I'm thinking about the way she looked at me in that room. I'm thinking about the fact that my father sold her like she was nothing more than merchandise.

"Where the hell you off to in such a hurry?" Catcher barks, his voice cutting through my thoughts like a knife.

I ignore them both, my focus narrowing on my sleek, black car waiting obediently by the kerb like a loyal dog. I tap the fob, and the hazard lights flashing in unison with the synchronised beep-beep, a sound that feels obscenely cheerful given the darkness of my thoughts. Without breaking stride, I yank open the driver's door and slide inside, my movements sharp and aggressive, every motion infused with the rage that's threatening to tear me apart.

"Fuck!" The word rips from me, a growl more than a curse, a sound that's barely human. I grip the steering wheel, my knuckles turning white from the force, but I manage to restrain myself from taking my fury out on it. Not yet. I need to get to the warehouse. I need to confront my father. I need to know if what Alba told me is true.

Aurelio slides into the passenger seat while Catcher folds his massive frame into the back, filling the vehicle with his imposing presence, his sheer size makes the car feel smaller, more claustrophobic. Aurelio has a rigid set to his jaw, his eyes flicking to me then away like he's watching a live wire sparking, and he's afraid of what might happen if he makes the wrong move or if he says the wrong thing.

"Shit, Gabe—" Aurelio starts, but I cut him off before he can finish, my voice sharp enough to draw blood.

"Shut it!" A warning they both know better than to ignore, a command carrying the weight of my authority, the weight of my fury and the weight of everything I'm feeling right now.

I can't hold it back anymore; it's as if my skin is too tight and something has to give, as if I'm going to explode if I don't release some of the pressure. I rear back and slam my fist into the steering wheel with everything I have, putting all of my rage, all of my pain and all of my betrayal into a single moment of violence. The horn blares, a long, angry wail voicing my fury, screaming into the night like a wounded animal.

"Fuck!" It rips from my chest, raw and bloody, a sound that doesn't feel like it belongs to me.

Aurelio flinches, his entire body recoiling from the violence of my outburst, but Catcher doesn't even blink, used to outbursts like these, maybe even expects them. He's a fighter after all, someone who understands rage, understanding the need to break things when the world becomes too much to bear. The car shakes with the violence of my punch, the sound bouncing around us, filling the space with its sharpness and the rawness of my emotion.

I can almost taste the anger as I pant through clenched teeth, trying to breathe through the chaos that's consuming me, trying to hold onto some semblance of control, even though I can feel it slipping away.

Aurelio looks at me, his frown deep enough to bury secrets in, his eyes searching mine for some kind of explanation, some kind of understanding. "What the hell happened back there?"

"That woman..." My words come out choked, strangled by the chaos inside my head, the weight of what I've just discovered and the knowledge that everything I thought I knew about my family is a lie. "That woman is... she's..."

Catcher's low and dangerous growl rumbles from the back seat, a sound that's filled with understanding and with recognition. "The one who knew my name? The pretty little thing with the doe eyes and fire hair?"

I nod, the muscles in my jaw twitching with tension, with the effort it's taking to hold myself together and to keep myself from screaming. "Yeah... she's Alba."

The silence that follows is heavy and suffocating, thick enough to choke on. I can feel Aurelio's eyes bearing into me, but I can't bring myself to meet them. I can't face what I might see there—the shock and disbelief, the horror of what this means, the implications of what I've just revealed.

"Alba!" I repeat, saying her name again as if it might somehow change the reality of the situation, as if saying it twice might make it less true, less devastating and less final. But it doesn't. Her name hangs in the air between us like a curse, a bomb that's just detonated and we're all waiting to see what the fallout will be; a death sentence.

Catcher lets out a low whistle, the sound oddly respectful, and oddly sad. "Damn, Gabe. Alba? Your Alba?" There's something in his voice that I haven't heard before, something that sounds almost like sympathy, almost like understanding.

Aurelio's curse is slightly harsher in the ranks, his voice sharp with disbelief and anger. "What the fuck,

Gabe? Alba? Are you sure? Are you absolutely sure it's her?"

"Of course I'm fucking sure!" I snap, my voice rising as my hands grip the steering wheel so hard I think it might break. "I know her face, Aurelio. I know her eyes. It's Alba. It's definitely Alba."

It snaps me out of the haze that Alba's name has spun around my head. I feel the car shudder with the force of my grip on the wheel, feel it bending slightly under the pressure of my hands, feel the rage building inside me like a pressure cooker about to explode.

"I know," I say, my voice low and dangerous, a warning to both of them that I'm on the edge, that I'm about to do something that might be irreversible and it might change everything.

Catcher leans forward, stretching his tattoos into elongated shapes, his massive frame filling the space between the front and back seats. "She ran away, vanished into thin air. None of us has sniffed a trace of her in many years. How the fuck is she here working for Dan? How is she here at all?"

"Working? You call that working?" I could still see her, trapped in that bed, trapped in that room, trapped in a world in which she does not belong. "Slaving more like. She's not working for Dan. She's owned by Dan. She's property. She's merchandise."

Alba, my Alba, tangled up in a nightmare I should've protected her from, a nightmare that I've been a part of, a nightmare that I've been perpetuating. I slam my fist against the steering wheel again, harder this time, the horn blaring again as another scream of rage, despair and betrayal explodes.

"Listen," I say through clenched teeth, my voice shaking with the effort it takes to hold myself together, to keep myself from completely losing it. "She... she told me something…" My hands tremble with the thought of what I'm about to unload, the weight of the secret that Alba has entrusted me with, the knowledge that my father really is a monster. "She says my dad sold her. She doesn't just work for Dan; he fucking owns her!"

Aurelio's face, usually a stoic mask of indifference, contorts with disbelief as his brows shoot up so high, they almost disappear under his dishevelled hair. His mouth falls open, and for a moment, he looks like he's been physically struck, like the words I've just spoken have knocked the wind out of him. "Come again?" he asks with scepticism and what seems like a note of dread, as if he's hoping he's misheard me, like he's hoping what I've just said isn't true.

"Sold her, Aurelio. Like she's property, like she's nothing," I say, each word a hammer blow, each word driving home the reality of what my father has done. "My father took Alba as payment for her father's gambling debt and he sold her to Dan. He traded her like she was a commodity, like she was nothing more than a business transaction."

In the back seat, Catcher shifts, his usually playful features now a grimace, a mask that looks almost like pain. "What? No," he interjects, his voice carrying a note of disbelief, a desperate hope that what I'm saying isn't true. "I mean, Luca's a heartless bastard when it comes down to business, but this... this is a whole new level of fucked up. He wouldn't... not Alba. He's not that crazy, right?"

"Wouldn't he?" I can feel the betrayal curling inside me, coiling around my heart like a snake's poison, like something destroying me from the inside out. To think my own father, cold as he is, would trade Alba for money, would sell the girl I loved like she was nothing more than merchandise. "My father is capable of anything, Catcher. Anything. If it means keeping his empire unchallenged, if it means maintaining his power, if it means settling a debt, he'll do it. He'll do it without hesitation. He'll do it without remorse."

"Luca Gallo's capable of anything," I say, the name of my father leaving the taste of an ashy bitterness in the back of my throat, like everything that's rotten and corrupt in this world. "Especially if it means keeping his empire unchallenged. If Alba's right, then he's crossed a line there's no coming back from. He's crossed a line that I can't forgive. He's crossed a line that means I can't be his son anymore."

The words hang in the air between us, and I can feel them settling, the weight of what I've just said and the reality of it crashing down on all of us. I'm saying that I'm willing to turn against my own father, that I'm willing to betray my own blood and to destroy everything I've been building towards for the sake of a girl who might not even want my help.

Silence falls like a shroud over us, the only sound the ragged breathing from each of us as we grapple with the revelation, each of us trying to process what this means, what this changes and what will be required of us. It's a moment of reckoning, one where the rules of our world will be rewritten in the darkest ink imaginable—our loyalty to blood, to family, now has a question mark that hangs over everything.

"So what do we do?" Aurelio asks, his voice quiet as his eyes search mine for some kind of answer, some kind of direction. "What's the play here, Gabe?"

I hit the ignition button and the Mercedes roars to life, the engine purring like a predator waking from sleep. It's a guttural sound, like the rage inside of me snarling at the injustice of the world, like my fury has been given a voice and a form. "There's only one way to find out," I say as I flatten the accelerator and put the car into a ferocious wheelspin. The car lurches as we peel away from the kerb, the tires screaming against the asphalt like wounded animals.

"Fuck, Gabe, slow down!" Aurelio screeches, gripping the dashboard as if his life depends on it—which is not far from the truth. My mind is not the most stable right now, and my driving reflects the chaos inside me, the storm that I've become.

"Can't," is all I say, my voice flat as my focus narrows to the road ahead, to the warehouse that's waiting for me and the confrontation that's about to happen. "I need to know. I need to see the proof. I need to look my father in the eye and ask him if he did this."

As we speed towards the warehouse, the cityscape turns into a blur of grey and black, the lights and buildings pass by in a haze of motion and speed. My thoughts are a tempest, each one more treacherous than the last, contemplating the possibility that my father traded Alba's soul for money, that he had sold the girl I loved like she was nothing more than a piece of property, that he had done this and never told me, never warned me, or even gave me the chance to save her.

We skid into the warehouse grounds, the headlights cutting swathes through the murky gloom, illuminating the darkness like a knife cutting through flesh. Pulling up out the front, my eyes catch the glint of watches and the dull sheen of holstered guns—my dad's security, the men who guard his secrets, the men who protect his sins. The men who will soon be mine.

"Come on," I mutter, killing the engine, and on the brink of killing anyone who stands in my way at this point. I'm done with subtlety. I'm done playing the game. I'm done pretending that my family is anything other than what it is—a collection of monsters who prey on the weak, who destroy the innocent and who profit from suffering.

Catcher's hand is already on the handle before the car fully stops, his massive frame unfolding from the back seat like a predator preparing to strike. Aurelio is right behind him, his face set in a mask of determination that is tinged with dread, the knowledge that what we're about to do might change everything, might destroy everything and burn it all down.

We step out, our shoes crunching on the scattered gravel loudly against the stillness, the sound echoing across the empty warehouse grounds like a warning, a death knell. My heart hammers, fuelled by adrenaline, fury, and the need to know the truth. There's a desperate hope inside of me that Alba is lying, that my father didn't do this and that there's some explanation that makes this all make sense.

But I know better. I know that Alba wouldn't lie about something like this. I know that she has no reason to lie, telling me the truth was the most dangerous thing she could have done, she's risked everything by telling me.

I lead the way, my back straight and my steps sure, even though inside I'm a fucking mess, even though inside I'm falling apart, even though inside I'm dying. I'm the heir to the Gallo empire, and I'm about to walk into my father's warehouse and demand answers that might destroy everything I've ever known.

"Evening, Mr. Gallo," one of the guards nods, his expression unreadable, his eyes carefully neutral. He's seen me angry before, but he's never seen me like this, never seen me this close to losing complete control, never seen the kind of rage that I'm barely containing.

"Move!" I snap, not bothering with formalities, not bothering niceties that usually govern these interactions. His eyes widen a fraction, but he steps aside, opening the path to the belly of the beast, to the heart of my father's operation, to the place where all of his secrets are kept.

Inside, the warehouse looms large and silently, a cavern of secrets and sins; a monument for everything rotten and corrupt in this world. We walk along the aisles, dust and old metal filling the space while the air smells of death, despair and broken dreams. This place holds many memories, none of them good, and yet I'm back again, chasing the ghost of a girl whose smile lights up the darkest corners of my soul, whose laugh can make me forget about all of this darkness and whose love could have saved me if only I'd been brave enough to let it.

We push forward, ready to tear down heaven and hell to uncover the truth, to find the proof that I need, to confirm what I already know in my heart to be true.

The door to my father's office bursts open under the force of my shoulder, the hollow bang echoing throughout the sterile quiet like a gunshot in a declaration of war. My blood is boiling as I storm across the room, heading straight to the place where my father keeps his most important secrets, the place where he keeps the evidence of his crimes, the safe.

"Come on," I mutter, spinning the dial, my fingers moving with the muscle memory of someone who's done this before, who knows the combination by heart. The tumblers click, and twist the handle and swing the door open, revealing rows upon rows of manila folders, each one a story of a woman's suffering, each one a record of my father's cruelty.

"Alba..." My fingers run over the labels until I find the right file, the file that contains the proof I'm looking for, the file that will confirm what Alba told me. My hands are trembling, not from fear but in pure, undiluted rage; a rage that threatens to consume me completely.

I whip the folder out, almost tearing it in my haste, and flip it open. Papers. Photos. Documents. Her face stares back at me, the beautiful eyes that have haunted my dreams and are now screaming betrayal from a grainy photo, eyes that are filled with fear, desperation and a pain that I can't bear to look at. Sold. My Alba, traded like merchandise and documented like a business transaction, recorded like she was nothing more than a line item in a ledger.

"Fuck!" the word a raw strangled sound, launching from my throat, a sound that's barely human. I can't breathe; it's as if my ribcage is constricting, squeezing tighter with every heartbeat, as if my body is trying to protect itself from the knowledge that I'm receiving, as if it's trying to shield me from the truth.

"Jesus, Gabe..." Catcher's voice is a distant growl, but it's the contents of the folder that have me reeling, that details that have me falling apart, that have me losing my grip on reality. Contracts, dates, payments—all with my old man's signature scrawled at the bottom like a regular business deal, like he was just conducting normal business, like he wasn't selling the girl I loved into slavery.

My stomach clenches, and I double over, vomiting gin into the nearest bin, my body rejecting the knowledge, as it tries to purge itself of the poison I've just ingested. Everything spins—the room, my thoughts, reality comes crashing down on me like a tidal wave, an avalanche causing the end of the world.

Catcher's heavy hand lands on my back, firm and grounding, reminding me that I'm not alone, I have people who will stand with me even as my world falls apart. "Shit, Gabe, what you gonna do?" His voice carries a rare concern, but beneath it, an edge of fury that matches my own, a fury directed at my father, at the injustice of the world and at the fact that Alba's suffered while I've been living in luxury.

"Something," I gasp between heaves, my voice raw as my body shakes with the force of my emotions. "I'm going to do something. I'm going to burn this whole thing down…"

I wipe my mouth, standing upright, and snatch the folder back. I clutch it to my chest like it's the most important thing in the world, because it's the key to everything, it's the proof that I'm going to need to justify what I'm about to do.

Chapter 16

Alba

Sunrise spills across the room in a lazy, amber cascade that tinges everything with a diluted honey hue. My eyelids flutter open reluctantly, sleep still trying to anchor me into my unconscious, a blessed state where I don't have to think, don't have to feel, don't have to be aware of what I've become. For just a moment, in the space between sleep and waking, I'm free. But then reality crashes down on me like a tidal wave, and I remember where I am, who I'm with, what I've become.

Dan.

I can feel him breathing steadily beside me, his chest rising and falling in a rhythm that seems to sync with the pulse of the city outside, of a world that's moving on without me, that continues to exist while I'm trapped here in this bed, in this room, in this life. While the sheets feel cool against my skin, there's a warmth radiating from the man I'm pressed against, a warmth that feels suffocating, that feels like it's consuming me, that feels like it's burning me from the inside out.

I shift slightly, a movement almost imperceptible, trying not to wake him, so I can buy myself a few more moments of relative peace. But the bed creaks beneath me, a sound that feels so impossibly loud against the quiet of the morning, a sound that announces my movement to the world, announcing my presence and announcing my captivity.

His heavy and possessive arm slides over my waist, drawing me closer into the circle of his embrace. Dan's presence is as commanding as it is comforting, a constant force in my world of precarious alliances and persistent threats. His touch conveys ownership, a subtle reminder that I am his in a way no one else can claim, I belong to him, I am his property, his possession to do with as he pleases.

I exhale softly, feeling the faint brush of his stubble against the nape of my neck. The weight of his arm across my body is like a chain, a shackle that binds me to this place, to this life and to this existence. Then, as if to assert his authority, even while asleep, he stirs behind me. There's no mistaking the intent behind the movement as he pokes my back with his penis—a silent but unmistakable demand that doesn't require words, that doesn't require an explanation, it only requires obedience.

For a moment, I close my eyes again, not in submission but in brief respite to gather my thoughts, trying to find some small corner of myself that hasn't been destroyed, that hasn't been consumed, or been completely annihilated by this life.

My give-and-take arrangement with Dan has taught me a lot about the balance of power and the virtues of desire, or rather, the illusion of desire, the performance of desire and the way that desire can be manufactured, sold and traded like any other commodity.

Slowly I turn, my face soaking in the morning light as I face my owner. I feel something inside me die just a little bit more. I've done this so many times that I can do it without thinking, without feeling and without being mentally present in my own body. It's become automatic, like breathing, blinking, and like all the things that keep us alive without requiring conscious thought.

I know the texture of his skin beneath my fingers without looking, the warmth radiating from him in the cool dawn air, the way his body responds to my touch, the way he moves when I touch him. The soft rustling of sheets is the only sound as I shift, acknowledging the unvoiced expectation that lingers between us, the expectations to do what I'm told, to perform, and to be grateful for the opportunity to serve him.

My hand grazes over the contours of his chest as I trace the path down his body with an intimate knowledge that comes from nearly a whole year of silent communication, from a year of learning his body, learning his preferences, learning exactly how to touch him to get the response he wants. There's a terrible intimacy in it, a closeness that feels obscene, feels wrong, like a violation even though I'm the one doing the touching.

To others, he might have appeared as just another man in the vulnerable throes of sleep, revealing nothing of the complexities that lay beneath his slumbering facade. But to me, he's my current owner, the one who holds the contract to my life and body, he owns me in a way that's more complete than any legal document can ever convey, he has consumed me so completely that I'm not sure there's anything left of me anymore.

In this quiet hour, I contemplate the nature of our interactions, the strange dance that we've been performing for so long, I can't remember what it feels like to be anything other than this. There had been a time when I thought perhaps there would be more than this ritual that has become so ingrained in our existence, when I thought perhaps that he might see me as something more than a body to be used, I thought perhaps that there might be some kind of connection between us beyond the purely physical.

Yet, with each passing day, the reality becomes clearer, I have never witnessed him actually have sex with someone or surrender to the carnal desires that seem to govern the world we inhabit. It's always just this—his cock in my mouth, his pleasure, his release, and then nothing. No reciprocation. No tenderness. No acknowledgment that I'm a person, that I have needs, that I have desires, that I have a soul that's slowly being destroyed by this life.

And so, I acquiesce, not out of defeat but in an understanding of the role I play, the role I've been forced into, the role that I can't escape. I descend along his body with a grace that speaks of many such mornings spent in a similar repose, with a practiced ease that makes me want to scream, to claw my way out of my own skin, and to disappear completely.

This is not love, or lust. It is something else entirely. This is survival. This is the price of staying alive; the cost of breathing, of existing, of continuing to move through this world, even though I'm not sure why I bother anymore.

His shallow and expectant breathing interrupts the silence of the room, I feel his body move and the sheets rustle as he shifts into a more favourable position, preparing to receive what I'm about to give him. It's always blow jobs with him, always the same ritual, always the same performance that I've perfected over the years.

My fingers wrap around him as I do what I was bought to do. I start to suck him off, the act itself has become mundane with its repetition, but mentally it is no less compelling, no less soul-destroying and no less devastating to the little that remains of my humanity.

It's been 13 years of this; 13 years of waking up in someone's bed, of performing for them, of being used, consumed, and slowly erased from existence, I'd perfected the ability to disassociate, to do it with no feelings and no attachments.

And then Gabe walked into the Red Room, and everything's changed. Gabe, with his dark hair and his piercing blue eyes, with his face that I haven't seen in 13 years, with his voice that I'd recognise anywhere, with his presence that awoke things I thought I'd learnt to suppress— hope, longing, despair, all mixed together into something that's threatening to destroy me completely.

But he walked away. He looked at me and he chose to walk away. He couldn't even bear to touch me, couldn't even bear to look at me, to acknowledge that I'm a person, that I'm the girl he once loved, that I'm Alba and not just Anna, not just a body to be used or a piece of merchandise.

I feel the last remaining pieces of hope shatter and fall

away. I feel the girl I used to be—the girl who loved Gabe, who believed in him, who thought he might save me—die completely.

There is no salvation coming. There is no rescue, no escape. There is only this; this endless cycle of being used, consumed, and slowly erased from existence. There is only the empty sadness for a life that's been stolen from me, a life that I'll never get back, a life that I'll never be able to reclaim.

I am Alba Baker, and I am nothing. I am no one. I am just a body, a mouth, a vessel for other people's desires and other people's needs.

And I will remain this way until the day I die.

Chapter 17

Gabriel

The sun hasn't even climbed high enough to cast a shadow over the Gallo estate, yet there I am, clutching the damnation of my soul in a manila folder thick enough to choke on. I move across the polished marble floors with purpose, my footsteps echoing throughout the halls. I could've stormed into his office the moment those files imprinted into my retinas in the warehouse, but I chose to let the rage simmer under my skin, until it felt like acid coursing through my veins, until it became something I can use, something I can weaponize.

"Morning, Gabe," the guards nod as I pass, I don't reply as their eyes flick to the folder under my arm. My mind is hell-bent on a confrontation and these guards do not want to feel my wrath.

I push open the door to his office without knocking. Luca Gallo, The Don, is enshrouded by the morning light filtering through the blinds as he sits at his desk like he owns the world, like he's untouchable, like he hasn't destroyed everything I've ever cared about.

"Got something for you, Papa," I say, making my voice hoarse with the remnants of last night's whiskey and smoke still tart on my tongue. I should have come earlier, instead of torturing my own psyche by waiting. But there's a method to my madness—one final play before all hell breaks loose. It's about seeing that look in his eyes when he realises I know. It's about savouring the taste of revenge; even if it's against my own blood.

Luca's eyes narrow, burning through me with a calculated gaze that has broken even the strongest of men.

"Jesus, Gabe," he says, an amused smirk tugging at the corners of his mouth, " Sembri essere alla fine della camminata della vergogna." *You look like you're on the tail end of the walk of shame.*

A bitter laugh scrapes its way out of my throat. "If only it were that simple, Papa." My reflection in the glass behind him is a mockery; a bastardised version of myself, with my tie askew and hair a bird's nest. My once pristine tailored black suit is now crinkled and hanging off my frame.

"You smell like you've been living in a brothel," he says casually, but I catch the sharp flicker of his eyes as he takes in every detail. He knows; the old man always fucking knows when something is off.

"Wouldn't be the worst of it," I say. The file burning against my side, a physical brand for the rage coiling tightly around my heart. Today, the truth will bleed, and I'll be the one holding the blade.

I slump into the chair across from him. My hand, steady despite the tremble of fury beneath my skin, slides the file across the polished mahogany that separates me from him. He looks at the pile of papers like it's a severed head.

"What's this?"

"Take a look," I say, watching as his fingers, adorned with rings that have broken multiple noses and jaws, pry open the manila folder. It's almost artistic, the way his brows draw together, confusion playing across features that mirror my own.

He scans the first photo, then the second. I detect the moment realisation dawns; his head cocks to the side, an animalistic tilt that makes my skin crawl. "What?"

The single word hangs between us, charged with accusation and disbelief. It's not a question so much as a challenge, one I'm more than ready to meet head-on.

"Don't play dumb with me, Papa," I say. "That's Alba." The name feels like barbed wire on my tongue, each syllable a memory of a girl I spent years chasing, a girl I thought was dead, a girl I've been mourning for 13 years.

"Alba?" He feigns ignorance, but his eyes, those dark mirrors of deceit, can't lie to me. Not anymore. I know him too well. I know when he's lying. I know when he's hiding something.

"Her father said she ran away," I say, my voice getting louder, getting sharper. "You told me not to chase her, and Mum, she had the gall to call her family trash, saying she left me like I was nothing but garbage to her." My fists clench at my sides. Every muscle in my body tensing for a fight that's been brewing for longer than I can remember. "But here we are. The truth is as ugly as sin—you sold her, didn't you? To settle her dad's filthy gambling debt."

The silence that follows is deafening, filling with the unsaid and unforgivable; the calm before the storm.

The frown on my old man's face could crack marble as he leans back in his chair. "Non l'ho venduta, figliolo mio." *I didn't sell her, son.* "Your mother and I, we thought she'd really skipped town."

"Ran away?" I lean forward, my hands flat against the cold surface of his desk, ready to pounce. "You didn't put much effort into finding her!" My voice spikes with scorn, mocking his pathetic excuse.

"We did," he says, a muscle twitching in his jaw. "We paid her father a visit. Place was deserted. No point chasing ghosts, Gabe. Plus I've never seen this file."

"Chasing ghosts," I say, snorting at the irony. "That's rich, coming from you." I push off the desk, pacing the length of the room, the tension so thick it could strangle us both.

"Her dad moved on. Packed up and vanished into thin air, just like her. We saw how torn up you were," he says, his voice softer now, but it just pisses me off more. "Told you to let her go, for your own good. It was clear she took off and left you mate… Or so we thought."

"Took off?" My laughter is bitter and sharp. "That's bullshit and you know it." I stop pacing and turn to face him. "Alba would have never left me!"

"Life's a bitch, Gabe!" He shrugs, the casualness and sheer indifference ignites something inside me that I can barely contain. It's like we're discussing a deal gone south, not a life that's been shattered,

"This is bullshit!" I bellow, slamming my fist down on

the mahogany desk with such force that the framed family portrait falls over. "Vedi tutti i maledetti documenti che attraversano la tua scrivania, papà. Questo lo avresti visto!" *You see every damn file that crosses your desk, Papa. You would've seen this!*

He looks up at me, his steely eyes not even flinching from the impact. Calm as ever, he shakes his head in a slow and deliberate motion that grates on my nerves. "No, I don't," he says coolly. "I see what's handed to me. The rest are seen by Fabio."

"Fabio?" I stare at him in disbelief. "Since when does Fabio filter what reaches you? Since when did he decide what you should give a damn about?"

My father remains stoic, an immovable statue in the face of the torrent I've unleashed upon him. He doesn't understand the tempest inside me.

Alba is more than just a girl; she's my obsession, a fire that consumes me, the girl I've been searching for, the girl I thought was gone forever.

"Since he became my right hand," Luca replies. "Since I trusted him to handle the day-to-day, so I could focus on the bigger picture."

"Great fucking job! A real big picture you're painting here, where girls get sold off and somehow my Alba got thrown in the mix." My fingers itch for the cold metal of my gun, its weight a constant reminder of the power at my fingertips, the authority to deliver justice in a world sorely lacking it. But I hold back. Not yet. Not until I know everything.

"Watch your tone, Gabriel!" he says, but there's a crack

in the facade. Maybe he sees it now, the depth of my rage, the lengths I'll go to for Alba.

My fists are clenched so tight I can feel my nails digging into the flesh of my palms. The ticking of the grandfather clock in the corner echoing like a time bomb in my head. I need answers, and I need them now.

"Where the fuck is Fabio?"

Without a word, my father reaches for his phone with an air of reluctant authority. He dials quickly, his eyes never leaving mine as the unspoken challenge hangs heavy between us. My gaze doesn't waver, even as he speaks into the receiver, "Come to my office, now!"

Fabio is the kind of man who seems carved from stone —a fixture in our home, silent and immovable. The trust I have for him is rooted deep, etched into my being from years of shared bloodshed and secrets. But in this moment, the trust erodes completely. I realise that he's been the one filtering information, he's been the one deciding what my father should know, that he's been the one keeping Alba's file from reaching my father's desk.

The door swings open with urgency as Fabio enters the room. The light filtering through the blinds paints stripes across his face, making him look like a ghost; like something that's not quite real.

"Did you see this?" The file slides from my father's hand to Fabio's with a slickness that makes my stomach churn.

Fabio thumbs through it, his expression impassive as if he's perusing a mundane inventory list and not the record of a young woman's life that was bartered away like a poker chip.

"Yes," he says, devoid of remorse or surprise. "Her father sold her for her virginity to pay his gambling debt."

"Alba!" I shout. "Her name is Alba. Why did you sell her? Why didn't you tell my father? Why did you keep this from us?"

Time seems irrelevant in the ensuing silence as the question hanging between us like a guillotine blade poised to sever years of trust. My hand moves with a mind of its own, snaking to the holster hidden beneath my jacket, fingers wrapping around the cold metal grip of the gun nestled there.

In one fluid motion, I draw it, my arm steady despite the maelstrom of rage within me. Fabio's eyes widen, but he doesn't move, doesn't try to run, doesn't try to defend himself.

"Tell me, Fabio!" I demand, though I know no answer will quell the inferno searing through my veins. "Tell me why you did this. Tell me why you kept her from me. Tell me why you let her suffer."

His eyes meet mine, a glimpse of something fleeting within them—a twinge of guilt, perhaps, or sheer surprise at my audacity. It doesn't matter. In the space of a heartbeat, I squeeze the trigger, the gunshot a thunderclap shattering the silence.

Fabio's body crumples to the floor, blood blooming between his eyes. His life—a life I once valued—extinguished in an instant in retribution for the innocence he helped steal, for the girl he helped destroy and the years he stole from me.

"Gabe! For God's sake, Gabe!" my father bellows, his

voice a mix of horror and anger, "We don't kill people in the house."

"Since when?" I sneer, the gun still smoking in my hand as my chest heaves with exertion and fury.

I stand there for a moment, attention still locked on the warm gun in my hand. Then, with deliberate care, I lay the gun down on the polished wood of my father's desk, right next to the file that contains Alba's life; her suffering and her destruction.

"Gabriel!" His bellow chases me as I march towards the door, my declaration of revolt. The world outside the office seems paradoxical, the muffled reality of life before vengeance took hold.

"Gabriel!" There it is again, the desperation clear in his voice, like a plea that barely masks the authority he thinks he still has over me. It's almost laughable.

I don't break stride even as I reach for the door handle. "Gabriel!" The third cry is raw, edged with a paternal fear I never thought I'd hear. Luca Gallo, the unshakeable head of the Melbourne underground, reduced to fear by his own blood.

"No…" I mutter under my breath in contempt. There's no turning back after what I've done, no repentance or absolution waiting in the wings. Just a road ahead, that is paved with blood, vengeance and the desperate need to save the girl I love.

"Gabriel!" He's standing out in the hall now, I can tell without looking; the authority that once commanded me, now falls on deaf ears. My hand shoves the door open, a gust of wind sweeps into the suffocating room, offering a freedom I intend to welcome.

"Stop!"

But I don't stop. Not for him. Not for anyone.

"Gabriel!" His final, fractured call chases after me through the open door, but I'm already gone, swallowed by the corridor's gloom as the door slams shut behind me, sealing the fate of Fabio, Alba, and whatever shred of innocence remained within those walls.

Chapter 18

Alba

I stare down at the bacon sizzling in the pan. My movements are mechanical, yet mindful, as I flip the strips to crisp perfection, the eggs beside them just beginning to firm up with golden edges. I don't think about anything, I just cook. The rest is noise.

Dan sits at the table, reading whatever article has captured his attention on the iPad. That device is like a technological appendage for him, always within reach, feeding him information or serving as a conduit for his less than savoury dealings. I can tell by the furrow between his brows and the absent way he's twirling a silver fork between his fingers that he's engrossed in something.

I stare for a moment too long, tracing the lines of tension etched along his jaw, wondering what thoughts are brewing behind his dark, calculating eyes. But then, the shrill of his phone cleaves through the quiet, startling me from my reverie.

"Dan," he answers with cold neutrality. I listen, still busy cooking as my ears tune into the fragments of his conversation. "Yes..." His affirmation is curt, a verbal nod needing no further elaboration. "Ah, oh?" A flicker of surprise, perhaps intrigue, laces his tone now. And then, "Really?" It's spoken with a note of incredulity that rarely makes its way into Dan's well-guarded expressions of emotion.

Whatever news the caller imparts seems to stir something within him; a subtle shift in his posture, the slight widening of his eyes and maybe even concern. Or is it an opportunity? With Dan, it's often hard to discern.

As I place the breakfast items on a plate, I can't help but wonder what machinations spin behind each uttered syllable. I've learnt to read him over the past year, learnt to anticipate his moods and to know what he wants, before he asks. It's a survival skill, like learning to hold my breath underwater.

"Here we are," I say as I place the breakfast in front of him, the savoury aroma rising between us in our untraditional domesticity. It's almost like we're a real couple; except for the fact that I'm his property and he owns me in every way that matters.

Dan glances up at me, a glint of something unreadable passing through his eyes. "How much?" he asks, his tone casual, yet underscored with a steel that belies the simplicity of the question.

The words slip into the air, mingling with the steam from the eggs, and a shiver traces my spine. There's no innocence in the inquiry, nothing that pertains to the cost of groceries or the trivialities of everyday expenditures. This is the language of deals and debts that I'm all too familiar with; yet forever bound by.

He taps a rhythmless beat on the edge of the tablet, the sound punctuates the stillness before he continues. "I could be convinced for 500,000 and a replacement?" The nonchalance in his voice jars against the astronomical numbers, the concept of human worth distilled into digits and cold negotiation.

My throat tightens around a response that will never come, the notion of 'replacement' coiling within me like a serpent. I know what that means. I know what he's saying. He's negotiating my sale like I'm a piece of merchandise, nothing more than a commodity being traded and exchanged.

Instead, I retreat silently back to the counter, my hands finding solace in the mundane task of wiping it down. The motion is automatic, practiced, something I can do without thinking, without feeling, without being present in my own body.

In the end, what is one more transaction to the likes of Dan? And yet, to me, it's everything—another link in the chains that bind me, each deal a reminder of the thin veneer of control I clutch at in a world where power is the only true master.

"Okay, deal," Dan says, clipped and decisive, before he hangs up. A deal sealed, another page in this ledger of lives turned with a finality leaving no room for second thoughts or regrets.

My heart thuds uneasily as I busy myself with the cleaning, the lemon-scented cleaner momentarily over-powering the lingering aroma of breakfast. The cloth in my hand gliding across the surface, each pass an attempt to scrub away the dread creeping into the edges of my consciousness. But the dread doesn't go away. It never does.

"Anna," Dan says, pulling me back from the refuge of routine. His tone is a herald to the words that soon fall from his lips, cold and as unyielding as steel. "You need to pack your stuff. You have a new owner. He will be here in an hour to pick you up."

The air in the room seems to constrict, pressing against me from all sides. Time, once a relentless march, now feels like a languid stream, each second bloating further with the gravity of his decree. A new owner. The phrase echoes within me, but I don't feel anything. I'm too numb. I've been numb for so long that I'm not sure I remember what feeling feels like.

I've been sold. Again. To someone new. Someone I don't know. Someone who will do things to me that I can't anticipate, can't prepare for, can't escape from.

But I don't feel anything.

"Understood," I reply, the word a shard of glass on my tongue. I don't allow the tremble in my hands to show the turmoil that threatens to rise within me. With calculated steps, I move past Dan, granting him nothing more than a fleeting glance as I resign myself once again to the hand I've been dealt.

"Hey, Anna," Dan calls out as I'm walking away, and I pause, turning back to look at him. There's something almost like sympathy in his eyes, which is strange because Dan doesn't do sympathy. "Whoever he is, he's paid a lot for you. Try not to disappoint him, yeah?"

It's almost funny, in a dark sort of way. He's warning me to behave for my new owner, like I'm a possession needing to be kept in good condition. Like I'm not a person, I'm just a thing to be used and passed around.

"I won't," I say, my voice flat and my face blank. "I never do."

I retreat to the sanctuary of my room, closing the door behind me like a punctuation mark at the end of yet another sentence in the story of Alba Baker. The room is sparse—a bed, a mirror, a small dresser with a few changes of clothes. Everything I own fits into a single bag, and can be packed up and carried away in an hour.

I pull out the bag from under the bed and start throwing things into it. Clothes. Toiletries. The few personal items I've been allowed to keep. My movements are automatic and practiced. I've done this before and I'll probably do it again.

As I pack, I catch my reflection in the small mirror hanging opposite my bed. The face staring back at me is composed, tranquil even; it bears no trace of the soul screaming for liberation from this relentless purgatory. I don't recognise myself anymore. I'm not sure I ever will.

How ironic it is, to crave an end from those who see ending lives as little more than a pastime. In the quiet of my room, surrounded by the muted evidence of my captivity, I allow myself a thought so dangerous it feels like a betrayal of my own will to survive.

Maybe one day, one of them will find the mercy—or the cruelty—to just kill me.

But even that thought doesn't stir anything in me. I'm too numb. I've been numb for so long that numbness is all I know.

The hour passes quickly. Too quickly. Before I know it,

there's a knock on the door, and Dan's voice calling out, "He's here."

I pick up my bag and walk out of the room, not looking back. There's nothing to look back at. There's nothing here that belongs to me. There's nothing here that's mine.

Chapter 19

Gabriel

My hands gripping the steering wheel so tightly I think it might break. I've been planning this for hours, ever since I left my father's office with Fabio's blood still fresh on the floor. I contacted Dan first thing this morning, told him I wanted to buy Alba, told him I could move her today. He didn't ask questions. Men like Dan never do—they just see the money.

13 years. It's taken me 13 years to find her, and now I'm finally going to bring her home.

Alba emerges from the house, and my breath catches in my throat. She's so thin, so frail, like a strong wind could blow her away. Her skin is pale, her eyes hollow, and I can see the damage that 13 years of captivity has done to her. But then her eyes meet mine for a fleeting second, and in them, I see everything that needs to be said. This isn't just a rescue—it's a reckoning. A chance to right a wrong in a world that's gone so off course; even the compass is spinning out of control.

Dan appears behind her, a slimy smirk plastered across

his face like he thinks we're old friends catching up over a fucking beer. "Gabriel," he says, his smirk widening. "Right on time."

"Dan," I reply, with no warmth in my greeting. My jaw is clenched so tight I can barely speak. I want to kill him. I want to wrap my hands around his throat and squeeze until he stops breathing. But I need him alive for now. I need him to believe that this is just a business transaction, that I'm just another buyer, another man looking to own Alba for a while.

"Hope she didn't pack too heavy," Dan jokes, nodding at her meagre belongings with a chuckle that sets my teeth on edge. I eye the pathetic excuse for luggage Alba clutches in her hands. It's laughable, really. The girls back at the warehouse travelled like they were never coming back, with bags full of clothes and shoes and jewellery. But Alba? She has nothing but this sorry excuse of a bag, this small canvas thing that looks like it could fit in the palm of my hand.

I look from the bag to her face, and something inside me breaks. This is what they've done to her. They've reduced her to nothing, stripping her of everything and leaving her with barely anything to her name.

"Jesus Christ. That's all you've got?" I ask, unable to keep the edge out of my voice.

Her nod is small, almost lost in the grandeur of Dan's clown show of a mansion. She doesn't speak. She just nods, her silence louder than any words could ever be.

"Alright, let's get this shit done," I say, my hand outstretched. Dan shakes it, his grip slimy, like everything about him. I want to pull my hand away and wipe it on my jeans, to do anything to get the feel of him off my skin. "Aurelio will be here within the hour," I continue, squeezing his hand a little tighter than necessary. "He wants to know your type. Got a preference?"

Dan smirks, a devilish glimmer in his eyes, ready to place his order as though he were at a drive thru. Disgust urges me to lash out, but discipline stops me. I need him to believe this is real. I need him to think I'm just another buyer, just another man in the system.

Dan scratches at his stubble, eyes skirting the sky as if the answer is scrawled in the clouds. "You know what? I've not had a Thai lady yet..." He lets the words linger, as though he's doing me a favour by being culturally diverse. "Might be nice to branch out, you know?"

"Done," I say with a fake smile, my skin crawling at the transaction. It's a necessary evil for what I need. I flick my hand towards my car, my voice firm, no bullshit. "Get in, Alba!"

She hesitates for a split second, looking between me and Dan, as if torn. I can see the fear in her eyes, the uncertainty; the question of whether this is real or just another nightmare. Then, with the smallest of steps at first, her pace quickens, and her long hair cascades behind her like a flag of surrender, like a sign of hope, like the first real thing I've seen in 13 years.

She slides into the back seat like it's a refuge, and something inside me settles.

She's here. She's safe. She's finally safe.

The bag she clutches is dwarfed by the space, as if to mock the life she's been reduced to. But that's about to change. I'm going to fix this. I'm going to give her back everything that's been taken from her.

"Always a pleasure doing business with you, Gabe," Dan says, his smirk telling me he thinks he got the better end of the deal. If only the bastard knew. If only he understood that I'm not just taking Alba—I'm taking everything from him, I'm destroying him, I'm going to make him pay for every second she spent in his hands.

"Likewise," I lie, turning my back on him. I stride to the driver's side of my Mercedes and climb in. The familiar scent of luxury wraps around me like a hug from an old friend, but it feels hollow now. Nothing feels real anymore, except for the knowledge that Alba is here, she's finally here.

I start the engine and pull away from the curb, my eyes flicking to the rear-view mirror to check on her. She sits on the back seat, small and fragile, clutching the pathetic excuse for a bag, like it's the only thing keeping her tethered to reality.

"Seat belt," I bark at Alba without turning to look at her. Safety first, even when your life already hangs by a thread. The click of the buckle tells me she complies. Good girl.

"Fuck!" I hiss, slamming my foot down on the accelerator before the gate has fully swung open. Gravel spats out from the rear tyres, a fitting salute to the shambles we're leaving in our wake. I drive fast, my hands tightening on the wheel as my mind racing with everything I need to do, everything I need to fix.

"Where to?" Alba asks sheepishly, her voice small and

uncertain, like she's afraid of asking the wrong question, afraid of what the answer might be.

"Home," I say, my voice softer and gentler now. "I'm taking you home, Alba."

I glance at her again through the rear-view mirror. She's so thin, so frail, so broken. But there's still a fire in her eyes, still that spark of defiance that I remember from when we were young. That spark is still there, thank fully, and I'm going to nurture it, I'm going to protect it and I'm going to help her find her way back to herself.

She has nothing but the small bag, and I hate it. Alba loved to collect things when we were younger. Her room was always tidy, but she always had random things she found—rocks and shells and bits of ocean glass and old coins. She had a way of finding beauty in broken things, of treasuring the discarded. And now she has nothing, and I want to fix that. I want to give her back everything that's been taken from her. I want to fill her life with beautiful things again.

Chapter 20

Alba

The drive from Dan's house has been silent and tense, I sit in the back seat of this expensive Mercedes, clutching my pathetic bag, trying to process what's happening. It's Gabe. The boy I loved 13 years ago, the boy who broke my heart in the Red Room, the boy who walked away from me like I was nothing—he's the one who bought me. He's the one who came to Dan's house after negotiating for me, like I am a piece of merchandise, like I am something to be traded and exchanged.

What does this mean? Is this revenge? Is he going to hurt me? Is he going to use me like all the others? Or is there something else happening here, something I can't quite understand, something that doesn't fit into the framework of my existence?

We pull through gates into a driveway, and the car comes to a stop. Gabe gets out, opening my door, and I follow him out of the car on shaky legs. He leads me toward the house, and I keep my eyes down, not wanting to look at him, not wanting to see the coldness in his eyes, not wanting to confront the reality of what's about to happen.

The first thing I notice when I arrive—how could I not?—is the size of the place. This sprawling structure is at least six times smaller than the home he grew up in and seems modest in comparison to where his parents lived. But it's still massive, intimidating and a fortress that speaks of power, wealth and control. It's different from his family's palatial estate, less ostentatious, more grounded, but still undeniably the home of a powerful man.

My gaze drifts past the grand staircase, through the archway that frames views of the sprawling grounds outside. The house is an expansive suburban dwelling that stretches its arms wide but still roots itself within reach of the world outside its gates. It's still three times the size of a normal home, yet somehow more grounded than grandiose, like Gabe has tried to distance himself from his family's excessive wealth, while still maintaining the trappings of power and control.

The interior is all dark wood and leather, with high ceilings that make me feel small and insignificant. The walls are lined with art—expensive art; the kind that costs more than I could ever earn in a lifetime. There are floor-to-ceiling windows and everything is pristine, everything is perfect, exactly what I would expect from a man like Gabe. But there's something cold about it all. There's no warmth here, no sense of home, no feeling of comfort. It's beautiful, but it's sterile, like a museum or a hotel, rather than a place where someone actually lives.

As I study the contours of the place, it strikes me just

how much Gabe has changed over the years. There's no trace of the boy who once roamed his family estate halls with laughter and mischief twinkling in his sapphire eyes. The boy I knew would have filled this space with life, energy and warmth. This man has drained it of all of that. This man is a stranger wearing the face of someone I used to love.

"Go take a shower," Gabe says, his voice cutting through my spiralling thoughts like a knife. There's an unyielding edge to his tone, brokering no argument. He jerks his thumb authoritatively down an expansive hall-way, a corridor flanked by doors that no doubt hold secrets. "You're filthy."

The word stings. Filthy. Because that's what I am now, isn't it? I'm filthy. Dirty. Contaminated by 13 years of being used, being touched, being destroyed, and Gabe can see it all. Gabe sees what I've become, and he wants me to wash it away.

I nod mutely, walking in the direction he pointed to.

"Turn left here," he instructs, devoid of the warmth I once knew, replaced by a steel authority that brokers no argument. It's jarring, to reconcile the boy who had shared secrets beneath the shade of old gum trees with this author-itative man, a man who now owns me, who now controls me, who now has the power to do whatever he wants with me.

We walk down the hallway, and he opens a door to revealing a guest room. It's stark in its simplicity—a plain spare room, undecorated walls holding no hint of person-ality or comfort. There's a bed with white sheets, a wooden dresser, a small desk in the corner. Theres an open door leading to an ensuite bathroom, with sterile white tiles and chrome fixtures. It's clean, functional, and completely devoid of any warmth or character.

The room looks like an afterthought, much like how I feel under Gabe's scrutinising gaze. As a child, he filled spaces with laughter; now, he seems to drain them of everything but functionality and necessity. There's an unsettling efficiency to him that makes the girl I used to be—a girl who basked in his kindness—feel like a stranger in my own skin.

His presence lingers in the doorway, watching as I survey the room. I can feel his eyes on me, assessing me, evaluating me, trying to figure out who I am now, what I've become and whether I'm still the girl he loved or if I'm something else entirely. I don't even know how to answer that question, because I don't know who I really am anymore.

"Will this be sufficient?" His tone suggests the question is merely a formality; I know better than to express any discontent. This is his house, his rules, his game. I'm just a piece on his board now.

"Perfect," I reply, my voice small and meek. "Thank you."

He nods once before leaving. I listen to the receding sound of his footsteps, wondering what's going to happen next, wondering what he wants from me, wondering if this is mercy or just another form of hell. The uncertainty is almost worse than the pain. At least with Dan, I knew what to expect. With Gabe, everything is unknown, everything is unpredictable, everything is terrifying.

With a sigh, I approach the ensuite bathroom. The marble countertop is lined with small bottles of wash products—shampoo, conditioner, body wash, all expensive brands, all generic and impersonal. Nothing to suggest luxury or care, just the bare minimum to cleanse oneself. It's more than Dan ever provided, but it's still cold, still impersonal, still a reminder that I'm not a person here, I'm just a possession.

I strip away the layers of fabric clinging to my skin, as the steam from the hot water begins to fill the room, blurring the reflection in the mirror. For 13 years, I've perfected the art of obedience; it's become second nature, a survival mechanism. But here, in this steam-filled sanctuary, a rebellious spark flickers to life within me.

The water is hot, and it cascades over my shoulders in a benediction, as I almost sag under the heat. The feeling doesn't last long. The reality of my situation comes crashing back down on me. Gabe owns me now. Gabe, the boy I loved, the boy who broke my heart, now owns me like I'm a piece of property. And I have no idea what it means, no idea what he wants from me, no idea if this is mercy or just another form of torture.

I lather my hair with shampoo, allowing myself to indulge in a fantasy, imagining telling Gabe to fuck off, telling him that I won't obey him, telling him that I'm not his to own. The thought is both terrifying and exhilarating. I know it's a fantasy, a fleeting sense of control in a world where I have none. But with Gabe, because of our shared history and the semblance of understanding between us, I feel I have the licence to push the boundaries more than I could with Dan. Not too much, just a little. I'm still at

Gabe's mercy, but the noose around my neck is not as tight as it was with Dan.

There's something different about being owned by someone you used to love. It's more complicated, more painful, more confusing. With Dan, it was simple—he was a monster, and I was his victim. But with Gabe, it's blurred. He's both the boy I loved and the man who now owns me. He's both my saviour and my captor. He's both the answer to my prayers and the source of my deepest fear.

Eventually, the water runs clear, the last traces of soap disappearing down the drain as I turn off the shower, a reminder that moments of solitude are precious and few. As I reach for a towel, I steel myself for the inevitable return to reality and to a role I have not chosen but cannot seemed to abandon.

The towel is plush and soft, so soft that it almost makes me want to cry. I wrap it around my body and look at my reflection in the mirror. My face is gaunt, my eyes hollow, my body skeletal. I barely recognise myself. The girl I used to be is gone, replaced by this hollow shell, this broken thing, this piece of merchandise.

But as I look at my reflection, I see something else. I see a spark. A small, fragile spark of something that might be hope, or defiance, possibly the last remaining piece of the real Alba that hasn't been destroyed. It's small and frag- ile, but it's there. And it's stronger now than it was before, because Gabe is here, because the boy I loved is here, and maybe, just maybe, there's a chance that things could be different.

"Get it together, Alba," I mutter, wrapping the plush

fabric around my body. My reflection, now clear in the dissipating steam, holds a look of something I haven't felt in years—something that might be hope. No matter what version of Gabe confronts me next, no matter what he wants from me, no matter what he plans to do with me, I will meet him with an unwavering spirit that refuses to be completely broken.

I just have to figure out what he wants. I just have to figure out if buying me was an act of mercy or just another form of possession. I need to figure out if the boy I loved is still somewhere inside this man, or if he's been completely consumed by the darkness.

Chapter 21

Gabriel

I'm sitting at the dining table, my fingers drumming against the dark wood as I wait for Alba to emerge from the bathroom. 30 minutes. She's been in there for 30 minutes, and I'm trying not to think about what she's doing, trying not to think about the fact that she's naked in my house, trying not to think about the fact that I've spent 13 years searching for her and now she's finally here. The anticipation is killing me, the uncertainty eating me alive, and I'm caught between wanting to see her and wanting to give her space, between my desperate need to know she's okay and my desperate need to not push her too hard.

My phone buzzes on the table, and I ignore it. Catcher's probably wondering where I am, wondering why I haven't shown up at the warehouse, wondering if I've lost my fucking mind. But I don't care about my legacy right now. I don't care about the business, don't care about the empire; don't care about any of it. All I care about is Alba, the fact that she's finally here, finally safe, and finally mine to protect.

The thought makes my chest tighten. She's finally here. After 13 years of searching, after 13 years of dead ends, false leads and desperate hope; she's finally here. And I have no fucking idea what to do with her, no fucking idea how to help her, no fucking idea how to be the man she needs me to be.

I stand up, walking over to the window and look out at the garden beyond. The sun is starting to set, painting the sky in shades of orange and pink, and I'm trying to calm myself down, trying to prepare myself for whatever comes next. I need to be strong for her. I need to be stable. I need to be someone she can trust, someone she can lean on, someone who won't hurt her the way everyone else has.

The door to the hallway opens, and I turn around. And I feel my breath catch in my throat, but not for the reason I expect.

She's wearing a teddy. A tiny piece of lace and satin that barely covers anything, leaving her exposed, vulnerable and... wrong. So fucking wrong. My eyes trace over her body—her thin frame, her pale skin, the way the fabric clings to her like a second skin. And I feel two things at once: a surge of attraction making my dick hard, and a wave of disgust making my stomach turn.

Because this is what they made her wear. This is what they conditioned her to wear. This is what she thinks she's supposed to wear for me. This is the uniform of her captivity, the symbol of her enslavement, the physical manifestation of everything that's been done to her.

My hands clench into fists at my sides, and I have to take a deep breath to keep myself from losing control completely.

"What the fuck are you wearing?" I ask, my voice sharp, cutting, and harsh in a way I don't intend, but I can't seem to help it; I'm not angry at her—I'm angry at the world, angry at the men who did this to her, angry at myself for not finding her sooner.

She flinches at my tone, and I can see the fear in her eyes, the way she shrinks back slightly and the way she's bracing herself for punishment. And that breaks something inside me, because she shouldn't be afraid of me. She should never be afraid of me.

"What I'm meant to wear," she says quietly, her voice small and uncertain, like she's asking a question rather than stating a fact. Like she's not sure if she's right, like she's waiting for me to correct her, like she's been conditioned to doubt herself so thoroughly that she can't even trust her own judgment anymore.

"Not for me, you're not," I say, my voice softer now, trying to convey that I'm not angry at her, that I'm angry at the situation, at the system, at the men who did this. "You can change in a minute. But first, we need to talk."

I'm battling with myself. My dick is screaming at me to look at her, to appreciate the way the teddy frames her body, to recognise that she looks absolutely fabulous in it, that the lace hugs her curves in a way that's both innocent and seductive. But my mind is screaming something else entirely—that this is how she dressed for her owners, that this is what they made her do, that every man who's ever seen her in this thing has used her, destroyed her, broken her into pieces.

The two thoughts are at war inside me, and I feel disgusted. I feel sick, like I'm going to vomit just thinking about all the hands that have touched her, all the eyes that have looked at her in this teddy and all the men who have taken what wasn't theirs to take.

I sit back down at the table and gesture for her to sit across from me. She moves slowly, carefully, like she's afraid of what's coming and she's bracing herself for pain. I want to tell her that I'm not going to hurt her, that I'm never going to hurt her, that I'm going to spend the rest of my life making sure that no one ever hurts her again. But the words stick in my throat, because I'm not sure she'll believe me, and I'm not sure I deserve her trust.

"I want to know what happened to you," I say, my voice rough and raw. "I want to know why and how everything. I want to know the whole story."

"I told you I was taken," she says quietly, her eyes downcast, her fingers twisting together in her lap.

"I know that." I reply, my voice rough. "But I want to know step by step. The whole story. Where you've been. Who owned you. Everything. I need to know, Alba. I need to understand what happened to you."

She takes a breath, and then she starts talking. She tells me about being taken from her home the same day we kissed, about the men who came for her, about the fear she felt as they dragged her away. She tells me about the warehouse, the auction, about being bought by Greenfield like she was a piece of merchandise, like she was nothing more than a commodity.

And with each word, I feel the disgust growing inside me. Not disgust at her—disgust at the world, at the men who did this to her, at the system that allowed it to happen, and my own family for being complicit in this horror;

weather it was known or not. My hands clench into fists, my jaw is tight, my breathing becoming shallow and rapid as she describes the things Greenfield did to her, the things his friends did to her, the things she was forced to do.

I can feel the rage building inside me, a living thing clawing its way out, demanding to be released. But I hold it back, because I need to hear this, I need to know what happened to her, because I need to understand the full extent of her suffering so I can make sure every man responsible pays with his life. She tells me about Greenfield's hands on her, about the things he made her do, about the way he looked at her like she was less than human. She tells me about the other men, about their faces blurring together in one monstrous visage, about the way they used and discarded her like she was nothing.

She tells me about the other owners, about the different places she was taken, the different men who used her. Each name is a knife wound, each story a reason to kill, each detail is another reason to burn the entire world down.

"I want to kill everyone who touched you," I say, my voice barely controlled, my hands shaking with barely contained rage. "Every single one of them. I'm going to find them, and I'm going to make them pay. I'm going to make them suffer the way you suffered. I'm going to make them understand what they did."

She gasps at me, her eyes wide with shock, and I can see her trying to process what I'm saying, trying to understand that I'm not angry at her, that my rage is directed at everyone else, at the world, at the men who destroyed her.

But she continues telling me her story, and I continue listening, the disgust continuing to build inside me until I feel like I'm going to explode, until I feel like I'm going to lose my mind completely, and I feel like the only thing that will make this right is vengeance, blood and death.

Finally, I can't take it anymore. The rage consumes me, the disgust overwhelming, the horror of what she describes is too much for my mind to process.

"That's enough," I say, standing abruptly, my chair scraping against the hardwood floor with a sound that makes her flinch. "That's enough. I thought I could handle it, but I can't. I can't listen to this anymore without losing my fucking mind."

I'm pacing now, my hands running through my hair, my mind spiralling with images of what's been done to her, with thoughts of all the men I'm going to kill, the desperate need to do something, anything, to make this right.

"Just tell me who owned you," I say, my voice low and dangerous. "I'll kill them. The rest can be left to imagination."

"Whatever you imagine," she says, her voice hollow and empty, like she's speaking from somewhere dark, broken and beyond repair that resides deep inside herself. "make it worse, because that's more the truth."

Whatever I imagine isn't worse than what actually happened. Which means what actually happened is beyond my comprehension, beyond my ability to process, beyond anything I could have anticipated. The horror of it, the depth of it, the sheer magnitude of her suffering is too much for me to bear.

I feel like I'm going to vomit, like I'm going to lose my mind. I feel like the only thing that will make this right is to find every man who touched her and kill them slowly, painfully and methodically; making sure they understand exactly what they did and exactly how much they're going to pay for it.

I walk to the kitchen, needing to get away from her for a moment, needing to get control of myself, to remember that she's not the enemy here. The enemy is out there, in the world, in the system that allowed this to happen.

"I'm going to get you some food," I say, trying to change the subject, trying to shift my mind away from the horror of what she's been through. "Are you hungry?"

"Whatever master permits," she says.

Master. She called me master. Like I'm one of them. Like I'm just another owner, another man who's going to use her and destroy her and throw her away. Like I'm no different from Greenfield or any of the other men who've touched her.

Something inside me snaps.

I reach for the closest object on the table—a glass—and I throw it across the room. It shatters against the wall, the sound loud and violent in the silence of the house, the glass fragments falling to the floor like tears.

"Master?" I shout, my voice raw with rage as my entire body shakes with the force of my emotions. "I'm not your fucking master! You're not my slave! For fuck's sake, Alba!"

I'm breathing hard, my chest heaves and my fists clench and I can see the fear in her eyes, can see her flinching away from me, can see her bracing herself for pain. And I hate myself for scaring her, hate myself for losing control and for not being able to hold it together for her sake.

"I'm not like them," I say, my voice quieter now but still raw, still filled with rage and desperation. "I'm not going to own you. I'm not going to control you. I'm not going to use you. Do you understand me? I'm not one of them."

I storm out of the room, unable to look at her anymore, unable to be in the same space as her without losing complete control, unable to be the man she needs me to be when I'm so consumed with rage that I can barely think straight.

"Clean that mess up!" I yell from the hallway, my voice echoing through the house, and I immediately regret it, immediately hating myself for it, immediately wanting to take it back. But I can't. I can't be around her right now. I can't be in the same room as her without losing my fucking mind.

I walk out onto the back patio and lean against the railing, my hands gripping the cold metal so tightly my knuckles turn white. The rage is still there, still burning inside me, still demanding to be released. But I can't release it. Not now. Not when Alba needs me to be stable, to be strong, to be someone she can trust.

I lean my head back and look up at the sky, trying to find some semblance of calm, trying to find some way to process the horror of what she's been through, trying to find some way to be the man she needs me to be.

Chapter 22

Alba

I stand there watching him walk away, my entire body frozen in place, unable to move, unable to think, unable to process what just happened. The sound of his footsteps echo through the hallway, growing fainter and fainter until he's completely gone, and I'm left alone with the shattered glass and my spiralling thoughts.

I place my hands on my hips and sigh, a long shaky breath coming from somewhere deep inside me. A single tear runs down my face, and I don't bother to wipe it away. What the fuck am I doing here? What is this? What am I to him?

Am I here for him? Am I another slave? The questions spiral through my mind, each one more terrifying than the last. Because he isn't treating me like the other owners did. He's not demanding that I perform, not forcing me to do things, not using me like I'm a piece of merchandise. But the way he demanded I clean up that mess—the way he yelled at me to do it—makes it sound like I am his slave, like I'm still owned, still trapped.

Fuck, I have no idea what I am to him.

I tiptoe around the glass, careful not to cut my bare feet on the sharp fragments. I open the cupboards one by one, searching for a dustpan and brush, my mind still spinning with confusion, fear and a desperate hope. When I finally find them, I pull them out and get to work, sweeping up the glass with methodical precision.

What other choice do I have? I can't refuse him. I can't run. I can't do anything but comply, anything but obey, anything but survive. So I sweep, and I try not to think about what it means, and I try not to wonder if this is mercy or just another form of torture.

The glass clinks into the dustpan, each fragment a small victory, each piece a reminder that I'm still here, still alive, still trapped in this beautiful prison. My hands are shaking as I work, my mind is racing with questions, and fears.

After I finish cleaning it up, and as I'm putting the dustpan and brush back in the cupboard, Gabe comes back. And I freeze, my entire body goes rigid, as my mind immediately prepares for punishment, for pain and the consequences of whatever I did wrong.

"Sorry I demanded that of you," he says, an honesty in his voice tinged with genuine regret and real remorse. "I shouldn't have done that. I'm sorry."

I don't know how to respond. No one has ever apologised to me before. No one has ever acknowledged that what they did was wrong. No one has ever shown me remorse, regret or genuine concern for my feelings.

"You may eat anything you want in this house, Alba," he continues, his voice steady and calm. "The fridge is always stocked, the cupboards are always full. You do not need my permission to eat. Please just eat. I won't stop you."

He runs a hand down his face, and I can see the exhaustion in his features, can see the way this is affecting him, the way he's struggling to be the man I need him to be.

"I'm going to be in my office," he says. "It's down the hall. Please change out of that outfit. I don't care what you wear, but lingerie isn't it."

And then he takes off, leaving me alone in the kitchen with my mess of thoughts.

I watch him leave, and I wonder if he hates the way my body looks now. Is that why he doesn't want me wearing the teddy? Is that why he's telling me to change? Maybe I'm not a sex slave, just a slave in general. Maybe he's not interested in my body, just in owning me, controlling me and keeping me trapped in this house.

The thought should be comforting, but it's not. It's just another layer of confusion, another question I can't answer, another piece of the puzzle that doesn't fit.

I open the fridge and the pantry, my mind already spinning with possibilities. I settle on two pieces of Vegemite toast, the familiar comfort of home, the taste of before, the taste of the girl I used to be. I can't eat a lot these days. Everyone has starved me over the years to keep me skinny and weak. Now I can only eat small amounts at a time, and even that feels like too much.

I make the toast and sit down at the table. I take a bite of the first slice, and the flavour hits me like a physical blow. It's so familiar, so comforting, so real. But after just one slice, I'm already feeling sick. My stomach is so small, shrunken from years of deprivation, it can barely handle the food.

I look at the second slice of toast sitting on the plate in front of me, and I feel a wave of panic wash over me. Why didn't I just make one? Why did I make two? What if I waste it? What if Gabe gets angry at me for wasting food? What if this is some kind of test and I'm failing it?

The fear is suffocating. I've been conditioned to believe that wasting food is a crime, that I should eat everything I'm given, that I should be grateful for whatever scraps are provided to me. But my stomach is screaming at me to stop, telling me I can't eat anymore, threatening to reject everything I've consumed.

I take another bite of the second slice, forcing myself to chew and swallow even though my body is rebelling against it. The toast feels like it's stuck in my throat, like it's choking me and it's going to come back up.

But I keep eating. I keep forcing it down. Because what other choice do I have? I'm terrified of wasting food. Terrified of disappointing Gabe. Terrified of what might happen if I don't finish what I've started.

Finally, I manage to swallow the last bite of the second slice. And immediately, my stomach really hurts. It's cramping and aching, threatening to reject everything I've consumed. I sit there for a long moment, my hands pressed against my stomach, my eyes closed as my mind tries to process the pain.

I've been starved for so long that my body has forgotten how to eat, deprived for so long that even small amounts of food feel like too much. I've been broken for so long that even the simple act of eating has become a source for fear, pain and confusion.

I stand up slowly and walk to the sink, rinsing off my plate, trying to compose myself and figure out what comes next.

Chapter 23

Gabriel

The morning sun is just beginning to break over the horizon when my phone rings. I'm still half-asleep, still tangled in the sheets, as I try to shake off the nightmare that's been haunting me all night. Alba. Her screams. Her tears. The things that have been done to her. The things I couldn't stop.

I reach for my phone, answering it, Matteo's voice cutting through the fog of my mind like a knife. "Gabe," he says, his tone sharp, impatient and gravelly with the weight of command, "we need to sort out the details for the next meet. It's on your turf this time."

I grunt a response, already pulling myself out of bed, and moving through the motions of getting ready for the day. My mind is still half-focused on Alba, and the fact that she spent the entire day yesterday in her room, while I worked in my office. I could hear her moving around, hearing her footsteps on the hardwood floor, her breathing through the wall that separates us.

But she didn't come out. Not until dinner.

And when she did, she picked at her plate like a bird, pushing the food around without really eating it. Alba used to love food. I remember that about her—the way her eyes would light up when she tasted something delicious, the way she'd savour every bite, and she'd ask for seconds and thirds without any shame or hesitation.

But that girl is gone. The girl who loved food is gone, replaced by this hollow shell of a woman who can barely stomach the thought of eating.

I hang up from Matteo and get dressed quickly, my mind already spinning with the details of the meeting, the politics of the underworld, the weight of the empire that's about to fall on my shoulders. But underneath it all, there's Alba. Always Alba.

I picture her door closed, a part of me aches to see her, to reassure myself that she's still here, under my roof, within my reach. But I can't afford distractions—not today. Not when I have to face the old man, not when I have to deal with the business, not when I have to figure out how to navigate this world without losing my mind completely.

The streets of Melbourne are waking up as I drive, the city stretching its limbs with the groan of traffic and the murmur of businesspeople starting their day. Buildings stand tall, watching as I navigate Melbourne's skeletal network. The sun climbing higher, painting the sky in shades of gold and orange. I'm trying not to think about Alba, trying not to think about the way she looked at dinner, trying not to think about the way she's slowly disappearing in front of me.

The old man will be at the warehouse. He's always there, perched like a decrepit vulture amidst the decay of his empire. We need to talk about the meeting of the seats, where the power plays of our countries underworld will come to a head. It's not just business—it's legacy, it's blood, it's everything.

Rubber on asphalt hums a monotonous dirge as I push the car faster, each turn bringing me closer to the inevitable. The sky brightens imperceptibly; a begrudging witness to the day's affairs. I pull up outside the warehouse, killing the engine and slamming my door with finality, facing my father's fortress; an imposing structure of steel and concrete. Getting out of the car, the air is crisp and bites against my skin. Security details dot the perimeter, with men who've sworn allegiance to my father and are now casting uneasy glances my way. They know what I've done. They can smell the change in the wind.

I offer no greeting—there's nothing to say to these minions. With a nod, they part before me, a silent admission of my place within this dark hierarchy. The dim interior swallows me as I step inside, fluorescent lights buzzing overhead like blowflies. The path to his office is etched into my navigational autopilot, a route marched often by duty and dread.

I bypass the usual pleasantries and the false camaraderie, moving with purpose, a silent chant to steel myself against the coming confrontation. His door is ahead, the threshold between what was and what will be.

I don't knock. The old man doesn't require such formalities—not from me. Pushing open the door, I step into his den, where pride and power encompass and suffocate me. He waits within, the architect of my torment and the keeper of my chains.

The door swings shut behind me with a sense of finality. He glances up, his predatory eyes bearing into me. A smile curls at the corner of his mouth in an omen more than a welcome.

"Nice to see you have come to your senses," he muses, dangerous undertones veiled by the warmth of his greeting.

My gaze hardens as I step closer. "I wouldn't say sense," I say. "But yes, I've calmed down now."

I stand before the man who sired me, shaped me into this semblance of control and cold calculation. Yet, my hands itch, a telltale sign of unrest. "I still don't forgive you," I say. "I find it hard to believe you had no idea. How can she slip through the books for resales without you knowing?"

He shrugs, the motion casual and dismissive. "I don't leave this office, son. I sit here and handle the paperwork, signing what needs to be signed." He gestures vaguely to the mountains of files crowding every surface. "I hardly ever read over the files as I trusted Fabio. I now see that was wrong; he wasn't trustworthy, and now I can't trust any of my men."

His confession hangs in the air, dressed up as an excuse. It's meant to be an olive branch, but it feels more like a thorned vine, ready to ensnare. I shrug in response, the motion doing nothing to lift the weight from my shoulders. "Well, I still don't forgive you."

He sighs, acknowledging the divide between us. Then, shifting gears, he leans forward with his elbows on the desk. "I heard you've bought Alba from Dan Johnson?"

"Yes, I have."

"Why?"

"Because she is mine, Papa," I say, my voice steady and certain. "Even if I never touch her, she is mine. She always was."

It's a truth I've known since the moment I laid eyes on her, a conviction that has burrowed deep into my bones. In this city, where power plays and violence go hand in hand, claiming something as your own is both a risk and a necessity. And Alba... she is the one thing I'm not willing to gamble away.

"Where is she now?" he asks.

"At home."

"Alone? Won't she run?"

I let out a breath that feels like it's been trapped in my chest for years. "It's okay if she does. She deserves the freedom. But I'm hoping she won't."

"Although I'll admit," I say, my hands curling into fists at my sides, "the thought of what has been done to her in the past is eating me alive. It makes me want to hide her away so no one can touch her again. It makes me want to burn down the entire world, so that no one can ever hurt her again."

My father sees right through the façade I've built up over the years. A smile plays across his lips, holding a semblance of warmth. "Yes, love is a funny thing," he says, his voice tinged with something I can't quite place. "You'll be okay, son. It will work out."

I'm not sure I believe him. I'm not sure anything will work out and I'm not sure I can fix what's been broken. But I nod anyway, because what else can I do?

"Also," he leans back in his chair, steepling his fingers, "where is the meeting happening?"

"Not sure. The warehouse will have a shipment in it at the time, so I was thinking of my place or yours."

"You're the boss soon," he says with a flicker of pride —or perhaps anticipation. "So, your house it will be."

I nod, a sense of the weight settling on my shoulders. The weight of the empire, the weight of the business, the weight of the responsibilities that are about to fall on me.

"Okay. I'll arrange it."

As I turn to leave, I realise I'm about to step into a role that will either forge me into a legend or break me entirely.

Chapter 24

Alba

I hear Gabe leave the house this morning, his car pulling out of the driveway with a finality that makes my heart race. He's gone. I'm alone. And for the first time in 13 years, I have the freedom to explore, to move around, to exist without someone watching my every move.

I emerge from the guest room slowly and cautiously, like I'm afraid someone is here hiding. My fingertips brush against the cool metal handles as I ease the doors open, revealing sparse furnishings and bland designs. I wander aimlessly, an intruder in a world that is distinctly not mine. The house is unassuming from the outside, but inside, it's a grand, modern five-bedroom sanctuary. Four rooms have been repurposed into sleeping quarters, but there's one room that's unmistakably Gabe's.

The moment I cross its threshold, the contrast strikes me. It's as if the sunlight hesitates to enter. The masculine and dark space is dominated by deep shades and heavy furniture; sleek lines of black timber stand in silent assertion. A bed, large and unapologetic, is made up with military precision, the dark sheets devoid of any frivolous touch.

It's a room that speaks of power and solitude—a fortress within a fortress. There's no trace of anyone else's influence. This room is Gabe's alone, sculpted by his desires and void of compromise. As I stand there, enveloped in the dim light, I know without doubt that only he could inhabit a space so commanding and so raw in its masculinity.

The realisation sends a shiver down my spine, not of fear, but of an awareness that behind the stoic façade of this man are layers yet to be uncovered, depths untold. And somewhere within me, a dormant force stirs—a blend of intrigue and trepidation at the thought of peeling back those layers. Gabe is a man cloaked in mystery, and standing in his most personal of sanctuaries, I feel both closer to and further from him than I ever have before.

I leave the starkness of Gabe's bedroom and drift down the hallway, my fingers trailing across the wall, feeling the texture of paint and the occasional framed picture. The air shifts as I move, mingling with a scent that is undeniably him—spicy undertones with a citrusy sharpness, a fragrance that seems to cling to the walls and seep into the very foundations of the house. It's distinctly masculine and comforting in its familiarity, unchanged by time or distance. Breathing it in, memories of a past I'm not sure I have permission to dwell on tug at the corners of my mind.

As if I'm compelled by an invisible force, I find myself standing before another closed door. This one swings open silently at my touch, revealing a space so different from the room I just left, it gives me pause. Here, soft light filters through the large windows, caressing the rich mahogany of a beautifully crafted desk that dominates the centre of the room.

Matching shelves line the walls, filled with a library of books that speak of a quieter side to Gabe—a side that thirsts for knowledge and perhaps solace found within the pages. The style is completely different from his bedroom, his domain of command, whereas this office is a sanctuary of thought and order. Elegant and business-like, every piece of furniture, every book, in its place, suggesting a meticulousness that borders on reverence for the rituals of work and the pursuit of wisdom.

I approach the desk, my fingers hovering before they settle on the smooth wood, tracing the grain that flows like a river through the landscape of the desk's surface. This room holds a different kind of power—it's not the overt strength of Gabe's private quarters, but rather the subtle influence of a mind that strategizes behind the scenes, one that plays the long game with patience and precision.

A heavy leather chair sits behind the desk, and I imagine Gabe sitting there, lines of worry and concentration crinkling his brow as he delves into the world's complexities. The dichotomy of the man is laid bare in these contrasting spaces—the darkness that lurks within, and the intellect that seeks to mask it.

It's all too easy to lose myself in the contemplation of who Gabe Gallo truly is—a man split between the brutality his role demands, and the potential for something more profound, something innately human that he clings to amidst the bedlam of his life in the mafia.

But I need to know. I need to know if he's a monster or not. I need to know if he's going to hurt me or help me. I need to know what his intentions with me are, what he wants from me and what I actually am to him.

I stand still for a moment in Gabe's office, allowing the cool silence to wash over me. It's an unexpected sanctuary amidst the chaos that his life has to be. But as I turn away, I see a small, framed photograph on the shelf—a woman with kind eyes and a smile that seems both gentle and knowing. Her arm is linked with Gabe's, both frozen in a moment of shared happiness.

A sharp and sudden pang of jealousy claws at my chest. It's ridiculous and unwarranted. Yet it's real. The unbidden question arises, does Gabe have a girlfriend or wife? Is she the reason this room holds such warmth, the undercurrent of love that I can almost reach out and touch?

My fingers brush against the cool glass of the frame, tracing the outline of their connected figures. If he does have someone, what would she think of him buying me, a woman from his past who has reappeared like a ghost? Would she see me as a threat, a spectre of a time before her? Or maybe she'd dismiss me, confident of her place by his side, secure in a love that has weathered storms I know nothing about.

The thought stokes the embers of jealousy into a slow burn. I can feel the heat of it colouring my cheeks, the irrational anger mingling with an inexplicable sense of infidelity. I don't have any claim on Gabe—never have. Yet the idea of him with someone else gets to me.

But I push the jealousy aside and continue exploring. I need to understand this house, to understand Gabe and to figure out what he wants from me before I make my next move.

I walk down the hallway and find the front door. My heart starts racing as I approach it. This is it. This is my way out. I reach for the handle and turn it slowly, carefully; half-expecting it to be locked and half-expecting alarms to go off.

But it's not locked. The door swings open easily, revealing the street and the world beyond. Freedom.

I stand there for a long moment, staring out at the world I've been denied for 13 years. I could walk out right now and disappear into the city. I could be free.

But I don't. I close the door and turn back to the house.

Because I need to know. I need to know if Gabe is a monster or not.

And the only way to find out is to stay. To watch him. To learn about him. To figure out if he's different from all the other men who've owned me, or if he's just another predator wearing a different mask.

So, I continue exploring. I walk through the kitchen, noting the abundance of food, the well-stocked pantry, the full refrigerator. I walk through the living room, noting the expensive furniture, the artwork on the walls, the books on the shelves. I walk through the hallways, noting the photographs, the decorations and the small touches that make this house a home.

And with each room I explore, I'm building a picture of who Gabe is. I'm trying to understand him. I'm trying to figure out if he's a monster or not.

The front door is unlocked. I could leave anytime I

want. But I won't. Not yet. Not until I know for sure what he wants from me.

If I run now, if I leave without knowing, then I'll never know. I'll spend the rest of my life wondering if I made the right choice, wondering if he was different.

And I can't live with that uncertainty, or the doubt.

I need to know.

Chapter 25

Gabriel

I pull into the driveway and feel a flutter of anticipation in my chest that I haven't felt in years. I'm excited to see her. Fuck. After 13 years of searching, 13 years of despair, 13 years of believing I'd never see her again, she's here. Alba is here. In my house. Under my roof.

I've spent the entire day at the warehouse, dealing with business, my father, and the endless complications of the empire that's about to fall on my shoulders. But the whole time, my mind has been on her. On Alba. I need to show her that life can be more than just survival, more than just existing, or just getting through each day.

I turn off the engine and grab my keys. I've been worried about her all day.

But as I step through the front door, the silence creeps in first. The house is too quiet. Too still. Too empty.

My excitement evaporates instantly, replaced by a cold, creeping dread that starts in my chest and spreads through my entire body like ice water poured through my veins. The silence is wrong. It's the kind of silence that comes with absence.

She's gone.

The thought crashes through my mind with devastating certainty. She's left. She's run. She's decided that staying with me is too risky, too uncertain, too terrifying. And I can't blame her. I can't blame her for running. I can't blame her for choosing freedom over the uncertainty of staying with me.

But the thought of losing her again, after just getting her back, is suffocating. It's crushing. It's destroying me from the inside out.

I move quickly through the house, my heart pounding in my chest, my hands shaking as I check the security system. I pull up the footage from the cameras positioned around the front and back of the house, my eyes scanning frantically for any sign of her leaving, any sign of her escaping.

Nothing. The cameras show nothing. No one has left through the front or back. The cameras would have caught her if she walked outside. But that doesn't stop the panic from clawing at my chest, doesn't stop the fear from consuming me, doesn't stop the desperate need to find her from overwhelming every rational thought in my head.

Maybe, she found another way out. Maybe, she climbed the fence. Maybe, she did something I didn't anticipate. Maybe, she's already gone, disappeared into the city, lost to me forever.

I race through the house, my footsteps echoing through

the hallway as I head straight for her room. I need to see her. I need to know she's still here. I need to know that she hasn't abandoned me.

I reach her door and push it open, the relief that floods through me is so intense that I almost stumble. She's here. She's sitting on the edge of her bed, just sitting there quietly, her hands folded in her lap, her eyes staring at nothing. She's here. She hasn't left. She hasn't run.

But something is wrong. Something is deeply, fundamentally wrong. She's sitting in the darkness of her room, in the quiet isolation, and she's not moving, not speaking, not doing anything. She's just sitting there like a statue, like a ghost, like she's not really here at all.

I frown, looking at her like she's lost her mind. "What the hell are you doing?" I ask, my voice rough with the remnants of the panic and fear that's still coursing through my veins, rough with the desperate need to understand what's happening inside that beautifully broken mind of hers.

She looks at me, and there's something in her eyes that I can't quite identify. It's not fear. It's not anger. It's something else. Something deeper. Something that speaks to the 13 years of captivity, to the 13 years of abuse.

"Why are you sitting in here in the quiet?" I ask, trying to understand what's going on, trying to figure out how to help her and to bridge the gap between who she was and who she's become.

"I'm used to it," she says quietly, her voice small and uncertain, like she's afraid that answering me is going to get her in trouble, like she's afraid that I'm going to punish her for being in her room, like she's afraid that she's done something wrong.

She's used to silence. She's used to being locked away. She's used to isolation. She's been conditioned to seek out the quiet, finding comfort in the darkness, to believe that being alone is safer than being with other people. And the realisation of what that means, what that says about what's been done to her, what that reveals about the depth of her trauma, makes my rage burn hotter than it ever has before.

I'm going to kill them.

But I can't do that right now. Right now, I need to focus on her. Right now, I need to help her understand that she's safe, that she's not alone and she doesn't have to hide in the quiet anymore.

"You can do what you want, Alba," I say, my voice steady despite the rage building inside me, despite the desperate need to protect her, despite the overwhelming desire to reach out and fold her into my arms "Watch the TV. Read a book. Go outside. Listen to music. Do whatever you want. This isn't a prison. You're not trapped here."

She nods slowly, but I'm not sure she believes me. I'm not sure she understands that she's actually free to do whatever she wants. I'm not sure she comprehends that I'm not going to lock her away, that I'm not going to force her to do anything, that I'm not going to hurt her.

The realisation that she's been so broken, so conditioned, so destroyed that she doesn't even understand what freedom looks like, is almost too much for me to bear. I want to pull her into my arms, to hold her and tell her that everything's going to be okay. But I'm terrified that if I touch her, if I get too close, if I try to comfort her, I'm going to make things worse. I'm terrified that my presence is going to trigger her, that my touch is going to remind her of all the men who've hurt her, that my attempt at comfort is going to feel like another form of violation.

So I step back. I create distance. I give her space.

"I'm going to start dinner," I say, trying to shift the energy in the room, trying to give her something normal to focus on. "I've also got bags in the car for you. Clothes. I guessed your size. I hope they fit."

I turn and walk out before she can respond, my mind already spinning with worry and concern and desperate hope that maybe, just maybe, I can be the man she needs me to be. After what she's been through for the last 13 years, she's going to be a little crazy. Maybe she needs a therapist. Someone who specialises in trauma. Someone who can help her process what's been done to her and who can help her heal in ways that I can't.

But first, I need to get her to eat. I need to get her to understand that she's safe. I need to get her to believe that I'm not going to hurt her.

I head out to the car and grab the bags, my jaw clench- ing. I'd placed a few orders for click and collect, which I sent one of the lackeys to pick up for me. She needs clothes and stuff that belong to her, things that will help to make her feel like herself again, things that will remind her of who she was before the darkness consumed her.

I got her jewellery, perfume, and other random things. I got leggings, tracksuits, t-shirts, jeans, and dresses—the type of things she liked when she was 17. I'm not sure she likes the same stuff anymore, but I didn't know what else to get. I tried to think about what Alba would have wanted, what will make her feel comfortable, what will help her feel like herself again.

I bring the bags inside and set them on the table, my hands moving with purpose as I start preparing dinner. I need to keep busy. I need to keep my mind occupied.

I pull out a pot and fill it with water, setting it on the stove to boil. The water starts to heat, steam rising from the surface.

I grab the pasta from the pantry and the beef from the fridge, my movements automatic and practiced. A simple pasta and beef soup. Nothing fancy. Nothing that requires too much thought or attention. Something warm and comforting, that says I care about her, that I'm thinking about her, that I want her to feel safe and cared for.

I start chopping the vegetables—onions, carrots, celery. The repetitive motion is soothing, grounding, as it helps me focus on something other than the fear and anger that's still lurking in the back of my mind.

I need to fix her. I need to help her heal. I need to be the man who saves her.

But what if I can't? What if I'm not enough? What if I make things worse? What if my presence, my touch, my attempt at help, only serves to remind her of all the men who've hurt her?

Adding the beef to a separate pan, I let it brown, as the scent of cooking meat fills the kitchen. I add the vegetables to the pot of boiling water, watching the colours brighten as they soften, watching the soup come to life.

The aroma of beef and herbs makes my own stomach grumble. I haven't really been eating myself since she got home. The stress of getting her home has been a little unbearable, but I'm going to make it work. All I can do is try. All I can do is show her, day after day, that I'm not a monster. I'm not going to hurt her. I'm going to help her heal.

Even if it takes the rest of my life.

Chapter 26

Alba

The hours roll into days, there's not a lot of change on the surface, but underneath, everything has changed. Gabe goes to work in the morning, and I watch him leave from the window, my heart does something strange that I can't quite understand. Then when he comes home in the evening, the first thing he does is go into the kitchen and start cooking. He cooks for me. Every single day, he cooks for me.

It's such a simple thing, a basic act of care, but to me, it's revolutionary. No one has ever cooked for me before. No one has ever put thought or effort into feeding me, nourishing me, and making sure I have something warm and delicious to eat. The men who've owned me before just gave me scraps, just enough to keep me alive, using food as a tool of control and punishment.

But Gabe cooks. He makes pasta, soup, stir-fries and things I've never even heard of before. And every night after dinner, he sits on the couch with his laptop on his lap, alternating between working and answering so many calls. It's crazy how he deals with everything. I'll never understand how he manages it all—the business, the empire, the constant demands for his time and attention. But somehow he does it, and then he's present with me, before he goes to bed, then wakes up and does it all over again.

He answers calls constantly. His phone rings nonstop, and he takes them all, speaking in a voice that's cold and commanding; nothing like the voice he uses with me. I hear him talking about shipments, meetings, people I don't know and things I don't understand. I hear the mafia in his voice, the darkness and the man he's become because of his family, because of his blood, and the world he was born into.

A few days ago, he brought me a phone. He took time to show me how to use it, showing me how to open it, navigate the internet and how to do things that people who've been free their whole life take for granted. And then he explained to me that if I leave the house, I need to take it with me, so he can pick me up if I need help. The implication clear—I can leave whenever I want. The door is unlocked. The phone is just a safety net, a way for him to know I'm okay if I decide to go.

I'm starting to realise that I can leave if I want and I'm starting to want to. I'm starting to see the fresh start, a life without chains and bars, the possibility of being someone other than what I've been forced to become. Gabe hasn't shown me any harm at all, and it's been nice. It's been more than nice. It's been healing in ways I didn't expect.

I'm seeing more and more of the boy he used to be peeping through the gaps of the man he's become. I see it in the way he looks at me, when he thinks I'm not watching. I see it in the way he cooks for me, with such care and attention. I see it in the way he respects my boundaries, the way he gives me space, never pushing me further than I'm willing to go.

But he's still the son of the mafia, the son of the man who trafficked me. He is still complicit in the system that destroyed me; even if he didn't know about me specifically. And I think I need a fresh start. One where I can be me. One where I can work out what I want in life, who I want to be and what kind of person I want to become.

Gabe offered to get me a shrink the other day. He said he would help me find one to talk to, that it might help me process what's been done to me, might help me heal. But I asked him not to. I don't want to relive my past. I don't want to dredge up all the trauma, pain and horror. I want to leave it exactly where it is—in the past, where it belongs.

The clothes he bought me were a little big at first, but with the constant food he's been feeding me, I've managed to gain a few kilos in weight. My face doesn't look so gaunt now, thankfully. My body is starting to look like it belongs to a person again; not just a skeleton wrapped in skin. I'm starting to look like Alba again, or at least like a version of Alba that could exist.

Gabe had a TV brought into my room, explaining to me how to watch Netflix and stuff. That's where I am now, in bed flicking through the shows, trying to find something that doesn't make me want to scream. I used to adore crime books and movies, but now I can't stomach them. The violence, the darkness, the depravity—it's all too much. It's all too real. So, I watch a lot of comedy instead. Things that are silly and make zero sense, but the background noise is nice. The laughter is a nice distraction.

It's where Gabe finds me now, sprawled out on my bed, watching some ridiculous show about people doing stupid things for money. He leans against the doorframe, telling me dinner is ready. I get up and walk out to the table, finding a fresh new dish I haven't tried before. It smells incredible—something with garlic, herbs and something I can't quite identify.

Gabe is really a good cook. So much better than I'll ever be. And I find I now look forward to what he cooks for dinner every night. I find myself anticipating it, wondering what he's going to make, wondering if it's going to be something I love or something I'll need to learn to love.

We sit down and I start eating. I'm eating nearly half a plate worth of food now. It's progress. Real, tangible progress. My stomach handling more food means my body is healing. My mind is starting to believe that maybe, just maybe, I'm going to be okay.

But tonight, Gabe places his fork down on his plate and says something that catches me completely off guard.

"I really do wish you would eat it all," he says, his voice careful but firm, "and stop moving it around the plate like it will magically disappear on its own."

I immediately feel the shame and fear rising in my chest, feeling the instinct to apologise and submit, to do whatever he wants. So, I say sorry to him, because that's all I know how to do. That's all I've been conditioned to do. That's all I've learnt in 13 years of captivity.

But he snaps at me, his voice sharp and cutting in a way I haven't heard in weeks.

"Stop being so submissive all the fucking time, Alba," he says, his eyes blazing with something I can't quite identify. "Tell me to fuck off. Tell me to go away. Tell me to shut up. I don't care. But stop doing what someone says. The old you would have happily told me to fuck off."

The words hang in the air between us, heavy with meaning and loaded with expectation. He wants me to fight back, to be defiant. He wants me to be the girl I used to be, the girl who had fire, spirit and the courage to tell people exactly what she thought.

I look at him, and for the first time in days, I feel something other than fear, gratitude or confusion. I feel anger. I feel indignation. I feel the spark of the old Alba starting to reignite.

"I'm not that little girl anymore, Gabe," I say, my voice steady and strong in a way I haven't heard it in years. "That girl is gone. She died a long time ago."

And I wait as the silence settles between us, sitting there and making itself known. It's heavy, thick and full of all the things we haven't said, all the things we're both afraid to say, all the things that hang between us like a sword.

He stares at me, his eyes softening as he takes in what I've said. And then he nods slowly, like he's accepting something he's known all along but needed to hear me say out loud.

"I know this," he says quietly, his voice gentle now, his eyes filled with what looks like sadness, understanding and a desperate kind of hope. "I know this, Alba. And I'm sorry. I'm sorry that I can't give you back the girl you were. I'm sorry that I can't undo what's been done to you. But I'm here. And I'm going to help you figure out who you want to be now."

And in that moment, sitting at his table, looking at his face and hearing the sincerity in his voice, I realise that maybe, just maybe, I don't need to leave. Maybe, I can stay. Maybe, I can figure out who Alba is now, in this moment, in this life, with this man who's trying so hard to be different from his father, to be different from the men who hurt me, to be something more than just another predator in a suit.

But I'm still scared and uncertain. I'm still not sure if I can trust him, if I can trust anyone, or even if I can trust myself.

Gabe stares me down through the silence, his eyes searching mine, like he's trying to read something written on the inside of my skull. And then he says something that catches me completely off guard.

"I have a meeting here with the rest of the seats," he says, his voice carefully measured. "Do you think you could help me?"

I blink at him, trying to process what he's asking. A meeting. With the heads of the mafia. In his house. With me.

"I added a few slacks and blouses in the bags of clothes I got you," he continues, "so, you could wear those? I'll need help dishing out the food, while I do the meeting. Aurelio or Catcher can help you too?"

Is he asking me to help him with the business that destroyed me?

"When?" I ask, my voice small and uncertain.

"Tomorrow," he says.

I just nod and say okay. Because what else can I do?

Maybe this is the moment where I realise that I can't stay. That I can't be part of this world. That I need to leave and find my own path, my own life, my own future.

Chapter 27

Gabriel

The morning of the meeting, I'm up early, moving through the house with a sense of purpose that I haven't felt in weeks. I'm nervous about this. I'm nervous about introducing Alba into my world, bringing her into the darkness, and showing her exactly what I am and what I do. But I'm also determined to show her that she's not something to be ashamed of, that she's not a secret, or something I need to hide away.

I start getting everything ready. The dining room—the one I never use, the one that's always felt too formal, too cold much like my father's house—needs to be transformed into a space where business gets done. I wish it was happening at my dad's place. He has more room, more space; more of everything. But it is what it is. This is what I have, and I'm going to make it work.

I move through the house, checking the table, making sure the chairs are positioned correctly, making sure everything is set up for the meeting. The heads are coming.

Aurelio, Catcher, and the others. They're coming to discuss business, to discuss the empire, the future of the organisation now that I'm taking over.

And Alba is going to be here. She's going to see me in my element. She's going to see the man I've become, the darkness I've embraced, the world I've built for myself.

I hear her moving around, and my heart does something strange in my chest. She's getting ready, putting on the slacks and blouse I bought for her. And I'm trying not to think about what she's going to look like, trying not to imagine her in the clothes, trying not to let my body respond to the thought of her.

But when she comes into the room, all my attempts at control completely fall apart.

She's wearing black slacks that fit her perfectly, hugging her curves in a way that makes my mouth go dry. And she's wearing a cream blouse that sets her red hair off so beautifully. She is stunning. Absolutely stunning. The kind of stunning that makes me want to pull her into my arms and claim her in front of everyone, the kind of stunning that makes me want to run my hands through her hair and cup her cheek, the kind of stunning that reminds me exactly why she's always been my weakness.

From day one she was mine. She just captivated me. There was something about her, something in the way she moved, the way she smiled, the way she looked at me like I was the only person in the world that mattered. And that hasn't changed. Even after 13 years. Even after everything that's happened. Even after all the darkness, pain and trauma.

She still captivates me.

I stop next to her as she helps me set up the room, making sure everything is perfect. I look down at her, and she stills, looking up into my eyes, and I can see the uncertainty there, the fear, the question of what I'm thinking, what I'm feeling, what I want from her.

"You look stunning today," I say, my voice rough as I try to control myself, rough with the desire I'm trying to suppress, the need to touch her consuming me. "You know this right?"

She blushes, and it's the most beautiful thing I've ever seen. The colour rises in her cheeks, and she looks uncomfortable, like she's not used to compliments and she doesn't know how to accept praise. The thought of all the *men* who've made her feel like she's not worthy of compliments, like she's not worthy of being told she's beautiful, makes my rage burn hot.

"Thank you," she says, her voice barely above a whisper.

I want to tell her more. I want to tell her that she's the most beautiful woman I've ever seen. I want to tell her that she takes my breath away. I want to tell her that I can't stop thinking about her, that I can't stop wanting her, that I can't stop needing her.

But I don't. I just nod and move on to the practical details.

"They're arriving at 11," I tell her, my voice shifting back into business mode, my tone more controlled and more distant. "The catering will be here at 10:30. They'll place it all in the kitchen, so all you need to do is walk it in at 11:30 and place it down."

She nods, absorbing the information, committing it to

memory. She's good at this. She's good at taking instructions, at understanding what's needed, at doing what's asked of her. But I don't want her to just follow instructions. I want her to think for herself. I want her to challenge me. I want her to be more than just someone who does what she's told.

But that's a conversation for another time.

"Catcher will help you, okay?" I say, making sure she knows she won't be alone, making sure she knows she has backup, making sure she knows that I'm not going to throw her into the deep end without support.

"Okay," she says, and there's something in her voice that sounds like resignation, like she's accepting a role in this world, like she's beginning to understand that this is what being with me means.

We go back to what we were doing, setting up the room, preparing for the meeting. But my mind is still on her, the way she looked in that cream blouse, the way her red hair catches the light, and the way she captivates me; she's always captivated me, and I know she always will.

And I'm wondering if she knows. If she understands that she's the reason I'm doing this. She's the reason I'm trying to be better, the reason I'm trying to change, the reason I'm fighting against the darkness that's trying to consume me.

She's always been the reason.

I move around the room, checking everything one more time to make sure everything is perfect. The table is set. The chairs are arranged. The room is ready. And Alba is ready. She's prepared. She's beautiful. She's here.

And in a few hours, the heads of the organisation are

going to walk through that door, and they're going to see her. They're going to see the woman I've brought into my world. They're going to see the woman I'm protecting. They're going to see the woman who is my weakness.

And I don't care one bit.

Chapter 28

Alba

T he clock strikes 11 am, and my heart immediately starts racing. The heavy thud of boots announces their arrival before I even see them. Catcher and Aurelio swing open the door with the casual authority of men who think they own the place, and I feel my entire body tense. This is it. This is the moment where I step into Gabe's world, when I see exactly what he is, and I begin to understand the full scope of the darkness that surrounds him.

My hands are shaking. I clasp them together, trying to steady myself, trying to appear calm and composed, even though I'm falling apart on the inside.

Catcher's towering frame looms over me the moment as he enters. The tattoos webbing across his skin appear alive, the dark serpents coiling under the surface, moving with every flex of his muscles. There's something powerful about him, something that speaks of violence and danger, but his eyes are kind when they land on me. He doesn't hesitate, stepping forward and planting a kiss on my cheek, the stubble on his face grazes my skin. The gesture is gentle, almost protective, and when he pulls back, there's genuine warmth in his expression.

"Sorry for grabbing you at the club," he says, his voice rough but sincere. "If I'd known it was you, I wouldn't have touched you. I didn't realise it was you until Gabe told me. I would never have done that if I'd known."

There's real remorse in his voice, real concern. He's not just saying what he thinks Gabe wants to hear. He actually means it. He actually cares that he grabbed me without knowing who I was, that he treated me like just another girl at the club instead of recognising me as someone important.

Before I can even muster a response, Gabe's voice cuts through the moment like a knife.

"You're still touching her now, dickhead," he growls, and there's something in his tone that makes my breath catch; a possessiveness laced with rage. A desperate need to keep Catcher away from me.

But Catcher just grins, his eyes twinkling with amusement rather than malice as he pulls his hand away from my arm, raising his hands in mock surrender.

"Relax, mate," he says to Gabe, his voice light and teasing. "I'm just saying hello to the girl. No need to get your knickers in a twist."

I want to reach out and touch Gabe. I want to put my hand on his arm and tell him it's okay, that Catcher doesn't scare me, and I'm fine. But I don't. I keep my hands clasped together, keeping my distance, keeping the wall between us firmly in place. Because I've made a decision. I've decided that I need to leave. I need to get away from this world, away from these men and away from the darkness that consumes everything around me.

Even if it means leaving Gabe.

Catcher's smile is genuine and warm as he heads off toward the dining room to help with the setup, his massive frame moving with a surprising grace. "Come on then, let's get this place sorted," he calls back to Aurelio.

Aurelio's approach is gentler and more sincere, a stark contrast to Catcher's boisterous energy. He offers me a smile that holds genuine warmth, despite the mischief dancing within his eyes. There's something almost familiar about him, something that speaks of a time before everything fell apart.

"We all missed you, girl," he says, and his voice is soft, almost tender. "Glad to see you're safe again. Gabe hasn't been the same since you went missing."

There's something comforting about Aurelio's familiarity, a fleeting moment of normalcy in a world that's anything but. It also terrifies me. Because if Gabe hasn't been the same since I went missing, that means he's been suffering. That means he's been broken by my absence. And the thought of being responsible for his pain, of being the reason he's been destroyed, is almost too much to bear.

But I can't think about that right now. I can't let myself feel that. Because if I do, I'll never leave. And I have to leave.

I stand there, caught in the crossfire of egos and old wounds, surrounded by men who see life as a game of chess, each move calculated, every consequence weighed. And through it all, I'm trying to hold onto the resilience that's carried me this far, the quiet defiance that speaks of my inner strength, even in the face of subjugation.

"Why you both gotta put hands on her…?" Gabe says, almost inaudible with all the noise of furniture being dragged and positioned, but I catch it—the venom and vitriol masquerading as jest. And I realise that he's not joking. He's not playing around. He's genuinely angry that Catcher touched me.

The realisation makes my chest ache. Because it means he cares. It means I matter to him, and it means that maybe, just maybe, he actually loves me.

And that's exactly why I have to leave.

Because I can't be part of this. I can't be the woman standing in the background of a mafia meeting, serving food to dangerous men, watching power shift and morality crumble. I can't be the girl who's always looking over her shoulder, waiting for the next disaster, bracing for the next wave of darkness.

I need quiet. I need peace. I need to be able to breathe without feeling like I'm drowning.

And then they arrive—Gabe's guests—a parade of power strutting into the den of the devil himself. I watch them file in, and my entire body goes rigid with fear. These are the heads of the organisation. These are the men who control Australia's underworld. These are the men who hold the power to destroy lives, to end people, to reshape the world according to their whims.

And they terrify me.

There's a woman among them, hanging off the arm of a man. She moves with a fluid grace that belies her true nature. Beautiful, slender and adorned with tattoos that speak of a story I don't know, she has an aura that seems untouched by the grime of this world. It makes me wonder what kind of woman flourishes in a world soiled by blood and greed. Does she see through the same lens of jaded cynicism that clouds my vision, or does she find beauty in the mayhem?

"Eleanor," she says as she glides past me, and the name suits her; it's elegant, soft and wrapped in a layer of mystery. I find myself momentarily lost in her eyes, even as they turn away to scan the room. And just like that, she's by the man's side again, her hand resting on his arm with a familiarity that speaks of a deep connection.

The man beside her is beautiful in a way that's almost criminal. His tall frame moves with an effortless charm, each step calculated and precise. Black hair styled to perfection, not a strand out of place, and tattoos creep from beneath the fabric of his suit, hinting at a wild side cloaked by tailored refinement. His smile is fleeting, as though he's well-versed in the art of keeping his emotions hidden, but for a moment, he directs it at me—a silent acknowledgment before following Catcher and Aurelio down the hall.

Trailing behind them is an older gentleman whose presence commands attention without demanding it. Rossi, Gabe calls him, and even the uncertainty of my memory can't diminish the importance of that name. His suit exudes wealth and power. Time hasn't been kind to him; the grey peppering his hair tells tales of stress and hardship, of decisions made and lives destroyed. And yet, there's an undeniable charm to the way he smiles politely at me, as if attempting to soften the edge of the criminal world we inhabit.

But I know better. I know their charm is a weapon. I know their politeness is a mask. I know beneath every smile there's a capacity for violence, for cruelty, for destruction.

Just before Gabe turns to follow them, he stops and looks at me, "Please, make sure you eat some of the food yourself."

I nod, quickly retreating to the kitchen where the scent of food wafts through the air, warm and comforting as it envelops my senses. The 30 minutes creep by slowly, each second laden with the weight of anticipation. My hands shaking as I prepare the dishes, arrange the bowls and get ready to walk into that room to serve the men. When it's finally time, I carry the dishes to the dining room, the rich aroma of chicken and mushroom risotto follows me like a ghost; like a reminder of the life I could have if I'd be brave enough to stay.

But I'm not brave enough. I'm too broken. I'm too damaged. I'm too terrified of what it means to be part of this world.

The steel in Catcher's eyes as he stands guard by the dining door sends a shiver down my spine, but when he looks at me, there's nothing but kindness there. The steam from the dishes undulates like spectral fingers, curling around my apprehension as I step forward. This is no ordinary meal service. This is a foray into the lion's den with porcelain and an entree as my only armour.

"Careful," Catcher grunts, but there's concern in his voice, genuine worry that I might hurt myself or drop something. He reaches out to steady me, his massive hand gentle on my elbow. "You good, Alba? You look a bit pale."

I nod, barely trusting my voice at this point. His concern and genuine care for my wellbeing, makes everything harder. Because Catcher is nice, kind, and shows me that not all of these men are monsters.

But they're still a part of this world. They're still a part of the darkness. And I can't stay.

Gabe's family's enterprises are managed with hushed tones and deals sealed with blood oaths. Yet here I am, after everything I've been through, in their presence, serving food that seems so mundane compared to the machinations at play. Looking around leaves me wondering why Gabe's father isn't presiding over the gathering, Is it a transfer of power? Has Gabe ascended to command? My mind reels with the possibilities, each more treacherous than the last.

With each step closer to the table where they all sit—a tableau of power draped in fine fabrics and sharper smiles —I feel the gravity of the room pull at me. The weight of their attention, the intensity of their focus, the sheer magnitude of their power. It's suffocating, overwhelming and everything I've been trying to escape.

I distribute the bowls methodically, my hands steady even though my heart is racing, even though I'm trying to appear calm, my breathing is shallow. As I reach Eleanor, she looks at me with soft eyes. There's a kindness in her gaze, something gentle that speaks to a part of me that's still human, still capable of connection, still capable of hope.

"Thank you," she says, her voice a soothing balm that makes me linger a moment longer than necessary.

"You're welcome," I reply, the words slipping out before I can catch them, wrapped in a warmth I hadn't expected to feel here.

She's a conundrum, wrapped in elegance and mystery. How does she fit into all of this? Her presence, somehow both commanding and gentle, sparks a curiosity within me that I can't quell. Is she merely an ornament to the man beside her, or does her calm demeanour mask a depth I'm yearning to understand? Is she trapped like I am, or has she found a way to thrive in this world?

Leaving the room, I find solace in a secluded corner to consume my own lunch.

And I make my final decision. I'm going to leave. Tonight. I'm going to take the phone Gabe gave me, I'm going to walk out the front door that he left unlocked, and I'm going to disappear. I'm going to find a new life, a quiet life, where I don't have to be afraid, I don't have to watch powerful men make decisions that destroy lives, where I don't have to stand in the background pretending that everything is okay. I can't be around men who sell women like me.

Even if it means leaving Gabe.

Even if it means breaking his heart.

Even if it means breaking my own.

Chapter 29

Gabriel

The meeting has been underway for about ten minutes by the time I finally get everyone settled around the table. The energy in the room is different now that I'm leading this instead of my father. There's an underlying weight to it, a responsibility now sitting heavily on my shoulders. But I push it aside and focus on business.

Before Alba comes in with the food, I need to get through the important stuff; The operational updates and the problems that need solving.

Matteo leans back in his chair and starts talking business. This is how we operate—straight into the work, no time for pleasantries or bullshit.

"The nightclubs are doing well," Matteo says, his voice carrying the confidence of a man who knows his operations are running smoothly. "The cross is pulling in record numbers. The new fit outs we did have been a hit. People are lining up around the block."

"Good," I say, nodding. "We need the revenue flowing. What about the shipment's?"

"Last drug shipment came through without any issues," Matteo says, his eyes gleaming with satisfaction. "Clean delivery, no hiccups. The new route we established is working perfectly. The cops didn't even sniff in our direction."

Aurelio nods in agreement, his expression satisfied. But Antonio, sitting across from me, furrows his brow. There's something bothering him, something eating at him; I can see it in the tension of his jaw and the way his fingers drum against the table.

"My shipments have been good," Antonio says, his voice measured, an undercurrent of frustration cutting through. "Mostly. But the last few... they've been stopped. Intercepted. And I can't work out why."

The room goes quiet. This is serious. Losing shipments means losing money, losing product, losing face.

"Stopped by who?" I ask, my voice sharp. "Cops? Rival families?"

"That's the thing," Antonio says, shaking his head. "Nothing's been found. No arrests. No bodies. It's like they just... disappeared. The drivers report that they were pulled over, the shipments were taken, and then they were let go. No violence. No threats. Just gone."

Matteo leans forward, his eyes narrowing. "That's not how the cops operate. They'd make a big show of it, arrests, press conferences, the whole thing. This sounds like someone else."

"Enemies?" Eleanor suggests, but there's doubt in her voice.

"Maybe," I say, thinking it through. "But if it was someone who disliked us, we'd know about it. There'd be retaliation. There'd be bodies. This is too clean, too organised."

"So, what do we do?" Antonio asks, the frustration now fully evident in his tone. "We can't just let this keep happening. We're losing too much product, too much money."

"We change it up," I say, my mind already working through the possibilities. "Change the delivery drivers. Change the routes. Change the men we're using. Mix it up so whoever's doing it can't predict our moves."

"What if it's a mole?" Matteo says quietly, voicing what we all think but don't want to say out loud. "What if someone on the inside is tipping them off?"

The suggestion hangs in the air like a blade. A mole means betrayal. A mole means someone we trust, has turned against us.

"We need to investigate," I say, my voice cold and controlled. "Quietly. Don't let anyone know we're looking. If there is a mole, we need to find them before they do any more damage."

"How do you want to handle it?" Eleanor asks. "Do we bring in someone from outside? Someone we trust completely?"

"No," I say firmly. "We handle this in-house."

Antonio nods, his jaw clenching. "I'll start pulling the records. I'll have the boys look into it, they only brought this up to me last week."

"Good," I say. "And in the meantime, we change

everything. Make it impossible for them to predict our moves."

Matteo runs his jaw, his eyes thoughtful. "This is going to cost us," he says. "We can't have anymore shipments detained."

"I know," I say. "But it's better than losing everything. And once we find the mole, we'll make an example of them. We'll make sure everyone knows what happens to traitors."

The room falls silent again, but this time it's a silence of men who understand the gravity of the situation, who understand that we're facing a threat from within our own organisation.

That's when Catcher appears at the door. "Food's ready," he says, his massive frame filling the doorway. "It's coming in now."

I nod, and a moment later, Alba appears with the first tray of dishes. Her eyes downcast, her movements careful and precise. She's trying to be invisible, trying to blend into the background, but I can't help but notice the way her hands shake slightly as she sets the bowls down in front of each man.

She moves around the table with practiced efficiency, serving Matteo first, then Antonio. Her red hair catching the light as she bends forward, and I have to force myself to look away, to focus on anything other than the way she moves, the way she breathes, the way she exists in this space.

When she reaches me, she hesitates for just a fraction of a second. Our eyes almost meet, but she catches herself and looks away, her cheeks flushing slightly. She sets my bowl down with the same care she's shown everyone else.

She finishes serving everyone and then shuffles out of the room, her eyes still downcast, her shoulders slightly hunched as if she's trying to make herself smaller, less noticeable. The door closes quietly behind her, and the room feels emptier without her presence.

For a moment, no one says anything. We all just sit there, the weight of what we've been discussing, the weight of the decisions we've made, settling over us like a heavy blanket.

That's when Eleanor rises with a dark fury and tempestuous energy. She makes no sound, but I sense the shift immediately. Her hand, swift and sure, reaches into Matteo's jacket and takes out his gun, setting my heart racing, especially when she takes the safety off.

"Jesus, Eleanor," I say, unable to keep the smirk off my face, despite the chill spreading through my veins. "You planning a coup or have you just missed me that much?"

"Cut the crap, Gabe," she says, arm unwavering as she trains the barrel right between my eyes. "Please tell me you have not bought yourself a fucking sex slave."

The accusation is part threat and part disgust. My raised brow is armour, a shield against the turmoil her words stir within me. I know what it looks like, know the quicksand pit it appears we're sinking into, and it burns like acid in my gut.

"Easy, Eleanor. Let's talk about this before you start redecorating the walls with my brains, huh?" I say, trying to keep my voice level and defuse the situation before it explodes in my face.

Eleanor's stare is a laser beam of fury. "Gabe, don't play stupid with me," she says, the gun in her hand quivering ever so slightly—a cobra poised to strike.

"Believe me, Eleanor, I haven't forgotten our chats," I say, trying to defuse her. The betrayal on her face stings because we've been scheming together to cleanse the family stain, to wash away the sins of the people trade. And here comes Alba, an unexpected curveball threatening to send Eleanor's trust—and my efforts—crashing down in flames.

That's when Matteo decides to chime in, the bastard. His eyes are two pits of dark hunger, feasting on the sight of Eleanor like she's about to be his last meal on earth. He palms himself through the fabric of his expensive suit, and he has the gall to purr at her, "Princess, if you don't want me to bend you over this table while everyone eats their lunch, I suggest you put the gun down."

I watch, incredulous, as she tilts her head, considering Matteo's proposition or threat—it's hard to tell with these two. Then in a gesture so loaded with tension and promise it could detonate the room, she slides her hand up her thigh. Christ, they're a match struck in hell.

"Matteo," I growl, "non stuzzicare la bestia." *Don't poke the beast.*

He just smirks, clearly enjoying the electricity between him and Eleanor.

"Your move, princess," Matteo taunts, the words dripping with a twisted reverence that only they understand.

"Keep your fantasies in check, Ricci," Eleanor shoots back, but her eyes swing to mine, demanding answers, demanding truth.

"Easy there," I say, palms up in surrender to the barrel of Eleanor's gun; the metallic gleam a reminder of how quickly things can turn deadly. "Let me explain." I nod towards her seat, my face set in earnest urgency.

Her dark and stormy eyes bore into mine, but she relents, sliding back into her chair with the grace of a she-wolf, cornered by hunters. The gun staying within easy reach though.

"So, who is she?" Eleanor says. "Why is she here, why she's serving us food, why she's in your house."

"That's Alba," I admit, swallowing the lump in my throat as her image fills my mind. "She's the girl who disappeared when we were just kids, ripped right out of my life."

Antonio, always quick to sniff out bullshit, furrows his brow, no doubt recalling the days. "The one you turned the city upside down for? The one you had your old man scrambling through the gutters trying to find?" he says with a mix of scepticism and curiosity.

"Yep, that's her." I let out a long sigh as guilt presses down on me. "Fabio... that slimy son of a bitch, sold her right from under my father's nose. For her virginity." Saying it out loud feels like confessing to a sin I didn't commit but am damned for regardless.

Matteo, his own brand of crazy barely contained behind his shark-like eyes, curses under his breath. "You're fucking with me?"

"No, I'm not fucking with you. That fucker is now feeding the fish near St. Andrew's Beach." The room falls silent. "Alba's been in the trade for the past 13 years. And then one night at Velvet, there she was—looking like both a prayer answered and my worst nightmare rolled into one."

I let out a breath steeped in old ghosts and fresh hell. "I had no choice. I bought her freedom the next day, from that sorry excuse of an owner, Dan."

Eleanor mutters something under her breath. It's like trying to catch smoke with your hands, elusive and fleeting. I lean closer, unwilling to miss a syllable of her acid-tongued monologue. "What was that, Eleanor?"

Her eyes pin me with a glare that could stop a bullet mid-flight. "So, what you're saying is... you're her new owner? The girl you fell in love with when you were just a kid, is now your sex slave, your property?"

"Is that what you think this is?" I snap back, feeling the familiar rage beneath my skin. The very idea makes my blood boil. "I'm not her fucking master, Eleanor. She's free. I haven't laid a finger on her since I saved her from the hellhole of a club."

Eleanor's frown deepens. "All I hear is that you re-chained her to you? That about sum it up?" Her voice, sharp enough to slice through sinew, cuts me deep.

"Jesus Christ, Eleanor!" I say, frustration searing through me. "She isn't chained to me or anyone. She can walk out that door whenever she wants." But even as I say it, I know how it looks, how it sounds. Like a fairy tale gone rogue, the prince turned jailer.

"Doesn't look like it, Gabe," she says, her eyes narrowing into slits that could eviscerate a man from 20 paces. She has that look about her that says she knows all the secrets you don't want anyone to find out.

Before I can reply, Matteo steps in, his voice smooth as

the silk lining of his suit jacket. "Easy there, princess. Let it go," he says, spooning more risotto into his mouth. "The man's trying to do the right thing. That's more than most of us can say."

Her head whips round. "Don't, princess me, Matteo!"

Matteo continues to chew, slow and deliberatly, eyeing her with an expression that's half amusement, half challenge.

I lean back in my chair. I drift off, thoughts racing as I chew over Eleanor's words, the air still prickling with her fury and Matteo's cold amusement.

Does Alba think she's chained to me? No. I've housed her, fed her, been the fucking model of restraint since I snatched her from Dan's clutches. She's had more freedom under my roof than she's seen in years. Is she free, though? Really free?

My fists clench of their own accord. The idea that I've re-caged Alba after busting her out of that nightmare is insulting at best.

"She is still caged," Eleanor says with hints of disbelief, "by her knight in shining fucking armour."

"View it how you like," I say. "Anything is better than what she had to go through before."

"Better for you," she says, unflinching and unforgiving. "Now you have her all to yourself and can do whatever you please."

"Christ, Eleanor!" I shout, slamming my hands down on the table. "You think I'd do that? You think I'm that kind of monster?"

She doesn't answer, doesn't need to.

"Look, I want out of this shit just as much as you. And

Alba isn't a part of the game. She's not a pawn or plaything. She's..." I struggle for the right words. "She's a person, not property. Not anymore."

"Keep telling yourself that, Gabe," she says provocatively, though there's a hint that she knows I'm telling the truth.

Matteo nods slowly. "The man's serious about this," he says quietly. "I can see it in his eyes. He's not lying."

"Maybe not," Eleanor says. "But you better make damn sure you're not just swapping one set of chains for another. Because if you are, I'll put a bullet in you myself."

I run a hand through my hair. "This world we live in—it warps everything, taints it all."

"Maybe. Just make sure your 'rescue' doesn't turn into another prison," Eleanor says, and her words hitting me harder than any bullet ever could.

For a moment I wonder if she's right. If by saving Alba, I've just swapped one set of chains for another.

Matteo raises his glass again, this time in a more genuine toast. "To Gabe, the new head of the Gallo empire. May he make better choices than his father did. And may he figure out what the hell he's going to do about the girl before she figures it out for him."

The words hang heavily in the air with implication. Because Matteo's right. I need to do it before she makes the decision for me.

Chapter 30

Alba

The small bag sits on the edge of my bed, packed with the few things I've managed to gather from the closet I found earlier in the week. A couple of changes of clothes and the phone Gabe gave me. Not much, but enough to get me somewhere. Anywhere but here.

I stare at it for a long moment, my heart pounding in my chest like a caged bird desperate to escape. This is it. This is the moment I've been building toward since I realised I could actually leave. Since I understood that the door is unlocked, that Gabe isn't keeping me prisoner in the traditional sense, even if the chains of my past are still wrapped around my ankles.

The meeting today changed everything. Watching those people, I realised what Gabe really is. He's not the boy I fell in love with anymore. That boy is buried somewhere deep inside this man, trapped under layers of darkness, blood and the weight of an empire built on suffering.

I love him. God help me, I still love him. I can see the

truth in his eyes when he looks at me, can feel the genuine care in the way he speaks to me, the tenderness in his words when he thinks I'm not paying attention. But love isn't enough when the man you love is part of a machine that destroys people like me. Love isn't enough when staying means becoming complicit in the destruction.

They say you must love all of a man, not just the parts you like. But I can't do that. I can't love the part of Gabe that runs an empire built on human trafficking. I can't love the part of him that sits at a table with monsters, planning how to continue his job. I can't love the part of him that's becoming his father.

So, I have to leave. I have to get out before I lose myself completely in the fantasy that somehow, someway, we could make this work.

I was going to wait until Gabe went to work tomorrow, slip out during the day when he wasn't here to stop me. But after today, after serving those people, seeing the power in that room, and feeling the weight of what Gabe is responsible for—I can't wait. I need to go tonight.

I check my phone. It's almost midnight. Gabe walked to his room about 30 minutes ago. I give it another 10 minutes, just to be sure he's actually asleep and not just lying in bed thinking, before I move.

The rain outside is relentless, hammering against the windows like it's trying to break through the glass. It's perfect. The noise will cover any sound I make, and the weather will make it harder for him to follow me if he wakes up.

My hands are shaking as I pick up the bag and sling it over my shoulder.

I move to the door and open it slowly, carefully listening for any sound from Gabe's room. Nothing. Just the steady rhythm of the rain and the occasional rumble of thunder in the distance.

I tiptoe down the hallway, my feet silent against the cool tile. The house is dark, lit only by the ambient light from outside that filters through the windows.

The back door is at the end of the hallway, past the kitchen and past the dining room where I served those people today.

When I reach the back door, I pause. This is the point of no return. Once I disarm the alarm and open this door, there's no going back. Gabe will know I've left. He'll come after me. Or maybe he won't. Maybe, he'll let me go and move on to the next thing, the next girl, the next distraction.

The thought makes me sick, but I push it aside. I have to do this. I have to leave.

I move to the alarm panel and enter the code Gabe gave me. He told me it was in case of emergency, in case I ever needed to get out quickly. I don't think he meant for me to use it to escape from him, but here we are.

The alarm beeps as it begins to disarm—a loud, piercing sound that seems to echo throughout the entire house. My heart stops and I hold my breath, listening, waiting to hear Gabe's footsteps thundering down the stairs.

Nothing.

The second the alarm is fully disarmed, I don't wait to see if he's coming, I yank open the back door and bolt into the rain.

The rain soaks through my clothes in seconds. I'm wearing just a t-shirt and jeans, and I'm already shivering, but I don't stop. I can't stop. I run across the grass toward the back fence, my feet slipping and sliding on the wet ground.

The fence is low, maybe five feet tall, with a simple flat top. I can climb it.

I'm halfway there when I hear it.

"Alba!"

Gabe's voice cuts through the rain like a knife, raw, desperate and filled with something I can't quite name. Fear? Rage? Desperation?

I spin on my heel, heart lurching into my throat, to see Gabriel Gallo emerging from the darkness, his hood drawn up against the deluge. His piercing eyes seeking mine through the rain, a silent plea etched within their depths. In this moment, I see the depths of his internal tug-of-war, his struggle between the man he's expected to be and one that questions the morality of it all. And yet, I also know the darkness that dwells within him, a tempest just as fierce as the one raging around us—a man who revels in carnage and demands absolute dominion over all he deems his.

But I am no longer content to be deemed anything by anyone. I am Alba Baker, a woman whose soul has been forged in the fires of adversity, not to be extinguished by the first sign of resistance. So, with a breath that tastes of liberation and rainwater, I turn away from the man who claims protection as his prerogative and run towards an uncertain future; one that is undeniably, irrevocably mine.

Gabriel's voice, a thunderous call in the storm, spurs me on. The rain-soaked world blurring into a palette of greys and greens as I sprint toward the boundary that promises freedom—a fence obscured by the night's embrace. My lungs are burning, but fear is a powerful fuel, and desperation is an even more powerful motivator.

The large pot plants along the fence line loom ahead. My muscles coil in preparation to use one as a makeshift step, to vault myself into the sanctuary of the wilderness beyond.

Mud spatters against my calves, a grim reminder of how tenuous my escape truly is. The nature reserve beyond the fence singing a sirens song, its dark foliage waving like the arms of an old friend in the tempestuous night. I propel myself forward, my focus narrowing to the singular objective—the leap that will sever the ties binding me to this life.

But then, a surge of adrenaline shoots through me as I sense Gabe closing the distance, his very presence both comforting and suffocating. I know he can outpace me if given the chance. His footfalls are rhythmic; a predator's cadence, heavy against the soft ground. Panic licks at my insides, igniting a fire that fuels my desperate strides.

The gap between us dwindles with every heartbeat. I can feel the heat of his pursuit, the sheer force of his will emanating like a palpable wave crashing against my back. I push harder, legs straining, arms pumping, willing myself to become a blur amidst the rain and darkness.

Just as my fingers graze the rough texture of the terracotta pot, reality shatters and arms like steel bands wrap around my middle, halting my flight with an abruptness that rips a gasp from my throat. We skid together, a tangle of limbs and soaked fabric, the momentum too great, the rain-slicked earth too unforgiving. Gabe's hold is unyield-ing, a vice that clamping down on any sliver of hope I've nurtured.

"Alba," he says, a fierce whisper lost to the wind and pelting rain. There it is—the crux of our twisted bond, my name spoken as both a claim and a benediction from the lips of a man bound by blood to a world I yearn to flee.

Panic claws at my throat, each breath a battle in the vice of Gabe's arms. I fight with the ferocity of a cornered animal, my legs flailing, trying to find purchase on the slick grass beneath us. My fingers twist, grabbing at the iron strength encasing me, but it's like trying to bend steel with bare hands.

"Let me go!" I scream, my voice raw against the thrumming rain. "I need to go!"

The night air is thick with the scent of damp earth and the impending violence seeming to pulse from Gabe's very skin. His presence envelops me, not just physically, but in a way that makes me acutely aware of the dark energy he wields effortlessly. His aura painted with shades of power and control, and I'm suffocating under the weight of it.

"Never!" he says into my ear, his breath hot against my skin, sending shivers down my spine that has nothing to do with the cold rain. "I can never let you go!"

And there it is. The truth I've been running from. The reason I have to leave. Because Gabe Gallo doesn't let go of things he considers his, and no matter how much he tries to convince himself—convince me—that I'm free, the reality is that I'm just as trapped now as I've ever been. The cage is just prettier, the chains invisible, and the man holding them is someone I love.

I fight harder, thrashing against his grip, but he's too strong, too determined, too fucking possessive. His arms tighten around me, and I can feel the desperation in his touch, the way he's holding on like I'm the only thing keeping him tethered to sanity.

"Please," I whisper, and I hate how broken my voice sounds. "Please, Gabe. Let me go."

"No," he says, and there's so much pain in that one word, so much anguish. "I can't. I won't. You're mine, Alba. You've always been mine."

And that's when I realise the truth—he's not trying to keep me prisoner. He's trying to keep me from leaving him. He's trying to keep me from disappearing like I did 13 years ago. He's terrified of losing me again, and that terror is manifesting as control, as possession, as this desperate need to hold on.

Chapter 31

Gabriel

The moment the words leave my lips, Alba's body goes rigid in my grasp. Her eyes widen with a mix of fear and disbelief jolting through me like electricity, and I realise I've said too much, revealed too much and shown her the depths of my obsession before she's ready to see it.

"Why?" she asks, and her voice so small and so broken, that it nearly destroys me. "You don't even like me?"

I tighten my hold on her, feeling the rain soaking through her thin t-shirt, her body shaking against mine. "What do you mean?" I demand, an edge to my voice that I can't quite control. "I got you out of there. I brought you somewhere safe, didn't I? I've been taking care of you, feeding you, giving you everything you could possibly need."

"Safe?" She laughs, a bitter, broken sound that cuts through the rain. "Is this what you call safe, Gabe? Locked away in your world, under your control? You bought me, just like Dan did. You just wrapped it up in pretty words and a nicer house."

Her words hit me harder than any bullet ever could, and I feel the truth of them puncturing my chest like shrapnel. Because deep down, in the twisted depths of my heart, I know that my idea of safety is just another form of captivity. I know I've been selfish, I've been thinking about what I want instead of what she needs. But I can't let her see the weakness in me. Not now. Not when I feel like she belongs here with me, like she's the only thing that makes sense in this chaotically violent world I've inherited.

"Alba," I say, fighting to keep my voice even, fighting to maintain control when everything inside me is screaming to just hold her tighter, to never let her go. "I did what I had to do. For you. Can't you see that? I bought you to save you. I brought you here to protect you. Everything I've done has been for you."

But as I gaze into her eyes, I know she sees right through the lies I tell myself. She always does. And that's what scares me the most—she can see me so clearly, knows exactly what I am and what I'm capable of, and she's still trying to run.

"If I let you go, can you please not run?" I ask, and I hate how desperate I sound, how much I'm begging her with that one question.

She goes limp in my hold, the fight draining from her as if my words are a valve, releasing all the resistance she's been holding onto. "Yes," she whispers.

I hesitate, watching the wariness flicker across her face, the calculation in her eyes as she weighs her options. But a man is only as good as his word—even a Gallo—so I loosen my grip, releasing her. She stumbles back, free but trapped all the same, inside the invisible cage I've locked her in, and I know it. I know that no matter how much freedom I give her, she'll always be bound to me now.

The moment she leaves my arms, Alba turns, her eyes wild, and she screams—a raw, guttural sound that echoes through the night and reverberates through my entire body. It's a sound of despair and fury, rattling something deep inside me, something I've been trying to keep locked away since the moment I realised she was alive.

"You might have saved me from where I was, Gabe, but I'm still in a prison," she says, her voice shaking with emotion. "I'm still trapped. The only difference is that now I'm trapped by someone I love, and that's so much fucking worse."

My frown carves deep into my skin, rain dripping from my hair onto my cheeks like tears I've never let myself shed. "I've clothed you, given you a home, fed you..." I say, hating how pathetic I sound, like I'm trying to justify my actions by listing all the things I've done for her. "Isn't that enough? Isn't that proof that I care about you?"

Her laughter is sharp and bitter, cutting through the rain like a blade. "And all the while reminding me how horrible I am, how disgusted you are by what's happened to me. Don't think I don't know—it's your family's fault I was ever in that situation to begin with! Your father trafficked me, Gabe. Your family destroyed my life. And you think buying me back makes it okay? You think that makes you a hero?"

"Disgusted?" I shake my head at her, my dark hair sticking to my forehead, rain streaming down my face.

"You think that's what this is about? I'm not disgusted by you, Alba. I'm disgusted for you. I'm disgusted at what was done to you, at what my family did to you, at the fact that I couldn't find you sooner, that I couldn't protect you from all of it."

My chest heaves with the effort of keeping my temper in check, with the effort of not just grabbing her and forcing her to listen to me, to understand me, to see that everything I'm doing is for her.

"You use the women on the floor at Dan's club all the time, Gabe," she says, and there's accusation in her voice. "Your hand's have been all over them."

"Is that what this is?" My hands clench and unclench as I struggle to hold it together, as I struggle not to lose my mind completely. "You think I'm some kind of hypocrite? That I'm no better than the men who hurt you?"

"That's what it looks like," she says, the certainty in her voice destroys me.

"Shit, Alba," I say, wiping my face with the back of my hand. "Those girls—none of them are you. I never touched them, not really. I was just going through the motions, trying to feel something, anything, to fill the void that you left when you disappeared. But nothing worked. Nothing ever worked because you're the only one I've ever wanted."

"Doesn't make it right," she says.

"Maybe not," I concede, because I know she's right. "But this isn't about them. It's about you, Alba. Always has been. Since the moment I met you in kindergarten, it's always been about you."

Alba laughs mockingly, and it's like a punch to the gut.

"For someone so smart, Gabe, you can be so fucking stupid. You really can't see what you're doing, can you? You're not saving me. You're just replacing one cage with another."

A growl rumbles deep within me, and I feel the rage building, the darkness rising to the surface. But it's her next words that slice through all the bullshit, that cut me down to my core.

"Look at you. You're not the same person I knew all those years ago. I don't even know who you are anymore. The boy I fell in love with was kind, gentle, funny. He made me laugh. He made me feel safe. But you—you're mean, you're horrible, you're just like your father."

I wanted to yell, to tell her she's wrong, that I'm still Gabe Gallo—just hardened by life, by necessity and by the weight of an empire I never asked for. I want to shake her, to make her understand that I changed because I had to, because the world demanded it of me, because the only way to survive in this business is to become a monster.

"I want to run, Gabe," she says, and there's something wild in her eyes now, something desperate and determined. "I want to live my own life. I want to be free from you, from your family, from all of this."

"Alba—" I start to say, but she cuts me off.

"Don't," she says, with something wild in her eyes. "I know I'm disgusting now, ruined, not worthy of love again. I know this, okay? I know and I've accepted it. So just let me go. Let me disappear. Let me try to build something that's mine, something that isn't tainted by your family's blood."

A part of me wants to grab her by the shoulders and

force her to see herself the way I see her—as the most beautiful, strongest and most resilient person I've ever known.

"Alba, listen to me," I say, stepping toward her. "You're not disgusting. You're not ruined. You're the strongest person I know. You survived 13 years of hell, and you're still standing. You're still fighting. You're still you, and that you is worth everything to me."

"No! Just stop, Gabe! Just fucking stop!" she cries, and I can hear the desperation in her voice, the way she's begging me to let her go, to release her from the hold I have on her.

But I can't stop. Not now, not ever. Because despite everything, she's the one constant in my life. My obsession, my desperation, my Alba. She's the reason I get up in the morning. She's the reason I'm trying to be better than my father. She's the reason I'm still human at all.

And I'm not going to let her slip through my fingers.

I lunge forward, my fingers instinctively finding the warmth of her neck, and I drag her into me. Our lips crash together, a violent maelstrom of need and raw emotion. The rain pelts us unforgivingly, rivulets cascading down our faces, mingling with our breaths. As I trace her wet lips with my tongue, something within me snaps free—all the control I've been maintaining, all the walls I've built, all the darkness I've been containing.

"Alba," I rasp against her mouth, breaking the kiss just enough to speak, my voice rough and desperate. "You're none of them. You're not disgusting. You're not ruined. You're mine. You've always been mine."

My grip tightens at her nape, a firm assertion of what

belongs to me, what I've claimed, what I will never let go of.

"I've been in love with you since kindergarten," I say, and the words pour out of me like blood from a wound. "You were the only girl for me then, and nothing—I mean nothing—has changed. Not when you disappeared. Not when I thought you were dead. Not when I found you at Velvet. Not now. Not ever."

Her body trembles against mine, whether from the cold or the force of my words, I can't tell. But I don't stop. I can't stop. I have to make her understand.

"I bought you because you're my Alba, my soul mate, the fucking love of my life," I say, and I know I sound unhinged, obsessed, possessive. I know I sound like the monster she's accusing me of being. "The world could go up in flames around us, and I wouldn't blink—not with you here in my arms, not when everything I've ever wanted is finally pressed up against me."

For a moment, there's only the sound of rain hitting the ground, the rapid beat syncing with my racing heart. I'm laid bare, the truth erupting from me like a force I can no longer contain. It's raw, it's ugly, it's possessive and obsessive and everything she's afraid of—but it's also the purest thing I have. It's the only truth that matters anymore.

"I love you, Alba," I whisper against her hair, holding her so tightly I'm afraid I might break her. "I've always loved you. And I will spend the rest of my life making sure you never forget it."

Chapter 32

Alba

Tears blur the edges of my vision, a scalding reminder of the mix of emotions swirling inside me—rage, love, desperation, hope, all tangled up together until I can't tell where one ends and the other begins. "Where did we go so wrong, Gabe?" I ask, and my voice is broken, shattered, barely recognisable as my own.

Gabe's arms encircle me tighter, a fortress of warmth in the cold uncertainty of the moment. His embrace feels like the final piece of a puzzle that I've been trying to solve with trembling hands and a battered heart. "Come inside, Alba," he murmurs against my hair, and there's such desperation in his voice that it nearly undoes me. "Come back, please. I need you. I always have."

His confession seeps into my skin, kindling embers of hope I thought had long since died. Gabe needs me— words that should feel like chains, yet somehow they ring with the melody of liberation. It's a contradiction that makes my head spin, that makes me question everything I thought I knew about love, freedom and what it means to belong to someone.

The strength of his hold on me lessens as he steps back, and I immediately miss the warmth of him. His hand reaches out, his palm open and inviting in a silent offer laid bare in the moonlight. "I'm not going to make you," he says, his eyes searching mine for a sign, for any indication of the choice that lies before me. "You're free, Alba. You're free to run or come home with me. I want you in my life, but I will never cage you. You're free to come and go."

Freedom—a word laden with dreams unfulfilled and paths untraveled. Gabe offers it to me, not with the weight of expectation, but with the gentle grace of a soul who understands the cost of its absence. The darkness around us seems to lean in, waiting for my verdict, and I feel the weight of this moment pressing down on me like a phys-ical force.

"You're free to come and go," he repeats, the words echoing like a mantra, a spell to dispel the ghosts of a past that cling to me with icy fingers. Can I step into the future he paints with such tender strokes? Can I trust the man whose very world represents everything I've once sought to escape?

In Gabe's outstretched hand, I see not just an invitation, but a vow—a pledge to rewrite the narratives that have bound us to roles we no longer wish to play. And I'm terri-fied. I'm absolutely terrified because I know that if I take his hand, if I choose to stay, I'm choosing a life that's anything but simple or safe or predictable.

My eyes flit to the fence that marks the boundary between his domain and the unfathomable breadth of freedom. I could climb it. I could run. I could disappear into the night and never look back. No one would stop me; Gabe's already made that clear.

But what is freedom, truly, when it beckons with the allure of the unknown? My heart thrums erratically, a caged bird uncertain if the sky is a promise or a peril. Will I always wonder if? The question plays in my mind, a spectre of doubts and what-ifs. To run would be to sever the last thread tying me to my past where Gabe is both the storm and the sanctuary.

Memories flicker like old film reels—laughter mingling with tears, tender touches shadowed by clenched fists. How can one reconcile the duality of a man who has known every contour of my soul yet belongs to a world that feasts on brutality? How can I love someone whose family destroyed my life?

I close my eyes, letting the scent of rain wrap around me, an embrace as uncertain as the future. With each heartbeat, I feel the pull of the life I could claim beyond the fence, vibrant and uncharted. Yet, intertwined with the lure of liberty, is the undeniable aura of Gabe's presence—the boy I fell in love with all those years ago, the man he's become; the contradiction of him.

"Okay," I say, and the word feeling like it's being torn from my chest. "Take me inside."

The words slip from my lips, a surrender to the enigma that is us. In this moment, with the decision made, it feels as though something has calmed within me. There's no grand epiphany, no resounding clarity—only the quiet acceptance of my own desires, my own choice, my own agency.

I run, not away from the choice, but towards the embodiment of all my fears and longing. Into Gabe's arms, I flee, seeking refuge in the paradox he represents. As his arms encircle me once more, I wonder if this is my own twisted version of freedom—where the bars of my cage are forged from love, loyalty, and the haunting hope for redemption.

"Take me home," I reaffirm, owning the decision that will either define or destroy me. With Gabe, there's no middle ground, only the precipice upon which we've skirted, and I'm choosing to jump.

Gabe's arms become my world, his strength an unyielding force as he lifts me effortlessly from the sodden earth. The downpour that has soaked through our clothes seems a distant concern as we cross the threshold of his imposing home. His steps echoing against the floor, as he walks us in, and I'm acutely aware of how small I am in his arms, how fragile, and how I'm completely at his mercy.

The back door swings shut with the gentle nudge of his foot, sealing us away from the storm's plaintive cries. My toes touch the cool and solid floor beneath me, but before I can process the transition, Gabe is busy at the wall panel, reprogramming the alarm. His movements are precise and practiced—a routine etched into muscle memory.

Once done, he turns to me, his hand outstretched in a silent invitation hanging between us. I place my trembling hand in his, skin to skin, a current of something ineffable passes through our touch. He draws me close, and there it is—that juxtaposition of tenderness and tenacity that so defines him. With deliberate care, he begins to peel away the layers of my drenched clothing, each piece discarded to a pile on the floor.

"If I ever do anything you don't like, tell me to stop," he says, and his voice is so gentle, so careful, that it breaks something inside me. "I'll always stop for you. I promise you that, Alba. Your comfort, your safety, your consent—it's everything to me."

He pauses, his eyes holding mine with an intensity that borders on reverence. "But please know this—I need you. I've waited 13 years to find you again, and now that you're here, I feel almost complete. Like I can finally breathe again."

I know of Gabe's contradictions, of the blood that stains his hands even as they seek to heal. Yet here, in the sanctuary he offers, I find myself caught in his presence, unable to deny the pull of desire long buried beneath layers of survival, trauma and fear.

I stand, exposed not only to the chill of the room but to the scrutiny of a man who navigates shadows with the ease of one born to darkness. But when he looks at me, all I see reflected in his eyes is a fierce protectiveness and a vulnerability that belies his hardened exterior. This man, who is set to inherit a legacy of immense power, is offering me a choice—to gamble on love in a world where the stakes are life and death.

A quiver runs through my body, not from the cold clinging to my damp skin, but from the realisation of autonomy flowering within me. For the first time in so many years, the chains of my past don't weigh upon my decisions. It's a freedom that terrifies, just as much as it exhilarates. Lifting my arms, I surrender to the moment, to

Gabe's tender ministrations as he peels away the soaked fabric clinging to my frame.

"Tell me if it's too much," he says softly, and I can hear the concern in his voice, the way he's trying so hard to be gentle with me, to not hurt me, to give me back some semblance of control.

But it's not too much; it's just enough to feel like I'm reclaiming parts of myself long forgotten; parts that belong to me and no one else. As each garment falls to the floor, a layer of my old life sheds with it, leaving me bare, vulnerable, and yet empowered in my nakedness.

I'm stripped of pretences, every scar on my body a testament to the hardships I've endured. Gabe's touch is hesitant as his fingers trace the roadmap of pain etched into my skin. His eyes never leave mine, even as he speaks with unexpected empathy.

"I know what my family does for a living," he says, and his voice is rough with emotion. "I've always known... and I've benefitted from the money we make. I've lived off the suffering of people like you, Alba. I've worn the wealth that came from your pain."

There's a tremor in his voice, a crack in the façade of the mafia prince standing before me. Guilt? Regret? I can't quite decipher it, but it warms something inside me to see him acknowledge this world's darker corners, to see him grapple with the sins of his lineage.

"But I've never seen this side of it—the destruction it can bring," he continues, his fingers tracing a particularly jagged piece of scar tissue on my ribs. "Not like this. Not until you. And I can't unsee it now. I don't want to unsee it."

In his gaze, I find none of the dominance or demanding nature that others fear in him. Here, in this intimate space where the shadows of our past mingle with the dim light of the present, Gabe is simply a man grappling with the sins of his lineage—a man yearning for absolution that I'm unsure I can give but am willing to explore.

I lean into the warmth of his touch, my breath catching in a quiet sigh. "It's okay," I say, the words tumbling out in an attempt to soothe the tumult etched across his face.

"No, it's not," he says, and there's so much conviction in his voice, such determination. "I'm going to be running the whole operation, Alba, and I plan to change it. I have to end all this madness. I can't allow it to continue."

The fire in his eyes burns with a ferocity that startles me and ignites hope where I thought none could be kindled. He speaks of power, control and overturning a tainted legacy. The vulnerability lacing his words reveals the weight of the crown he's poised to wear, a responsibility he bears with a reluctant sense of duty.

"I will not let this happen to anyone else again," he says, imploring me to understand his declaration. "I promise you, Alba. I'm going to burn it all down if I have to. I'm going to dismantle this empire brick by brick, if it means saving even one person from what happened to you."

At that moment, there's a shift in the air, the possibility for redemption, or perhaps the fantasy of it. His lips brush against mine, a kiss charged with the promise of change, tender and imbued with an urgency that speaks volumes. It tastes like hope, desperation and love all mixed together; and I'm drowning in it.

As our mouths part, the remnants of his pledge linger on my lips, a bittersweet taste of what could be. Can one man turn the tide on a history written in blood? Can he carve out a new path when every step is stained by the sins of the past?

Gabe's touch is gentle, but the grip he has on my hand is unyielding—a silent affirmation that he intends to try, regardless of the cost. And as I stand naked before him bearing scars that are both an indictment and a challenge, I feel optimistic about the future for the first time in 13 years.

"Gabriel," I whisper, his name is a soft exhale, a prayer for the man who holds my battered heart, and the boy who once dreamed of a different world—one without the cruel edges that have defined our lives.

His answer is in the steady beat of his heart against my own, the warmth in his embrace, and his unwavering blue eyes, promising a fight not just for power but for atonement. I realise that maybe, just maybe, we have a chance. Maybe, we can build something beautiful from the ashes of our broken pasts.

Maybe, love is enough after all

Chapter 33

Gabriel

I step back from Alba, the heat in the room cranking up a notch as I shrug out of my hoodie, feeling the tension between us like a living, breathing thing. Without hesitation, my hands go to my pants and slide them down over my hips. My cock bobs free, hanging proud and curved, and I watch her eyes roam across me, leaving a scorching trail that sets my skin ablaze.

When her gaze catches on the dark swirls and patterns that ink my skin, I see her swallow hard, and fuck, that simple gesture nearly undoes me.

"You've got a lot of ink now," she says, her voice soft and curious, and there's something in her tone that makes my chest tighten.

"Part of the life," I say with a lopsided grin, shrugging as if the layers of ink don't carry a story for every scar hidden beneath. Her eyes tell me she reads them like the chapters we've missed in each other's lives, and I'm grateful she's not asking for all the details right now. I don't think I could handle telling her about every kill, every sin or every moment I've spent in darkness thinking about her.

"Does it hurt?" she asks, a tentative curiosity in her eyes that makes me want to pull her close and never let go.

"Less than not having you did," I say with raw honesty, the words heavy with meaning hang between us,.

My hands ache to touch her, to trace every curve and commit it to memory like a sacred text. I lean down, my lips barely grazing hers. "Tell me to stop if you need me to stop," I breathe against her mouth, ready to pull back at a moment's notice if she gives the word. I mean it. I'll stop if she asks. Even though it might kill me.

Her response isn't spoken, but the nod that comes is as loud as a church bell in my head. "I want you to touch me, Gabe," she says with a bravery that knocks the breath from my lungs.

Fuck. My heart stutters, then slams against my chest like it's trying to break free. This is my Alba, the girl who's haunted every fucking dream and every waking moment since she vanished from my life. The love of my life, standing before me, asking for my touch.

"Jesus, Alba," I say, the world around us narrowing until there's nothing left but the pulse of our hearts and the heat of our bodies as they're draw together like magnets. She's the ember that ignites my soul, and I'm ready to burn.

With an urgency thrumming through me, I sweep Alba into my arms, her body light against my chest. She clings to me, her breaths in tune with the pounding of my heart as I carry her through the dimly lit hallway. The door to my room a gateway to the reckoning we've both been skirting around for far too long.

The moment I cross the threshold, the world outside ceases to exist. It's just her and me—the past and the present colliding with the force of a thunderclap. I lay her gently on the bed like she's the most precious thing I've ever touched. Because she is.

I drink in the sight of her, lying there on black sheets that make her skin glow like she's carved from moonlight. Scars lace her flesh, telling tales of a survival no one should have had to endure. But they don't make her any less perfect. If anything, they add to her story, showing the depth of her strength that will forever leave me in awe.

There's something about her fiery red hair fanned out across my pillows that short-circuits my brain. Red—the colour of passion, of sin, of Alba—my ultimate weakness. Since she disappeared from my life and took my soul with her, no other redhead has come close to touching me. I've always known, deep down in the marrow of my bones, that no one would ever compare to her. No one.

Her eyes watch me in silent invitation, sparking a hunger in my gut that threatens to consume us both. This is it. There's no turning back now.

Alba's light as a feather touch, trails down my ink-laden skin, heavy with intent as each line of my muscles tense under her exploration. "You're beautiful, you know that?" she whispers, and I can't help the raw chuckle that escapes me, a sound more akin to a growl.

I hover over her, arms planted on either side of her head, my ink telling stories of pain and power, of a life drenched in both blood and desire. "No, Alba," I say as my lips brush against hers, "you are the one who is beautiful. You're the most beautiful thing I've ever seen."

She smiles at me, and it's like the sun's breaking through the clouds after a lifetime of darkness. I want to memorise this moment, this exact second where she's looking at me like I'm not a monster, like I'm just Gabe, the boy she fell in love with all those years ago.

"I need to fuck you now, Alba," I say, my voice rough and desperate. "I can't wait. I've waited 13 years for you, and I can't fucking wait another second."

My grip tightens around my cock, flesh hot and pulsing with a hunger that's been gnawing at me since she walked back into my life. It's been consuming me, burning me from the inside out, and I'm done waiting.

She looks up at me with a heat mirroring my own, and nods—a silent acquiescence that fuels the fire. "Gabe... I —" Her words dissolve into a breathless sigh as I cut her off with my mouth on hers.

"Shh," I murmur against her lips. "I'm not letting you go ever again. You're mine, Alba. You've always been mine. And the first time I fuck you, I want to feel every single inch of you. I want to mark you, claim you and make sure you know that you belong to me."

Her submission is the kindling, and my resolve is the match. There's no space for hesitation, only the blistering need to reclaim what's always been mine. I'm poised at the gates of heaven, ready to worship at the altar of Alba's body once again.

Alba's nod is all the permission my aching body needs. "Take me," she whispers, and those two words are my undoing.

I align myself to her, the head of my cock nudging at her entrance, and I have to pause for a second because I'm already on the edge, already about to lose it just from the anticipation of being inside her.

"Fuck!" The word slips from my lips like a prayer as I push into her slowly. Heat envelops me, tight and not nearly slick enough, but it's Alba and nothing has ever felt so right. Her walls stretch around me, gripping me in a welcome that sends shivers up my spine.

She's not as wet as I want her to be, but patience has long since been burned away by desire. I can't wait, and the way her body yields to mine arouses me even further. I want to go slow, want to savour this, want to make it last, but my body has other ideas.

"Christ, Alba," I groan, burying myself to the hilt within her. "I just need you, need to feel you. Need to know you're real, that this is real."

"Gab…" Her voice breaks off as I pause, savouring the sensation of being inside her after so long. She's tight around me, and I'm fighting for control, fighting not to come right now like some inexperienced kid.

"Later," I say, my voice strained. "Right now, I just need my girl. I just need to feel you around me."

The softest moan comes from Alba's lips, a sound that could make angels sin. I wrap my mouth around hers, hungry for every part of her. Our kiss is a gentle clash of desperation, a contrast to the slow, deliberate movements of my hips. My hand wanders, fingers tracing the delicate curve of her breast, teasing her nipple into a hardened peak.

"Fuck, Alba!" My self-control teeters on a knife's edge. Her tight warmth clenched around me is too much, too intense. Every stroke feels like a revelation, skin on skin, no barriers, nothing between us but sweat and heat and the overwhelming need to be as close to her as humanly possible.

I know I'm going to be quick, I can't help it, not with the way she's wrapped around me. The sensation is other-worldly; the primal instinct to claim her obliterates any last vestige of restraint. Her grip on me tightens, pulling me deeper, and that's all it takes. The rush hits me like a freight train, and I come with a low, guttural curse, spilling inside her in an act of possession that leaves me reeling.

"Shit, Alba!" I pant, the aftermath of my release coursing through me as I pull out, leaving a part of me behind. Her gaze, heavy with desire, meets mine as I slide down her body, my eyes never leaving hers.

"Oh, I'm not done yet," I say with the promise of more, of everything I have to give. "Not even fucking close. I'm going to spend the rest of the night worshipping you, making up for every second we've been apart."

I settle between her thighs, my shoulders pushing her legs wider as I take in the sight of her. She's glistening with my release, and I can't help but lean down and taste her. The moment my mouth makes contact, she gasps, her hands flying to my hair.

"Gabe!" she cries out, and the sound of my name on her lips like that is better than any drug I've ever expe-rienced.

Chapter 34

Alba

My spine arches instinctively, a silent ode to the raw heat that envelops me as Gabe's mouth descends in an unapologetic claim. There's a depravity in the way he devours me, a ravenous hunger that ignites my flesh and makes me feel alive in a way I've never felt before.

The room fills with the scent of sin, my senses drowning in the intimate taboo of tasting himself mingled with my essence. He looks at me, heavy with desire, as our flavours meld together upon his tongue—a wicked concoction of us that seems to draw me even closer into the heart of this fervid moment.

"Fuck, Alba," he murmurs against me, and the vibration of his voice against my most sensitive flesh sends shivers racing up my spine. "You taste like heaven."

As if compelled by an unseen force, his fingers penetrate me with an urgency that leaves no room for doubt or hesitancy. They move with a rhythm that feels almost primal, driving in and out as though they're staking a claim on the very core of my being. When he curls them just so, striking that secret place inside me that I didn't even know existed, a surge of pleasure jolts through me, demanding my breath and my focus.

"Oh God, Gabe!" I cry out, my hands flying to his hair, gripping him closer. I've never felt anything like this before—this overwhelming sensation building inside me, threatens to consume me entirely.

Gabe accelerates his pace, fingers pumping with a fierce intensity that stirs the depths of my consciousness. His mouth works in tandem with his hand, and I'm drowning in sensation, in the feeling of being completely and utterly worshipped by this man who's supposed to be a monster but feels like my salvation.

The precipice looms, a tantalising edge that I'm careening towards with reckless abandon. Gabe's teeth graze my most tender flesh, sending shockwaves of pleasure that radiate from my core to the tips of my tingling toes. When his mouth clamps down, a scream claws its way out of my throat, unbidden and raw. The walls of my body grip his invading fingers in a vice, pulsating around him as if to keep him there, locked within me forever.

"Alba!" he says through gritted teeth with an insatiable hunger that echoes the darkness I've come to crave. "I want another one. Come for me again, baby."

His command is more than words; it's an invocation, summoning forth another deluge of sensation. He plunges back into me with renewed fervour, three fingers this time —a relentless force driving into my quivering depths. With the gentlest breach, his smallest digit presses against a new gate, easing into the forbidden recess. "Fuck!" I moan with a breathless sigh, for it feels so scandalously good, so impossibly intimate.

Orgasms were never something I sought—phantom pleasures I'd heard whispered about but never dared to chase. Years of hollow encounters, where I played the part expected of me, left me numb, indifferent to the notion of true ecstasy. But here, beneath Gabe's masterful touch, I'm reborn in the throes of genuine passion. Each deliberate stroke of his fingers stirs a revelation within me, blossoming into an epiphany; what I feel now is both heaven and bliss entwined.

It's as though every nerve ending has been awakened by Gabe's hand alone, each one singing in chorus to the melody of our carnal symphony. His presence is a paradox —both a threat and a sanctuary—and in this moment, I willingly play along, entranced by the power he exudes and the control he effortlessly wields over my body and soul.

Gabe's tongue, relentless and fervent, glides across my clit. He laps at me with the fervour of a man starved, his fingers delving deeper still—rhythmically thrusting, curling to coax that part within me into rapture. My core tightens with each press of his fingertips, an ascending pressure that promises a fall as sweet as it is inevitable.

"Ah, Gabe..." I gasp on the cusp of pleasure he orchestrates so skilfully. Each time he hits that divine spot, my body sings a little louder and grows a little wetter, a sensation that becomes a crescendo into something unfamiliar— a strange and overwhelming tide that crashes over me.

And then, without warning, euphoria bursts forth like a dam breaking. The sensation is startling, akin to losing control completely, except this loss is pure bliss. I shatter, coming apart beneath his mouth and hands as waves of pleasure gush from me. My vision fades as I focus on the ecstasy that wracks my frame and leaves me breathless.

"Fuck!" The word is torn from the depths of my soul, and I'm shaking, trembling, completely undone.

Beneath the surging pleasure, I'm dimly aware of Gabe's head rising from between my quivering thighs. His face is drenched, eyes alight with a mix of awe and wicked satisfaction. "Holy shit, Alba!" he says, his grin devilish, "you gush so perfectly for me."

The pride in his voice ignites something within me—a flame of possessiveness I've never known. The fact that he's proud of me, that he's celebrating my pleasure, makes my heart swell in a way I can't quite explain.

"Fuck, I need to drink that next time," he says, climbing up the length of my trembling body. And before I can catch my breath, he sinks back into me, filling me to the brim once more.

"Ah, yes..." I moan, still reeling from the aftershocks. His presence inside me is both a salve and a spark, reigniting the embers of my desire even as I bask in the afterglow of release. With Gabe, it seems there's no respite—only the perpetual climb towards another peak, another shattering high.

"Mine," he says fiercely as he moves within me, each stroke deliberate and purposeful. There's a reverence in the way he speaks, a certainty that transcends the lust-fuelled haze surrounding us. And I'm caught in the whirlwind of passion and power that is Gabe; I can only hold on and savouring the ride.

"Yes," I whisper, running my hands down his back, feeling the muscles flex and move beneath his skin. "I'm yours, Gabe. Only yours."

The raw sensation of Gabe inside me, his every movement magnified by my over-sensitised flesh, draws me closer to climax again. My back arches off the bed as he lifts my hips, angling himself deeper, each thrust hitting deeper inside me in a way that makes me see stars.

"Alba, you feel incredible," he says, his voice rough with desire. "So fucking tight around me. So perfect."

His hand slips between our fevered bodies, igniting sparks as he circles my swollen clit. Another surge of pressure builds within me, an impending storm summoned by the relentless movement of his fingers. I'm tight around him, so achingly tight, each ridge and vein of his cock a brand upon my inner walls.

"God, you're going to make me lose it," he says, his breath hot against my skin. "You're mine, Alba. Only mine. No one else gets to touch you like this. No one else gets to see you like this. You're mine, and I'm never letting you go."

His declaration is a dark promise, one that wraps around me like velvet chains, binding me to him in ways that terrify and thrill me in equal measure. I should be scared. I should run. But instead, I'm holding him closer, pulling him deeper, wanting more of him.

I gasp, caught in the rising tide as he plunges into me with renewed fervour. He's relentless, a force of nature that will not be denied, and I'm adrift in the tempest of his passion. With every stroke, he drives us both closer to the edge, to that precipice where ecstasy and agony blur into one.

"Say it!" he demands, his eyes burning into mine. "Say you're mine, Alba. I need to hear you say it."

"I'm yours," I say, and I mean it with every fibre of my being. "Only yours, Gabe. Always yours."

That's all it takes. An explosion of white-hot pleasure rip's through me, my body convulsing as I release. I hear the slap of skin, the splash of my own release, and Gabe's guttural cry as he finds his own climax, joining me in the chaos of our union.

We're lost together, two souls entwined in the darkness, and I've never felt more found.

And as we cling to each other, spent and panting, I understand that this is what it means to belong to someone who wields power like a weapon but cherishes your submission like the rarest of treasures. This is what it means to be truly seen, truly known and truly loved.

In the aftermath, our breaths are ragged symphonies playing in the silence of the room. Gabe's weight presses down on me, a comforting anchor in the storm he's just steered us through. I'm still trembling from the intensity, my senses raw and heightened to every nuance of his touch.

He leans over me, his chest heaving with exertion as he looks at me. His lips brush against mine, tender despite the fervour that still lingers between us. And then, he utters words that cleave through the haze enveloping my mind.

"Marry me, Alba," he says, with such earnestness in his voice, such desperation. "I can't live another day of my life without you. I don't want to. I want to wake up next to you every morning for the rest of my life. I want to build a life with you, a real life, away from all of this darkness. I want to be the man you deserve, and I want you to be my wife."

Startled, my eyes widen as I study his face, half-expecting him to laugh and reveal it was a joke. But there's only earnestness—a plea wrapped in a vow. "What?" I ask, my voice barely a whisper.

His fingers trace the contour of my jaw, leaving a trail of heat in their wake. "I'm not joking," he says, his stare piercing through me. "You're mine, Alba. I will never live another day without you by my side. Marry me. Please. Make me the happiest man alive."

The unyielding demands of his dangerous life in the mafia fall away. At this moment, there's only Gabe with his unwavering gaze and the palpable truth of his words. It's a proposal devoid of pomp but laden with our inter-twined fates.

"You're mine," he says, marking me in a way that tran-scends the physical realm of our connection. "And I'm yours. Completely and utterly yours."

And I realise then, with the clarity of dawn breaking the night's hold, that this man has laid himself bare before me. This is not just a question; it's the offering of his heart, the one that beats with the rhythm of power and vulnera-bility, of control and morality.

"Yes," I say, and the word feeling like it's been ripped from the very depths of my soul. "Yes, Gabe. I'll marry you. I'll spend the rest of my life with you."

"Mine," I say. The word is a promise, a surrender, and a claiming all at once. Because in this maelstrom of love and darkness I have found my place. I've found my home. I've found my forever.

And as Gabe pulls me close, kissing me with a tenderness that belies the intensity of what we just shared, I know that no matter what comes next, no matter what darkness we have to face, we'll face it together. We'll face it as one.

Because I'm his, and he's mine, and that's all that matters.

Chapter 35

Gabriel

Consciousness creeps back to me, and I'm instantly aware of the warmth wrapped around my body. Alba's soft curves press against me, her head rests on my chest, her leg a possessive drape over my thighs. The gentle rise and fall of her breath seeps through my skin, calming the usual storm that rages within me.

I'm struck by a moment of absolute shock—the realisation that she allowed me to touch her. After everything she's been through, after 13 years of having her body violated, used and destroyed, she let me touch her. She melted into me. She came apart beneath my hands, mouth and body, the weight of that gift and trust, nearly crushes me.

I would have lived with her for the rest of my life without ever touching her again. I would have been happy just to have her in my space, breathing the same air, existing in the same world. If she never allowed my skin to touch hers again, I would have married her and loved her forever anyway, because that's what she deserves—a man who loves her without condition, without expectation.

But she did allow it. She allowed me in, and she had melted into me in the end, and if that was the only time she ever lets me touch her that way, I will still marry her and love her forever anyway. Because what matters isn't the sex—it's that she trusted me enough to let me close.

Just thinking about touching her last night causes my dick to stand up, demanding I wake her and claim her with the hunger that hasn't been sated, despite last night's intimacy. God, I want to feel her again, to lose myself in the sweet oblivion she offers. But there's something sacred in this stillness, in the quiet embrace of dawn as her body's entwined with mine. So, I fight the urge, choosing to keep Alba close just a little while longer.

My hand, scarred and calloused from years of less tender embraces, stretches out to snag my phone off the bedside table. The screen lights up, two missed calls from my dad, and four from Aurelio and heaps of unanswered messages.

"Fuck!" I mutter under my breath. Catcher's name appears on the many notifications, each message punctuated by an urgency that spells trouble. The bastard never can let me have a morning to myself.

Catcher:

Need to see you

Shit's going down

Get your ass here

. . .

CATCHER CALCONE, THE MAN WHO'D FACE THE DEVIL WITH a smirk, can't handle his own demons without stirring up hell. I sigh, knowing whatever he's cooked up will be nothing short of chaos. With him, it always is.

I need to deal with whatever mess he's gotten himself into this time, but I want a pause button on life, just a few more silent beats with Alba and no Catcher, no calls to violence. Just us and the illusion of peace in a world that has none to offer.

My bedside clock reads 8 am, and I do a double take. Shit, it's way past the hour I'm usually up and about, marching through the warehouse doors. But this morning, Alba's warmth has replaced the cold bite of responsibility, her body a living shield against the demands waiting outside our door.

"Damn!" I say, realising today isn't going to be any kind of normal. My old man and Aurelio wouldn't ring me unless the fires of hell were licking at their heels, and here they are, missed calls glaring at me from my phone screen. Trouble is brewing, boiling over probably, and I'm still in bed, tangled up with Alba.

I try to gently detach myself from her embrace—the last thing I want is to wake her—but life has a cruel sense of humour. Her eyes open, clouded with sleep and edged with the remnants of her dreams.

Alba's "sorry" comes out muffled against the sheets as she starts to peel herself from me, her movements hesitant and fragile. I'm not having any of it. My arm shoots out, strong and sure, pinning her back down with a firm gentleness that speaks of my need to keep her close. "No, stop…" I command. "Sleep in, relax. I have to hit the warehouse. I'll be back soon."

"Oh, okay," she says, and I can see the shift in her eyes, just the mention of the warehouse has her on edge.

"Hey, look at me," I say as I cup her chin, lifting her gaze to mine. "I've got to see Dad and Aurelio. Catcher's stirring shit up again, and I probably have to smooth things over before they blow up." I soften my grip, trying to pour reassurance into every syllable. "But listen, I'm not selling any girls today, Okay? Please don't be scared."

Her eyes search mine, hunting for the truth beneath my words.

With her chin still perched on my hand, Alba's nod is slight but certain. "Okay," she whispers.

"Good. Because I want you—no, I need you—to be anything but meek with me." My thumb brushes against the softness of her lower lip. "The Alba I saw last night, the firecracker who matched me, passion for fury—that's who you really are. With me, let that part out. Be yourself. Be the girl who told me to fuck off when we were 17. Be her again."

A smile cracks the edges of her usual reserve, brightening those eyes that always seem to see straight through me. "Okay," she says again, stronger this time, rough around the edges but honest and real.

I lean in then, not just with my body but with everything I am and seal my vow with a kiss that tastes of beginnings and wild, reckless hope. Pulling back just enough to hover over her lips, I say, "Alba, I promise you, I'm going to dismantle the human trafficking ring. All of it.

Once I take over, once my old man hands me the seat, it's done. I know I said this last night, but I'm serious, Eleanor and I, we've been scouting different ventures. I just have to play the dutiful son until he gives me the reins."

Her body tenses beneath me, and I hold eye contact, unflinching, willing her to see the sincerity etched into every line of my face. "It's gonna happen. I swear on my life."

Her eyes widen as she processes the weight of my revelation. The shock on her face is a clear signal that I've dropped a bombshell that shatters everything she thought she knew about me—and my bloodline.

"Your father... he built his whole empire on that," says Alba.

"Yeah, he did. But under my reign, I'll forge something different, something clean. An empire that'll keep you safe and our future secure." My words are an ironclad promise, a declaration of war against the very roots from which my family tree grew.

It's time to give her something to hold onto—a glimmer of normalcy in our lives.

"Speaking of futures..." I say, the corner of my mouth twitching into a half-smile. "Mrs. Gallo, today's agenda also includes making some important plans."

"Plans?" Her brow furrows in confusion, not yet connecting the dots.

"Marriage plans." I say, my mouth cracking the hugest smile at the thought of her really being Mrs. Gallo. "Do you want a church wedding, or something a little more exotic?"

Her smile breaks through the uncertainty, radiant as the

sun. "A private wedding is fine with me," she says. "I've had enough eyes on me over the years. I think I've had my fill of being watched."

"I enjoy watching you," I tease, the predator inside me stirring at the intimacy of the moment. "The way your body moves when you walk, the way your…"

"Shhhh," The resolve in her voice matches the strength in her smile. "Your eyes will be the only ones I'll accept from now on."

"Then mine is what you'll get," I say, sealing it with a kiss.

But as I pull back, my expression becomes more serious. There's something else I need to address, something that she has already said no to, but I just can't accept.

"There's one more thing," I say, and I can feel her tense again. "I'm getting you a therapist. A good one. Someone who specialises in trauma. I know you said no, but I think it will help."

"Gabe, no—" she starts to protest, but I cut her off gently.

"Alba, I know you don't want to relive your past. I know it's painful. But you need someone to help you process what happened, someone trained to help you heal. I can't do that for you, as much as I want to. You need professional help, and I'm going to make sure you get it." I brush a strand of red hair from her face, my touch tender. "I'll be there with you every step of the way. I'll hold your hand through every session if you want me to. But you're getting that shrink, even if you have to fight me on it."

She looks like she wants to argue, but I can see the

resignation in her eyes. She knows I'm right, even if she doesn't want to admit it.

"I love you, Alba," I say, and I mean it with every fibre of my being. "And part of loving you means making sure you get the help you need to heal. So yes, you're getting a therapist. And yes, I'm going to help you through the whole thing. We're going to do this together."

She nods slowly, tears glistening in her eyes. "Okay," she whispers. "Okay, Gabe. I'll do it."

"Good girl," I say, pulling her close and holding her tight. "We're going to get through this. Together. I promise you that."

Chapter 36

Alba

The world outside seems to dim as I roll over in Gabe's bed, the sheets still warm from where he'd lain. Sunlight filters through the half-closed blinds, casting golden stripes across his broad back. I watch him move with a fluid grace that belies his imposing frame, every motion calculated and sure. My eyes are drawn to the enormous Phoenix tattoo that covers his entire back, the intricately beautiful details seem to shift and dance in the morning light.

He reaches for his suit, a tailored piece that clings to him, emphasising the kind of masculine appeal that has become his trademark in the last 13 years. As he buttons up the jacket, the fabric speaks of power and poise, and I find myself thinking about what he said about dismantling the trafficking ring. About making sure it never happens to anyone else again.

The therapist idea still sits heavy in my chest. I know he's right—I can feel it in my bones that I need help processing what happened to me. But the thought of reliving it all, of speaking it out loud to a stranger, terrifies me in a way that even Gabe's darkness doesn't. At least with Gabe, I know what I'm getting. With a therapist, I'm walking into the unknown, and the unknown has never been kind to me.

But if he said he'll help, if he said he'll be there with me every step of the way, then maybe I can do this. Maybe I can trust him enough to let him guide me through the worst parts of myself. The idea is still scary, but it's a different kind of scary—the kind that comes with hope attached to it.

He turns, and even in the simplicity of the morning, he's the epitome of the enigmatic man that captured my heart so long ago. Leaning down, he presses a kiss to my forehead, a gesture both tender and possessive. "Don't forget to eat," he says.

His lips are a soft command, and in their wake, a revelation unfurls within me like the first bloom of spring. I realise, with a jolt that runs bone-deep, that I have never stopped loving Gabe. He's my first love, the kind of all-consuming flame that could never be extinguished or replaced. Even when I was running from him, even when I thought he was complicit in my suffering, some part of me was still his.

I lay in his bed, ensnared in the web of our past, present, and whatever future might exist for us. And amidst the chaos of emotions that threatens to overwhelm me, there's a singular, unshakeable truth: I never tried to let him go because some part of me knew he was as much a part of me as my own beating heart.

His lips graze mine in a fleeting kiss, sending a

cascade of butterflies rioting through my stomach. They're the very same ones that fluttered wildly when I was 16, sitting on the swing set at the local park, swapping promises under the cloak of night, while the rest of the world remained oblivious to our stolen moments. The memory, vivid and sweet, melds with the present, blurring the lines between then and now. Gabe always did have the power to make time stand still.

I watch him stride across the room, exuding the controlled power of a man who knows exactly what he wants and how to get it—the same determined gait that once led him away from me and into his father's empire. As he adjusts the cuffs of his suit, a symbol of his impending reign over a world shrouded in moral ambiguity, I realise something pivotal: I have chosen to remain here, in this space with him.

I'm not here because I can't escape. I'm here because I don't want to. Not anymore. It's an irony that brings a brief smile to my lips. After all these years of wanting to escape, I chose to stay the moment the opportunity arose for me to leave. He never locked me in, never demanded my fealty to his crown of thorns. Instead, he gave me the key, left the door ajar, and in doing so, granted me the most complex form of freedom—a liberty laced with love and lined with loyalty.

For the first time in my life, I feel safe. Happy. Content. And I'm starting to understand that maybe the only reason I wanted to run was because everything was so uncertain. I didn't know what Gabe wanted from me, didn't know if he was going to hurt me or help me, didn't know if I could trust him. But now that it's not uncertain anymore, now that I know he wants to keep me safe, I feel like I can let go and actually feel that safety.

I'm programmed by 13 years of being held captive, to only think people are out to hurt me. But Gabe isn't. He wants to keep me safe, and he's willing to prove it every single day. And I can turn that safety into anything I want. I can see it now—he would do anything I asked, he would do everything I wanted. All he wants is for me to be happy, to be safe, to be free.

And the thing is, I want to be part of what he's building. I want to be part of dismantling the machine that destroyed me, the machine that destroyed so many others. He's going to take down the trafficking ring, make sure it can't happen to anyone else and I want to be there when it happens. I want to see it fall. I want to be part of the wheel that pulls it all apart and makes it disappear.

It's sort of empowering, actually. For so long, I've been powerless, a victim of circumstances beyond my control. But now, with Gabe, I have the power to make a difference. I have the power to help stop what happened to me from happening to anyone else. I have the power to be part of something bigger than myself, something that actually matters.

The thought of the therapist doesn't seem quite so terrifying anymore. If I'm going to be part of this, if I'm going to help Gabe dismantle the trafficking ring, then I need to heal. I need to process what happened to me so I can be strong enough to face the people who did it. I need to be whole again, not broken and fractured.

I watch him stride toward the door, exuding confidence and power, and I feel a surge of something I haven't felt in a long time—hope. Real, genuine hope that maybe, just maybe, I can have a life that's more than just survival. Maybe I can have a life that's actually worth living.

"Remember what I said," Gabe calls out.

I nod, though he's already halfway out the door, not needing to see my affirmation to know it will be there. He trusts me to take care of myself, just as he trusts me to stay. And in that trust, there's an unspoken understanding: I'm free to roam, free to leave, and free to be me—within or without the walls of his domain. But where freedom beckons, so too does loyalty, for the devil I love is a certainty I can no longer deny.

"Mine," I whisper to the space he vacated, to the lingering scent of his cologne and the ghost of his touch. Always, I will remember—and always, I will choose this life, this man, with all the complexities and contradictions that come with him.

Chapter 37

Gabriel

The heavy door to the warehouse office groans on its hinges as I shove through it. Catcher and Aurelio are in front of what is essentially the throne of our gritty kingdom. Catcher's ink-covered arms are crossed at his chest, a scowl carved deep into his face, while Aurelio leans back, a silver lighter flipping between his deft fingers and that damn smirk playing on his lips.

My father, with his steel-grey hair and eyes that have seen more bloodshed than most armies, stands up from behind his dark wood desk. His towering frame moves with a predator's grace as he gestures towards the leather chair that might as well be a crown for all it represents.

"Son, this is your show," he declares. He steps back, hands clasped behind him, the very picture of relinquished control. But we all know better; this is a power move, one calculated to drop me right into the boiling pot. The weight of it settling on my shoulders like a lead coat.

I take a reluctant step forward, eyes darting between my two friends—or, more accurately, the two headcases

I've grown up with. "What the fuck have you done now?" I ask, already bracing myself for whatever insanity they've cooked up this time.

Catcher's jaw clenches, the tattoos on his neck rippling with the movement. His eyes, cold and reckless, meet mine, and I can see the madness within them—the kind that loves the violence and mayhem. It's the same look he gets right before he dives headfirst into a fight, and my stomach drops.

Aurelio, ever the charmer, simply exhales a stream of smoke, the scent of burnt tobacco momentarily overpowering the room's musty odour. He flips the lighter closed with a sharp snap, and I can see the tension radiating off him.

I run a hand through my hair as I brace for whatever insanity they've cooked up this time. It's never simple, never clean, but then again, nothing in our world ever is. "Well?" I prompt, my voice low and dangerous. "One of you better start talking, or I'm going to assume you've both lost your fucking minds."

Catcher leans forward, that predatory smile spreading across his face. "*Ho portato una ragazza,*" he says with a brazenness that makes my blood run cold. *I took a girl.*

My brows knot together, and I feel the familiar itch of incredulity scratching at my skull. "You took a girl? Who? And what the fuck do you mean you 'took' her?" I'm already moving toward him, my fists clenching at my sides.

Aurelio is next, dragging a hand down his face as if he could wipe away the weariness that clings to him. He exhales heavily, his breath a gust of last night's whiskey.

"The last week's shipment," he says, his voice strained. "It was processed and sent to auction yesterday, minus one girl."

"Christ!" My mind races, trying to piece together the implications of what Catcher has done. This is bad. This is really fucking bad. "Tell me you're joking!" I say, squaring my shoulders as if bracing for a blow. But Catcher just sits there, smirking like he's won the lottery, and my anger spikes to dangerous levels.

I lean forward, bracing my palms against the cold surface of what will soon be my desk. "So, you just grabbed one of the girls? Like she's some kind of stray cat?" I ask, my voice dripping with disbelief and barely contained rage.

Aurelio shifts in his seat, his discomfort palpable even without looking at him. Catcher just stares back at me, unflinching, and I want to punch that smirk right off his face.

"I have no clue where he's stashed her, properly at that fortress he calls a country estate…" Aurelio finally admits, and I can hear the frustration in his voice. He's just as confused and angry as I am.

"Fuck, Catcher!" I say, disbelief warping into anger. "Why the hell didn't you just buy her, mate?" What the fuck is he playing at… "You know the rules. You want something, you pay for it. You don't just take it."

His smile remains predatory and self-assured. "I'm not like you, Gabe," Catcher says with contempt. "Non compro le mie ragazze. La vedo, la voglio, lei è mia." *I don't buy my girls. I see it, I want it, she's mine.*

The audacity of the man has me clenching my fists to

keep from decking him. I want to hit him, want to make him understand how fucked up this is, but I also know that violence right now won't solve anything. It'll just make things worse.

"Jesus Christ!" I mutter under my breath. The rules of our world are simple and brutal, but even those have lines you don't cross. And Catcher just crossed about a dozen of them. "What's her name?" I ask as I rub my temples; like it can knead away the tension building behind my eyes.

"Posey Hudson," Aurelio answers, sliding a manila folder across the scarred surface of the desk. "Virgin. Worth a million at auction."

I flip the file open and stare down at the photograph clipped to the corner. A girl with haunted eyes and a wisp of a smile that doesn't reach them stares back at me. Posey Hudson. The dossier is brief but tells me everything I need to know; she's young, she's traumatised, and she's worth a small fortune.

"You have to pay for her, mate," I say, flicking the file shut with a snap. "Either buy her or let her go. Those are your options."

Catcher's face is stone—a cold, hard slab of indifference. "No."

I shake my head, the anger coiling tighter inside me. "This is stupid, Catcher!" Stupid doesn't even begin to cover it. It's lunacy, the kind that gets people killed. It's the kind of move that starts wars within our organisation. "You can't just take a girl from the auction. You know what that does? It fucks with the entire system. It makes people think they can do whatever they want."

"Look, I'll pay for her, mate," Aurelio interjects, his

voice strained but steady, trying to be the voice of reason while teetering on the edge of this madness with us. "Then we can all move on. No harm, no foul. We just buy her and pull her from the auction list and call it even."

Catcher casually shrugs, and I want to lose my mind. He shrugs off bullets and blood, so what is a girl's life to him? "Fai quello che vuoi, ma non-pagherò un dollaro per lei," he says with complete indifference. *Do what you want, but I won't pay a dollar for her.*

I stare at him, trying to understand what's going through his head. Is this about principle? Is this about proving something? Is this just Catcher being Catcher, completely fucking unhinged and dangerous?

"Take the money from my account, I'm done with this," Aurelio says as he stands, turning on his heel, and heading for the exit. The door slams behind him, echoing through the warehouse like a gunshot.

I turn to face Catcher, the weight of leadership heavy on my shoulders. He meets my gaze, a smug grin crawling across his face, and I realise this is what it means to be in charge. This is what it means to make the hard calls, to enforce the rules, to keep the empire running smoothly.

"First and only warning," I say, my voice low and deadly. "You do this again, you step out of line like this again, and I will end you myself. I don't care how long we've known each other. I don't care that we grew up together. You cross me, you cross the family, and there will be consequences."

He leans back against the chair, arms crossed over his chest like he hasn't just crossed a line you don't come back from. "Noted," he replies, nonchalant as ever. With a nod he stands and strolls out, his heavy boots thumping against the concrete floor.

I slump into the chair, feeling every inch the king of a crumbling empire. The leather is cold against my skin, and I wonder how many times my father has sat in this exact chair, making these exact kinds of decisions. How many times has he had to choose between loyalty and order? Between friendship and responsibility?

Across from me, the old man takes a seat, his movements slow and deliberate. "So, this is what this view looks like," he says, quieter than I've ever heard him. There's something almost melancholic in his voice, like he's remembering what it felt like to be where I am now.

"Touché," I mutter. The bastard has the nerve to smirk, like he's known all along how this would end—with me sitting on the throne I never asked for, staring down the barrel of a future I wasn't sure I wanted.

The silence is a blanket of tension you can almost see when the old man's hand shoots out, thumb jerking towards the door that just slammed shut behind Catcher. "You'll need to keep an eye on that one," he says, a warning that raises the hairs on the back of my neck. "E' una mina vagante." *He's a loose cannon.*

"On it," I sigh, the words tasting like ash in my mouth. Keeping tabs on Catcher is like trying to lasso lightning— futile and extremely dangerous. But it's my responsibility now. It's my job to keep him in line, to make sure he doesn't destroy everything we've built.

But before I can let that sink in, Dad looks at me, hitting me with the full force of his legacy. "The seat is officially yours, son. I'm done. From tomorrow, you will be head of the house."

I frown, incredulity tightening my features. "I still have five weeks?" The words are half statement, half question, my mind racing to catch up with the sudden shift in time-lines. I thought I had more time to prepare, more time to figure out how to do this without completely fucking it up.

"You're ready," he assures with a smile that carries more weight than a judge's gavel. It's not a suggestion; it's a decree, my coronation set in stone by the king himself. "You've proven yourself. You've shown me that you can make the hard calls, that you can lead and you can protect what matters."

I want to argue, want to tell him he's wrong, that I'm not ready for this. But I know it won't matter. The decision has been made. Tomorrow, I become the head of the house. Tomorrow, the entire empire falls on my shoulders.

Leaning forward, his voice drops to a conspiratorial hush. "Now tell me about Alba. What's happening with her?"

I meet his stare, feeling the burn of my own resolve. Alba. My Alba. The one thing in this dark world that makes sense, that makes me feel human, that makes me want to be better than I am.

"I'm going to marry her," I declare, and the words feel like a vow, like a promise I'm making not just to my father but to myself, to Alba, to the universe.

His reaction catches me off guard—a smile, wide and genuine, spreading across his weathered face. "Great news," he says. Relief washes over his features as if I've just handed him the keys to paradise. "I'm glad she's home, son. This is where she always belonged."

Something I can't quite grasp courses through me. In this dark underworld, Alba is the light that cuts through the gloom, the calm that soothes the chaos. And as I sit on the throne that will soon command an empire, it's her name that echoes through the chambers of my gunmetal heart. She's the obsession that anchors me, the desperation that drives me, and the violence that protects her will be my most sacred vow.

Tomorrow, I become king. But today, I'm just a man who can't wait to get home to the woman he loves.

Chapter 38

Alba Baker

4 Years Later

The first glint of dawn tiptoes through the curtains, and I'm pulled from the depths of sleep by the most intoxicating aroma—fresh tea and buttered toast, the scent of home and safety intertwined. I blink away the remnants of dreams, my eyes adjusting to the soft light filtering through the silk drapes, and there he is. Gabe stands silhouetted against the morning sun, his broad shoulders outlined in gold, as he places a tray on the bedside table with the kind of care that speaks to the tenderness he reserves for me in these quiet moments.

"Morning," I murmur, my voice still thick with sleep, still wrapped in the haze of dreams where he was mine in ways that go beyond the physical.

"Good morning, Alba," he replies, his voice the rolling timbre of distant thunder—soothing yet powerful, a sound that has become my favourite song. The way he says my name, the way it curves around his voice, makes my heart stumble even after two years of marriage.

I prop myself up on my elbows, the sheets pooling around my waist, and smile up at him. There's something profoundly ritualistic about this moment, one we've shared every single day since we exchanged our vows and I took his name, intertwining our lives irrevocably. The weight of that name, the weight of what it means to be Mrs. Gallo, still settles on my shoulders like a crown I never expected to wear but now can't imagine living without.

"Thank you," I say, reaching for the steaming mug he's brought me. My fingers wrap around the ceramic, feeling the heat seep into my skin, warming me from the inside out. It's more than just a beverage—it's a lifeline, a symbol of the normalcy we've carved out within the chaos, a small act of devotion that speaks volumes about who he is when the doors are closed and the outside world can't see.

Gabe watches me intently, his dark eyes tracking every movement I make, as if he's still afraid I might disappear, as if I might still run. After two years and everything we've built together, he still looks at me like I'm a miracle he can't quite believe is real. His lips curve in response to my smile, a silent acknowledgment of the private world we've created, the sanctuary that exists only for us.

I sip the tea—a perfect brew, light and rich, made exactly the way I love it because he's learnt every prefer-ence I have, every small thing that brings me comfort. This is how our days begin, not with orders or schemes, but with quiet moments steeped in domesticity, a lull in the perpetual storm that rages around us beyond these walls. It's our sanctuary, and as I sip from the cup, I know that despite the demands and dangerous deeds awaiting beyond our bedroom door, here I am safe. Here I am cherished. Here I am home.

Gabe's movements are methodical as he shrugs off his jacket, the leather falling away like he's shedding a layer of the darkness that clings to him outside this room. His white shirt follows, the buttons slipping free one by one from their holds, revealing the taut expanse of his chest, the defined muscles that speak to his power, his control, his dominance. But it's not the sight of his exposed body that causes my heart to stumble—it's the crimson specks marring the cuff of his sleeve, tiny drops of blood that tell a story I'm not sure I want to know.

My brow arches upward, a silent question lingering between us. He catches me looking, and in those dark eyes, I read a narrative that goes unspoken. There's a momentary weariness there, a heaviness that speaks of violence and difficult decisions, before he composes himself, pulling the mask back into place.

"An issue at Velvet," he says simply, as if blood on his cuffs is just another part of the day. "It required my attention."

"Is everything—" I start, only to be cut off by the shake of his head, a firm finality to the gesture that tells me not to push, not to ask for details I don't need to know. Gabe took Velvet off Dan years ago, pushed him out, and from what I've come to understand eliminated him from the earth, how I ever asked, but it's good to see the club is under new management, and run very differently than it had in the past.

"Handled," he assures, though the set of his jaw

betrays the effort it took. "Needed the king to step in and defuse the situation before it escalated."

I continue to watch him, my expression taut with concern as he sighs, the sound carrying the weight of the empire on his shoulders. "The twins were in town," he adds, a note of disdain threading through the words like poison through water. "They brought Mercy with them."

"Ah," I say, understanding dawning like a dark cloud. The twin sons are the heads of the Gold Coast Mafia, and their presence in Melbourne always spells trouble. Their names alone are enough to make people nervous, and the fact that they brought Mercy—their enforcer, their weapon —means whatever happened at Velvet was serious. "Okay," I concede with a smile, one that seeks to ease the tension etched into the lines of his face. It's a smile born of years shared, of secrets kept, of battles weathered side by side. "No more needs to be said."

The coolness of the room evaporates as heat emanates from Gabe's skin as he sheds his clothes, each garment falling away like layers of his complex life, revealing the man beneath the king. He moves with an authority that resonates deep within my bones—a silent assertion of his presence that leaves no room for doubt, no room for anything but him. The scars that mark his body tell stories of violence and survival, and I've learnt to read them like a map of his journey to this moment, to us.

"Put that tea down," he commands, his voice dropping to that low, dangerous tone that makes my entire body respond.

My hand pauses mid-air, the ceramic cup inches from my lips. I acquiesce immediately, placing the steaming mug on the bedside table, my heart already beginning to race in anticipation of what comes next. After two years of marriage, I still feel that flutter of excitement, that rush of need when he looks at me like this—like he's starving and I'm the only thing that will satisfy his hunger.

With the fluidity of a predator, Gabe closes the distance between us. His large and capable hands scoop me up into an embrace that envelops me entirely—body and soul. His hard length presses against me, and I can feel the evidence of his desire, the way his body responds to mine even after all this time. It's intoxicating, the knowledge that I affect him this way, that I have this power over the king of the underworld.

The growl that emanates from Gabe is feral, filled with a yearning that resonates deep within my bones, making me feel alive in ways I never thought possible. "I missed you," he says into my ear, his breath hot and heavy with want. "I need you. Now let me eat, because I'm starving."

He begins a deliberate descent down my body, his movements unhurried yet purposeful, as if he has all the time in the world and nothing matters but this—this moment, this connection, this intimacy that belongs only to us. As he journeys past the swell of my belly, the hem of my shirt catches, revealing the most intimate parts of me. He wastes no time, driven by a hunger that goes beyond the physical, a need that's almost spiritual in its intensity.

His tongue traces a searing path from my ass to my clit, each lap a testament to his mastery over my body, to the way he knows exactly how to touch me, exactly how to make me fall apart. "You smell so good," he says against my skin, sending shivers cascading through me like a waterfall of sensation. "And you taste even better. Like honey and home and everything I've ever wanted."

A gasp escapes my lips when I feel the firm press of his fingers at my entrance, teasing before slipping into me with a certainty that speaks of countless nights spent learning every contour of my being, every secret place that makes me come undone. The richness of his voice and the heat of his touch hold me captive, willingly tethered to the man who is both my husband and my king, my destroyer and my saviour.

"Alba, you're so wet," he says, pausing to taste me again, and I can feel the smirk on his lips as he savours me like I'm the finest delicacy. "Your sweetness, it's intoxicating. I could spend the rest of my life right here, between your legs, drinking you in."

The heat of his words wraps around me, sending ripples of need through me that make my entire body tremble. My hands find their way into his dark hair, my fingers threading through the strands as I try to anchor myself to something solid while he unravels me, piece by piece.

"I want to drink every last drop of you," he says, his fingers dancing inside me, stoking the fire he's kindled with his mouth, his words and his absolute devotion to my pleasure. "I want to taste you until you're screaming my name, until you can't remember anything but the feel of my mouth on you."

And then, a slow intrusion, another digit joins the chorus of sensations, slipping into my ass with a gentleness that belies the intensity of what he's doing to me. A gasp—sharp, unbidden—tears from my throat as I feel myself stretch and yield to him, accommodating him because I trust him completely, because I know he would never hurt me, because this is what love looks like when it's raw and real and absolutely consuming.

The delicate pressure is both startling and exquisite, another layer of pleasure that spirals outward from my core, building and building until I feel like I might explode from the sheer intensity of it all. My body is singing, every nerve ending alive and screaming for release, and he knows it. He can feel it in the way I'm clenching around his fingers, in the way my hips are moving against his face, in the way I'm whimpering his name like a prayer.

"Let go for me, Alba," he urges, his intense gaze penetrates all my defences, seeing straight through to the core of who I am. "Come for me. I want to feel you fall apart."

It's dual stimulation, a crescendo of overwhelming bliss that builds with each deliberate motion, each calculated touch designed to push me higher and higher. My climax looms, an imminent storm on the horizon, and with a final, loving hum against me, Gabe unleashes it. I shatter, fragments of ecstasy scattering like stars across the dark sky of my closed eyelids. My body convulses around him, clenching and spasming as wave after wave washes over me in a deluge of pleasure that threatens to drown me. And through it all, Gabe holds fast, drinking deeply, his own groans of satisfaction mingling with the symphony of my release.

I'm still trembling, still coming down from the high, when he gently turns me over onto my hands and knees. With an expertise born from years of intimate exploration, Gabe enters me slowly, deliberately, giving me time to adjust to him even though we both know I need him, that

I'm already ready for him. His fingers trace a scorching path along my spine before sinking back into my ass, and an involuntary shiver races through me, coiling tighter in my belly as he fills me completely, his presence undeniable, unyielding.

Moans slip from my lips, a surrender to the man who knows how to navigate the landscape of my desires with a conqueror's precision, the man who's spent two years learning exactly how to touch me, exactly how to make me feel like the most treasured thing in his world.

"Mine," he says, the word a declaration, a claim, a promise all rolled into one. His hand, solid and warm, wraps around the swell of my belly, the life within me stirring at his touch as if recognising the bond we all share—him, me, and the child growing inside me. "All mine," he continues, each thrust punctuating his words, driving deeper, making me feel every inch of him. "And now you're giving me something special. You're giving me an heir."

The rhythm he sets is unhurried, each movement a deep-sea current that pulls me under, drowning me in a sea of sensation. There's no rush, no urgency, only the inexorable push and pull of bodies entwined, of two souls that have been bound together since that first moment we met, since the moment he saw me and decided I was his.

Gabe's mastery over my body is not just physical—it's a psychological tether that binds me to him, rendering me powerless and yet more powerful than I have ever been. In his arms, the lines between right and wrong blur, and for a moment, there is only us; the king of the underworld and his queen, forging a new legacy from the ashes of the old, building something beautiful from the wreckage of our broken pasts.

"Mine," he whispers again, his rhythm shifting, the languid pace escalating as he drives into me with a fervour that matches the desperate beat of my heart. The intensity of his thrusts grows, each one sending shockwaves through my swollen body, and I revel in the raw urgency of our connection. Eight months pregnant, and my senses are heightened to an almost unbearable degree. My skin is a live wire, every touch sparking a fire within me that only he can stoke, that only he knows how to feed.

"Ah, Gabe," I gasp, my breath hitching as the coil inside me winds tighter, ready to snap. With each powerful stroke, he claims me all over again, and I'm lost in the sensation, adrift in a sea of endless desire that has no bottom, no end. My hands roam to my breasts, fingertips grazing the tender, sensitive peaks that are so much more responsive now that I'm pregnant. A pinch to my nipples sends a jolt straight to my core, and I shatter around him, convulsing in waves of ecstasy that seem to draw him deeper into me, that make him groan my name like a prayer.

"Alba," he grunts, the sound raw and guttural, a testament to his own nearing edge. His movements become frenetic, chasing his release with a kind of single-minded purpose that both thrills and overwhelms me. The pressure builds until it's all I can feel, all I can think about—until finally, I feel him tense, the warm flood fills me as he finds his own climax, drawn out by my body's insistent pull, by the way I'm milking him, by the absolute connection between us.

Panting and spent, Gabe withdraws and collapses onto the bed beside me. He reaches out, his arms strong and sure, drawing me down against the hard planes of his chest. His heart thunders against my ear, a reassuring drumbeat that grounds me even as my mind floats in the aftermath of what we've just shared. His hand settles protectively over our unborn child, and I feel the tenderness in that gesture, the way he's already devoted to this child, to us and to the future we're building together.

"We did it, baby," he says with an undercurrent of triumph that resonates deep within my soul. "I signed the last contract today. We officially own every single one. No more girls will be trafficked in my city. No more. It's done."

As he speaks, the significance of his words sinks in, painting a picture of a future that is both daunting and achingly beautiful. With that declaration, the Gallos are not just rulers of an empire—we are architects of change, crafting a world where darkness will no longer swallow the innocent whole, where girls won't be stolen, sold and broken, like I was.

"The Gallos are leaving a new legacy in place," Gabe says, his hand resting protectively over our unborn child— the heir to a throne built on both blood and hope, on redemption and second chances. "And just in time to welcome the new heir to the fold. Our son or daughter will inherit a world that's better than the one we found."

I nestle closer to him, the heat of his body a balm to the chill that has nothing to do with temperature. My life has always belonged to Gabe, entwined with his from the moment we met—a destiny that bound us together through shared vows and silent promises, through trauma and healing, through the darkness and the light.

"Forever it will remain," I say, knowing in my heart that whatever the future holds, we will face it together—as partners, as equals, as the king and queen of a new dawn, as the architects of a better world for those who dare to come after us.

And as the morning light continues to pour through the windows, bathing us in gold, I realise that I'm not just safe anymore.

I'm home.

I'm loved.

I'm free.

The End

Bonus Chapter - Gabriel

Naples is alive beneath the stars, the Mediterranean glittering like scattered diamonds as Alba and I walk along the waterfront, our fingers intertwined. The pizza we just shared was simple and authentic, the kind of meal that tastes better when eaten with the woman you've waited 13 years to marry. She's stunning tonight—wearing a cream silk dress that clings to her curves, her hair falling down her back like a waterfall. The way the moonlight catches her face, the soft smile playing at her lips, makes me feel like the luckiest bastard alive.

We got married 2 days ago at the registry office in Melbourne, just the two of us. No fuss, no spectacle, no one watching. That's what Alba wanted, and I would give her the world if she asked for it, so a quiet ceremony with just her and me was easy. She wore a simple white dress, nothing fancy; nothing that screamed bride. She just looked like Alba—my Alba—and when the registrar pronounced us husband and wife, I felt something shift inside my chest, something that had been broken finally clicking back into place. Then 2 hours later we boarded a private plane and flew straight into Naples.

Now, as we make our way back to the hotel, I can feel the anticipation thrumming through my veins. I've been planning this night for weeks, coordinating with the hotel staff, making sure everything is perfect. She deserves perfect. After everything she's been through, after all the darkness and pain, she deserves a night that's nothing but beauty, love and me worshipping her the way she was meant to be worshipped.

We step into the elevator, and I pull her close, my hand settling on the small of her back. She looks up at me, her eyes reflecting the soft light, and I can't help but lean down and kiss her. It's tender, unhurried, a promise of what's to come.

"I love you," I murmur against her lips.

"I love you too," she whispers back, and those words still feel new, still feel like a miracle.

When we reach our suite, I open the door and step back, letting her enter first. The room is dark, but as her eyes adjust, I watch her take in the sight before her. Rose petals cover every surface—the floor, the bed, the furniture —creating a landscape of deep crimson against the white linens. The air is heavy with the scent of roses, romantic and intoxicating.

"Oh my God," she breathes, her hand flying to her mouth.

I don't give her time to process. I grab her, pulling her against me, and kiss her like I've been dying to do all day. My hands tangle in her hair, and I pour everything into this kiss—all the love, all the devotion and all the promises I'm making to her in this moment. She responds immediately, her hands gripping my shoulders, her body pressing against mine.

"I hope you don't feel like sleeping tonight, my love," she says when we break apart, her voice husky with desire, her eyes dark with want.

A low chuckle rumbles from my chest. "Not a chance, Alba."

I start to strip her out of her clothes, my movements deliberate and slow. The silk dress slides down her body like water, revealing the perfection beneath. I kiss her shoulder as I let it drop away, then her collarbone, then the swell of her breast. Every inch of skin I expose, I worship with my lips, my tongue, my teeth.

She's breathless by the time I've removed everything, standing before me in nothing but the moonlight and rose petals. I take a moment to just look at her, to commit this image to memory—my wife, beautiful, brave and absolutely mine.

"Come here," I murmur, guiding her to the bed.

I lay her out carefully on the pristine white sheets, surrounded by crimson petals. She looks like a goddess, like something too beautiful to be real. I lean over her, my hand tracing the curve of her waist, and I tell her, "Look up."

She does, and I watch as her eyes widen, as a gasp tears from her throat. The ceiling above us is covered in glow-in-the-dark stars, creating a constellation of light in the darkness. It's like we're lying beneath the night sky, suspended in a universe of our own making.

"I love you, Alba," I say, and I mean it with every fibre of my being.

I kiss my way down her body, starting at her collarbone, moving across the swell of her breasts, down her ribs, across her belly. She's trembling beneath me, her hands threading through my hair, pulling me closer. I can feel her heart racing, can feel the anticipation radiating off her in waves.

When I reach the apex of her thighs, I don't hesitate. I part her with my fingers, exposing the glistening heat of her, and I lower my head. The taste of her is intoxicating—sweet and musky and absolutely addictive. I've tasted her countless times, but it never gets old, never loses its power to make me feel like I'm drowning in her.

"Take your suit off," she gasps, her hips bucking against my face.

I chuckle against her, the vibration making her whimper. "Not yet," I say, my voice rough with desire. "I need to taste you first."

I bury my face between her thighs, my tongue working her with expert precision. I know exactly how to touch her, exactly where to focus and exactly how to build her toward that edge. My fingers join my mouth, sliding into her heat, curling to hit that spot that makes her scream my name.

"Gabriel," she cries out, her body convulsing around me. "Oh God, yes, yes—"

I push her higher, driving her toward her climax with single-minded purpose. I want to feel her come on my tongue, want to taste her pleasure, to know that I'm the one bringing her this ecstasy.

"Come for me, *bella*," I urge, my voice muffled against her. "I want to taste it all."

She shatters, her body goes rigid as waves of pleasure crash through her. She's crying my name, her hands pulling at my hair, her hips grinding against my face as she rides out her orgasm. I drink her in, savouring every drop, every tremor, every gasp.

When she finally comes down, I climb back up her body, kissing my way across her skin. I settle over her, my body cradling hers, and I look down at her face. Her eyes are closed, her breathing still ragged, her cheeks flushed with pleasure. She's the most beautiful thing I've ever seen.

"I love you, Alba," I say again, because I can't say it enough, because I need her to know, because after 13 years of thinking I'd lost her, I need to remind myself that she's here, that she's mine, that this is real.

She opens her eyes and looks up at me, her gaze soft and full of emotion. She reaches up and touches my face, her fingers tracing my jaw, and she says, "I love you too."

Those 4 words—I love you too—are everything. They're redemption, forgiveness and hope, all rolled into one. They're the reason I survived 13 years of darkness. They're the reason I am tearing apart my father's empire. They're the reason I'm standing here, in this moment, as a man reborn.

I kiss her again, slow and deep, pouring all my love into it. And as we lie there surrounded by rose petals and glow-in-the-dark stars, I know that this is what forever looks like.

This is what love looks like when it's real, when it's earnt and when it's worth fighting for.

This is home.

About Cassandra Doon

Cassandra hates writing about herself in the third person, but here we are. With over 33 novels penned and no signs of stopping, she writes across multiple genres. Unable to be pinned down by just one, you'll find Fantasy, Dark Romance, Young Adult, and even a Detective series in the mix.

Having grown up in a small country town and later lived in the city, Cassandra found a perfect spot she likes to call an 'in-between place'—complete with rolling hills and just a stone's throw from the Gold Coast in Queensland Australia.

While she may have had social media in the past, Cassandra has since declared it's not for her. Her website is now the best place to find out what's happening in her world and to see what upcoming books are on the horizon.

Also by Cassandra Doon

The 4 Seats Series:

Matteo

Felix

Gabriel

Catcher

Ruhn & Frost

The 4 Seats Extended World:

Aces

Obsessed Shadows 

Adrian Romano

The Moretti Brothers (Coming Soon)

Standalone:

The Kings of Willows Peak

Damaged Goods 

Tuesday May

The Devils Cut

The Detectives Mate

Dark Dahlias Rite

A Field of Tulips and Bones

Follow Poppy

To Her

Blood moon

Unit 9

Broken Creek Ranch

The Dead Zone

Eclipsion (Coming Soon)

~

Oakland Harbour Series:

Missing

Found

Home

~

The Boys Series

The Boys Of Hastings House 

The Boys of Bittersweet College

The Boys of Nightsbane University (Coming Soon)

The Boys of Winchester U (Coming Soon)

~

Second Chances Series:

The Waterfall 

Wicked Bonds

Writhe (Coming Soon)

The Restaurant (Coming Soon)

~

Umbravivus Series:

The Lost Kingdom of Umbravivus (Coming Soon)

The Crowned King of Umbravivus (Coming Soon)

The Queen of Umbravivus (Coming Soon)

Butcher and the Witch Series:

Poison is always in the Prettiest Bottle

Candles make Great Alibis

Socials with a Slice of Pie

Also By C.L. Doon

The Rain Dang Detective Series:

Still Waters

Moving Waters (Coming Soon)

Standalone:

Second Chances at The Riverbend Café

Lavender (Coming Soon)

Also By C. Doon

Standalone:

Ravenwood Manor

Phantom Navis

www.ingramcontent.com/pod-product-compliance
Lightning Source LLC
Chambersburg PA
CBHW051120190726

48290CB00006B/1620